SHROUD OF BETRAYAL

A VIPER CLUB NOVEL – BOOK 1

LILIAN ROBERTS

Cover Design & Formatting by Paradox Book Covers & Formatting.

Self published - 2021.

This is the work of fiction. Names, characters, places, brands, media, and incidents are either the product of the author's imagination or are used fictitiously. Any resemblance to similarly named places or to persons living or deceased is unintentional.

PRINT ISBN 978-1-945415-24-1
EBOOK ASIN:978-1-945415-25-8

CONTENTS

PROLOGUE

*I*n 1815 Napoleon led his army of some 72,000 troops against the 68,000-man British army that included Belgian, Dutch, and German soldiers in the south of Brussels near the village of Waterloo, under the command of Arthur Wellesley, Duke of Wellington. The loss on both sides was immense. Ultimately, the Battle of Waterloo marked the end of Napoleon's storied military career.

After six years behind enemy lines, only four members of the British elite spy group "Viper" were finally heading home. Patrick Marcus Wingham, George Theron MacDougall, Michael Gregory Norman, and Edward Anthony O'Connel served his Majesty George IV as secret agents on French soil, under the leadership of the Duke of Wellington.

William Alexander Weldon, the fifth member of the group, was not with them. He lost his life during what they thought it would be a routine mission. Patrick and William had been best friends since they were in short trousers. Together, they joined the Calvary. They were given their orders in 1809 and left for France, along with three other men.

Prince Regent's prime minister carefully selected the group of five from the British nobility. Wealthy, powerful, and extremely qualified individuals. They were sent behind enemy lines and became one of the most impressive and fearsome spy teams in French history. Being brought together with a common interest and being part of this elite group became a tight link that held them together through many difficult times while on foreign soil.

Their directives were to infiltrate the enemy's ranks and seek alliances with French agents willing to provide them with information. They established regular channels of communication between them and London and started their work undercover. They became the well-known and fearsome group that the enemy named "Viper." Their name seemed to be chosen by the enemy because they moved undetectably, made calculated decisions, and delivered a venomous strike to the enemy lines before realizing they were compromised. The name was quite entertaining for the five friends, so they adopted it.

Andrew Fletcher managed the network behind enemy lines and thought the name "Viper" was apropos.

The Viper group had thoroughly developed a system for acquisition of surveillance to differentiate between mundane and significant intelligence to execute their target espionage operation successfully.

They vowed friendship, trust, and commitment to each other until death. In the past six years, they remained close like brothers and looked out for each other's wellbeing. Unfortunately, to Patrick's devastation, William lost his life in an enemy ambush.

Now only four out of the awe-inspiring five were boarding the ship bound for England. They had spent those six years successfully blending among the French locals and collecting valuable material that helped the British victory over Napoleon Bonaparte's forces at Waterloo in Brabant. Bravery marked them as heroes, and their bodies carried the signs of battle.

The ship sailed early in the morning. It was cloudy and cold, but only gentle waves slapped against the hull. The water seemed serenely blue, but more than halfway through the trip, the sea began to change moment by moment. It started to rain hard. Almost immediately, the waves increased, and the wind picked up. The turbulent waves hence the strong winds, became all the more violent. The ship shivered, rose, and dipped, seeming to swing end to end. The horizon disappeared in either direction, and the skies turned dark. The captain advised the small group of passengers to stay in their cabins until the storm passed.

Patrick remained calm as the wind wailed, the howling

storm ripped through the air, and the rain pounded the portholes of his cabin. Flashes of lightning that punctuated the dark sky made him wince. He lay in bed, placed his hands behind his head, and closed his eyes. He had crossed paths with death several times and had managed to stay alive. He was not afraid of a storm.

William's face emerged as he drifted toward sleep and blanked every other thought out of Patrick's mind. They grew up together almost, like brothers. They were raised in luxury and sent to the best schools with the rest of England's elite. With their astonishing good looks, they strolled the floors of the ballrooms stealing young ladies' hearts. They spent countless hours together, creating the most amazing memories, keeping each other's most intimate secrets, and bonding together by a beautiful friendship.

But William was now gone. At the memory of his best friend's body lying bloody and lifeless in the dark street, Rue Saint-Vincent in Paris, Patrick felt moisture in his eyes. The enemy murdered him during one of their missions. They all knew they might never go home, but one leaving the others behind with a huge void was kept away from their minds. They had been sure they would either die together or save each other from harm.

Grief dove deep into his bones and settled into his stomach. He felt pressure against his chest as if an iron hand seized his heart and tried to wrench it right out of his body. He missed him. There would never be new memories made with his best friend. They would never ride their gorgeous mounts across the beautiful fields surrounding their properties or enjoy hunting and fishing during summer's lovely days.

He would never have a trustful keeper of his secrets. But somehow, none of those things mattered any longer. William was dead, and Patrick felt a great chill burst forth from the depths of his heart. Life would never be the same.

The night William lost his life, the Viper group of four had attended an evening soiree with high ranked officials of the French government. William was chosen not to accompany the group. They had orders to follow five steps: planning and direction, collection, processing, production, and dissemination. William was to handle the information delivery.

The four men mingled with various guests and many friends they had assimilated while pretending very effectively to be part of the French nobility. Their fluency in the French language had been a great addition to their success. The arrangement between the five members of the group was that once there was information obtained important enough, they would quietly pass it on to William via messenger. In return, he would deliver it to the BMIC (British Military Intelligence Contact).

British Intelligence was involved in choosing how to process the information received from behind enemy lines, transforming the raw data into formats conducive to the production of functional intelligence, analyzing the data collected and turning it into useful surveillance, and finally disseminating data to the various military groups responsible for providing the enemy blows. The Viper group was responsible for the way they collected relevant intelligence.

The delivery would take place while exchanging pleasantries that seemed nothing more than a friendly conversation between acquaintances. During those short moments, they would chat in a quiet and urgent tone, and quickly they would move away to blend with the crowd. Their mission was to gather vital intelligence about military fundamental cordial positions and secret missions, from drunken French officials. This information would assist the British to arrange the delivery of their next blow to the enemy lines.

Patrick brought the champagne glass to his lips and took a sip while surveying Larue's crowded room. Larue was the Viper's French contact, and he had secured a servant's job for the evening. He was aware of each man's location around the court and ready to receive and pass on any information they handed him. When Patrick had all the details he needed, he motioned to Larue, and they met out in the garden away from any human eye. In the night's darkness, he handed Larue a small note and returned to the event making sure his absence had not been detected. Larue was to deliver the message to William.

This had been the routine of their covert operations, and it had worked splendidly to date. The enemy kept receiving deadly blows to their forces. During their most significant strategic endeavors, the secret codes were decoded, and they could not understand or uncover the betrayal. They were sure that this was the work of spies, but their efforts to unearth the infiltrator were futile. The squad's identity was cleverly concealed and deadly.

Later that evening, Patrick, who was in the middle of a conversation with a few officials, noticed Larue entering the courtyard. Larue was not to return following the note delivery to William. Patrick's eyes narrowed for a quick moment. He then inclined his head slightly to acknowledge him. His gaze swept the crowd briefly to locate his colleagues: George Theron MacDougall, Michael Gregory Norman, and Edward Anthony O'Connel. He was not surprised to find them staring above the crowd at the entrance. The sight of Larue sent a chilling sensation up and down their spines. Something was amiss. Patrick glanced back at Larue and raised a curious brow. A flood of thoughts raced through his mind, and he frowned inwardly. Larue moved toward the other side of the room, halting beneath the orchestra balcony next to the massive staircase that led to the upper floor.

Patrick excused himself politely and strolled across the dance floor in an unhurried manner. Reaching Larue's location, he didn't engage in conversation, instead he turned to face the opposite way pretending to observe the crowd.

"I will meet you at the garden house located in the back of this building," Larue whispered and moved away from Patrick, leaving the room without attracting any attention of the joyful guests.

He shot a glance at Larue's retreating back, and his gaze moved to the three men who were watching from across the room, wonder emerging on their faces. A slight move of Patrick's head alerted them toward the exit.

They exited the crowded room separately and stepped outside. The terrace was nearly bare as the last few couples moved inside at the music instruments' sound, starting again after a short break. A problematic feeling gripped Patrick as he crossed the large patio and reached the top of the steps leading down to a dark garden. He descended quickly and moved deeper into the night shadows to wait for his friends. It wasn't long, and one by one, they came down, heading in his direction.

"What's wrong?" George whispered.

"I don't know yet," Patrick replied. "Larue is meeting us at the small building in the back of the garden. But I have a feeling something has gone dreadfully wrong." Michael humphed, and Edward remained silent.

They all walked unnoticed into the night until they reached the small building. It looked dark and uninhabited. Their trained eyes noticed Larue crouched by a large tree toward the back of the building.

Up close, they stared at each other. "What is it, Larue?" Patrick asked.

Larue's voice quivered. "It was an ambush," he murmured.

"An ambush? What happened? Where is William?"

Larue paused for what seemed to be a lifetime. "William was killed," he said, and his voice broke.

Patrick's training prevented him from reacting

impulsively, but the powerful jolt that shook his body was very hard to mask. His shocked reaction held him to an eerie stillness.

The others exchanged stunned glances. A sick feeling enveloped Patrick, and bile rose to his throat. A thick silence fell between the five men, and disbelief painted their grim faces.

"How did you get away?" Edward asked, suspicion coating his voice.

Larue's brows rose in stunned surprise. He had reported directly to William out in the field for the past six years, passing valuable information between London agents. His jaw hardened, and he drew a sharp breath. His words came out hard and slow. "Do you think I had something to do with this?"

Edward started to express a sincere apology, but Larue raised his hand in silence motion.

"William meant everything to me. I don't have any family, and he was the only man who cared about me as a human being."

Edward wished he had kept his mouth shut. "I'm sorry, Larue, I was not thinking."

Larue continued as if he hadn't heard Edward's apology. "We saw a single man in the distance and were sure it was our contact. He was waiting at the same place as always. William told me to stay back and that he would be right back. I watched him reach the other side of the lonely road when several men came out of nowhere and jumped William. I drew back quietly; there were too many to tackle on my own."

"How many?" Patrick asked.

"I saw six. In a matter of seconds they appeared out of nowhere. William did not have a chance to defend himself. It looked like an enemy ambush, but I can't be sure. It could have been rogues, looking to hurt someone. They left his bloody and battered body in the dark street of Rue Saint-Vincent and walked away in clear celebration," Laure said in disgust, his voice a bare whisper. "I waited in the dark at a safe distance, and when they were gone, I moved only to find out that they had also killed Williams' contact. Both bodies were only a few centimeters apart. I moved both bodies to a safe location."

"Do you still have the information I gave you?" Patrick muttered.

"Larue pulled the paper from his coat pocket and handed it back to Patrick. "It was still in William's upper pocket. It is safe. I'm not sure what to think," he said.

The news disturbed them deeply. They had to go back inside and leave the soiree at different times. They could not afford to raise any suspicions and or have anyone associate them with each other. Larue left after he agreed to meet them in a couple of hours at the corner of Rue Carne and Rue Fleur to lead them to William's body. Larue nodded in agreement and disappeared in the dark.

Patrick was the first to feign illness. He arrived at his apartment, strode into the sitting room, and plunged onto a chair breathless. The thought of William's bloody and beaten body made his anger blaze. He dropped his face into his hands and spent a considerable amount of time alone in the dark. The pain was worse than he ever imagined. He was sure that he would never get over something so horrible and so devastating.

It had been about an hour when the first knock at his door pulled him out of his deep haze. Edward was standing at the door, expression grim. They exchanged a warm embrace as pain cursed through their bodies at the loss of their friend. George and Michael joined them a short time after.

Patrick pulled his watch out of his pant pocket and advised them that they needed to go. It was going to be a harrowing endeavor. Burying William's body was weighing heavy on each man. But they knew that there were no formal expectations on each regiment or base to honor its fallen in an honorable manner. There was no quick way to send the fallen bodies back home. The theory of transmittable diseases was a prevalent problem.

The meeting with Larue was glum. Larue had brought with him another British agent who led them to a remote cemetery for a respectful burial. Patrick paused to look at each man's stark face, dragged in a deep breath, and after a warm handshake, they departed, taking separate directions and disappearing into the night.

And now the Viper squad of four headed home without William. Patrick's thoughts turned to William's family. He loved them just as much as he loved his own family.

CHAPTER ONE

*G*regory Oswald Weldon, William's father, was the Duke of Brigshire and a very close friend of Patrick's father. William had received a letter of his father's passing two years prior, but this was war, so he was not permitted to go back home for the burial. He mourned his father's loss along with Patrick on enemy soil and tried to move on. William had two older brothers, Nicholas and Garrett, serving in the regency and a younger sister, Katherine. Nicholas was next in line, and he received his father's title. He would be named the Duke of Brigshire upon his return home from the war.

Patrick had been in love with William's young sister Katherine since he first set eyes on her at a very young age. He had decided that he was going to ask for her hand in marriage. He had a strong feeling that she felt the same way about him, but the war took him away before he had a chance to act on his promise.

Katherine had joined him and William in their childish games, and he had given her the name Kat. Patrick was sure that his love for her was not just a child's dream. As they grew a little older, propriety was so strictly supervised that he could not converse with her privately as a gentleman to let her know that he was madly in love with her. They danced a few waltzes together, but only under the strict supervision of the elders. He had not been allowed to call her by her first name in public for fear that he might damage her reputation.

She would now be twenty-two years of age and married to Lord Quinton. The thought made him cringe. He vividly remembered the letter that William had received from his family a year after they left home, telling him about her upcoming wedding. He would never forget the searing pain that raced through him at the news, and he spent many nights in misery. He cursed himself for not asking for her hand in marriage before he left, but now it was too late. William had been distressed as he'd been aware of his best friend's feelings for his sister, and he told Patrick he hoped that would return home before the wedding, and Patrick would offer for Katherine, and everyone would be happy.

The letter shocked both men because they knew Quinton a lot better than most. He was not the man William would have chosen for his sister. Nor would his father have chosen such a man for his daughter. Quinton was from a very wealthy and upstanding family in London, but he was well known for his gambling addiction, drinking, and bedding married women. Both William and Patrick speculated that one of the husbands considering his honor compromised, would challenge Quinton to a formal duel. What in heavens did Katherine find in him? Patrick often wondered. He had the looks, but he was not a good man. He knew Katherine well enough to know that she was not shallow to fall for just a man's looks. She was intelligent and quite particular about the people she chose to be friends with, so why Quinton? Duke Alexander Michael Bennett was Quinton's father simply known as Bennett. As a young lad he befriended Gregory Oswald Weldon, William's father and Henry Edward Wingham, Patrick's father. The three became best friends and remain particularly close during their school years at Eton College. Something happened that destroyed this amazing friendship and that something remained a mystery.

Patrick's forehead creased, and he pursed his lips in disgust. Well, there was nothing he could do about that. He frowned and shook his head, trying to push aside any thoughts about Katherine. He was now going home without William, and he would have to face things as they were.

Suddenly, he could sense the stillness of the ship and the quietness of his surroundings. He jumped out of bed and approached the porthole. Shirtless, he stood and stared, admiring the change in the sky. The rain had stopped, and he could see stars making their appearance, letting everyone know that the storm had passed. Patrick turned around and went back to bed. He was exhausted and needed sleep.

A soft female voice called out his name. Patricks' eyes snapped open. He sat up, leaned on his elbows, and jerked his head toward the sound, searching the darkness before realizing no one was there. It was quite dark in the cabin but for the insignificant light that slithered through the two portholes. What time was it? He sat at the edge of the bed and reached for his pants. He fished his watch out of a pocket and flipped the cover open. He walked over to the porthole and lifted it toward the light. It was 3:00 in the morning. What in the world? He took another quick look around the small room. That voice had to be a hallucination because he was utterly alone.

He walked back to bed and tried to fall asleep. The journey from France was long and tiring, and he was having difficulty sleeping. After tossing and turning for almost an hour, he gave up and got out of bed. He needed to get some air, so he got dressed, opened the door, and stepped out onto the narrow corridor. Turning, he strolled down and onto the deck. He drew in a deep breath letting the salty air sip through his lungs and slowly exhaled.

The night was crisp and breezy. The air carried the ocean's salt, and somewhere in the distance, his beloved land waited for him. He was homesick, and his heart was in turmoil, overwhelmed with the thoughts of William, Katherine, and the thousands of British casualties that covered the bloody French battlefields with a dark blanket of death.

As he crossed the extended deck and headed toward the railing, a shiver coursed through his body. He took a quick look around, but there was no one in sight; the deck was bare. He didn't wonder where everyone was. It was in the middle of the night, and passengers would be resting comfortably in their beds following the horrible storm.

Reaching the end of the deck, he closed his hands on the railing and gripped hard. He gazed out in the open across the dark horizon, trying to catch a glimpse of his beloved England.

His eyes moved slowly and focused on the rippling water of the massive wake created by the moving ship as it cleaved through the dark ocean. He rested his elbows on the railing, and his thoughts turned to his own family.

He was twenty-nine years of age and the oldest of three sons. He knew that his birthright would call for him to become the Duke of Scunthbury after his father Henry was gone, but that was the last thing he wanted to do with his life. It would be difficult to face his father and go against an English tradition carved in stone. It was his birth that ruled his destiny. Patrick's brothers, Christopher and Anthony, were twins, and both still attended Eton.

His mother, Olivia, Marianne O'Neill, was a beautiful woman from a prominent English family dominant in their part of the country for centuries. The marriage between his parents was not an arrangement. They met during the busy season in London and fell deeply in love.

His father laid claim for her hand within a short time. He used his power and title to call on her, and after the required time of courting and chaperoned carriage rides in the park, he asked her parents for her hand, and soon after that, they were married. Ever since that date, they never spent a day apart. Henry was aware of his wife's brilliance and beautiful gift of charm. People around them loved her, and that was an additional plus for their business dealings.

It was quite unusual since most marriages were arranged for money and station with love having little to do with the union. The extravagant balls were the right occasion for zealous parents to display their daughters as if they were animals for sale at stockyards. The young women had one purpose and one purpose alone: to catch a husband with a vital title and great fortune. But they could not show their eagerness in public. There were unspoken rules that they had to follow, and they could not veer outside those rules. Capturing the man's attention was done in an ingenious and conspiratorial way. Their appearance had to be close to perfect, from their gowns to the jewels to their attitude.

Patrick's mother, the very wealthy Duke's daughter, added a sizable amount to her husband's already established fortune. She was a magnificent woman who was adored by her husband. His father had been fascinated with her from the very first moment their eyes met across a busy ballroom, and he made sure that she knew that she was adored. He told her he loved her every single day for the past thirty-three years of their marriage. He was happy to let her help him with his business decisions because she was witty and smart. She was a woman who stood by her husband's side during all the business dealings. He respected her desire to be that woman to use her brilliant mind and run the house and the estate side-by-side with her husband.

She had been an excellent mother to the three boys. She

refused to have help in raising the children; she wanted to be hands-on in the raising of her boys. The children were left with help only when she had to attend specific engagements that required her presence alone or with her husband.

Yes, Patrick's parents were still madly in love, and that was the kind of marriage Patrick wanted for himself.

Anything his mother ever wanted his father was happy to provide. His love and affection showed in front of his children as he was a man of high principles, and he believed in raising men who would choose a wife to have and hold and protect with their life to the very end.

Patrick couldn't help the smile that jerked his lips upward as warm thoughts cascaded through him, creating a heartfelt need to be close to his parents once again.

As the last dark shadow disappeared behind the horizon, he pushed away from the railing and took a last look around, but all he could see was endless water. He smiled once again and returned to his cabin.

The moment that he heard the words, "We have arrived" and felt the human commotion, he was almost too overwhelmed with emotions to move. He walked outside and met his friends on the deck, moisture covering their eyes. They were home. The ship docked on the busy seaport, and they walked down the plank.

People were waiting and waving and screaming. There were laughter and hugs and overwhelming emotions surrounding the four men, but no one waited for them since they had not informed their families of their arrival day.

Patrick squinted at the buildings silhouetted against the intense sunlight. They walked forward, took a huge breath, and exhaled deeply. They smiled wide because they knew they belonged here. They stepped out onto their beloved land and walked across the street. They surveyed the surroundings and halted a few feet away and looked both ways. The roads were narrow and dusty, filled with people, shops, and coaches lined up waiting to take people to their destination.

They shook hands and exchanged warm smiles. They were now bound together by a strong friendship, which nobody would be able to penetrate. After agreeing to get together soon, they motioned to the coach drivers, and each took their separate way to their estates. Patrick gave the driver directions, climbed into the carriage, and dropped his bag in the opposite seat. The driver took off, and Patrick laid his head back against the soft squabs and closed his eyes. The carriage rumbled on at a steady pace, and as they got closer to the city and passed Hanover Square, they came to a crawl. London streets were often quite slow. It had been forty-five minutes since they left the docks, and the muddy coach considerably slowed as it crossed the large iron gate of Patrick's London estate. The cobblestoned driveway resonated beneath the horses' hooves, and shortly, the carriage stopped in front of his home on Oxford Street.

· · ·

Patrick stepped down, dropped a few coins into the driver's hand, grabbed the bag, and climbed the elegant home's marble steps. His excitement mounted, and his heart pounded in his chest painfully. He dropped the bag at his feet, and anxiously, he reached in his pocket for the key, but his pocket was empty. He frantically patted his coat, but there was no key. What did I ever do with the keys? He sighed out loud and raising his hand, he grabbed the heavy metal handle and gave it three firm raps. He started to pace back and forth until he heard slow footsteps approaching the door, and shortly after, it swung wide open.

Christian Walsh, the man who had raised him from a very young boy, a fine-looking, middle-aged man, impeccably dressed, stood in the opening ready to say something, but his mouth dropped, his eyes went wide, and his face lit up with excitement.

"Patrick, my boy!" he exclaimed, and reaching out, he pulled Patrick into a tight embrace. "Let me see you." He pulled back and gave Patrick a good look over. "Why didn't you send a letter that you were coming home? I would have sent the carriage to pick you up," he continued, rambling, unable to stop from the excitement. He then let go of Patrick and moved a few steps back to gaze at him once again.

Patrick stood there with a huge smile on his face. He had not been able to utter a single word, but he felt entirely blissful. Christian had been his butler since he was in short coats. Patrick thought of him more like family than his butler.

"Hi, Christian, yes, it's me, and I'm home. I didn't send

a note because I was unsure when I would get on the ship, and I didn't want everyone worried about my arrival."

Christian took a few steps back to let Patrick walk in. "Well, welcome home, my boy, take a load off. You'll find everything just as you left it. I'll have the bag sent up to your room. You go on upstairs, and I'll have the servants bring hot water for your bath.

Patrick nodded, overwhelmed with emotion. He started toward the staircase, but he stopped short. He turned around, and taking a few steps back, he pulled Christian in for another hug. "I'm sure happy to be back," he said cheerfully. "I've missed home." He then turned and climbed the stairs two at a time.

The feeling of being home was inexplicable. The British loss in the war had been immense, so he had been sure that he would not see this place again. Every soldier left home thinking they might not return alive.

After a pleasurable long warm bath and a hearty meal, he retired to his soft and comfortable bed. His contentment for being home in his bed was palpable. Not a single thought had the chance to cross his mind as he fell asleep the minute his head hit the pillow.

The next morning, he sent a message to his parents that he had arrived home safely and would be visiting their country estate in a fortnight.

He dressed leisurely and went downstairs for breakfast. He was famished. After finishing a hearty meal and a second cup of tea, he left the breakfast room and headed to the second floor. As he began to ascend the staircase, he decided that it was time to make plans. Today he would stay home. He would take no visitors and would reply to no messages until he had time to put his thoughts into order. He would take a walk around the garden and possibly lose himself in the fascinating book pages he started to read in France but never finished. He had not had this type of luxury for the past six years.

When he reached the landing, he drew in a deep breath, turned left, and strolled down the long hall until he reached his office door. He leaned against the door jamb as his eyes roved the room enthusiastically. He pushed away from the door and crossed the threshold. With his booted heel, he pushed the door shut behind him. His gaze drifted over the rows of leather-covered books with titles etched into the spines that lined the shelves covering all the wall spaces. The furniture was of rich dark woods and expensive fabrics. The large windows covered with heavy blue curtains poured to the floor and were corded with gold silk ropes. The room reeked prosperity. A feeling of warmth cursed through him. He was home, and he was grateful.

He shrugged out of his coat and flung it on the settee by the window. His eyes traveled across the beautiful gardens below. The lush green and the seasonal flowers held his gaze and almost mesmerized him. A smile painted his handsome face. Yes! He was home. He moved over to the glass cabinet and grabbed the decanter of brandy. He poured a glass, and after taking a swig, he walked back to his desk. Standing behind it, he looked down at the tray overflowing with invitations that had arrived early that morning. His mouth clenched into a straight line.

How in God's name did all these people find out that he was home? He sank into the comfortable chair and set the glass aside. He sighed, knowing that he would have to go through each of them and accept or reject. "No, no, no," he said out loud with sudden determination. "I'm in no mood to stand inside any ballroom and make trivial conversations with silly young girls. At least, this is what he thought of most of the crowds in the elite ballrooms ever since he was seventeen-years-old. He suppressed the oath that rose to his lips.

He was sure that none of these envelopes were important business notes. He had provided his solicitor's address to all the people he had essential dealings with before leaving for France. He was also sure that Jonathan had gone through each business note very carefully and had taken the appropriate action in his absence.

He leaned back and closed his eyes. Tomorrow he would spend a reasonable time going over his mail, and then he would visit Jonathan Walker, the family solicitor, to discuss the status of his affairs. He had left everything in his trustworthy hands six years ago. Next, he would set up meetings with his head foreman and his accountant. He had no plans beyond that point, and he didn't want to think of any either.

The face that suddenly appeared in front of him made him gasp. Kat's striking alabaster face made him squirm in his chair. He could vividly see her deep blue sapphire eyes that had haunted his dreams for the past six years, and her small perfect heart-shaped mouth with inviting pink lips that looked so soft and so kissable. He clearly remembered watching her sculpted body behind those elegant gowns that clung to her figure as she walked. When they were children, he used to be mesmerized by her silky hair that fell loose around her shoulders. The sun's rays created sparkling golden waves on her golden locks as she ran through the fields trying to get away from her brother and him. He gazed down at his hands bemused and wondered what it would feel like to run his fingers through that soft texture, and he shivered. He could still hear her mesmerizing laughter. Conflicting desires raced through his veins, and his heart throbbed at the thought of touching her. He frowned at his shameless thoughts, as she was now someone else's wife, and he had no right in thinking of her that way.

He tilted his head and focused on some of those little white cards on his desk, but it was a lost battle. Kat's presence was even more resilient now. The old anguish was back. She had married another man, and he never had the chance to let her know how he felt. Did she ever think of him as anything more than a friend?

How would he be able to control his emotions in a face-to-face situation? A sensation of unease prickled his veins. He shook his head, shot up off the chair, and took a deep breath to ease his thoughts. He felt the room closing in; he strode across the floor, not looking left or right until he reached the window overlooking his home's beautiful gardens, his distracted gaze idly stared. Wild thoughts ran through him, and he could not stop any of them from entering his mind. He had missed Kat dreadfully, and the fact that she was sharing another man's bed was shooting a raw, painful current through his spine. Pulling on the hinges with both hands, he pushed the windows wide open and drew in several breaths of fresh air. For what seemed to be an eternity, he stood unmoved and finally was able to breathe normally.

A gentle breeze touched his face. He took several deep breaths filling his lungs with the fresh air.

Maybe seeing her again and verifying that she was happily married to Lord Quinton would help him move on with his life. He let out a loud agonizing laugh, not believing a single thought he was having. He walked back to his desk and slumped down in his chair as if the entire obsessive struggle with his thoughts suddenly drained his body's life.

He was sure that he would never entertain the notion that Quinton George Bennett was the right man for Kat. He tried to push the disturbing idea to the back of his mind because he was sure that Quinton was unfit to be the husband of any decent woman. There had to be a reason that Kat married him, and God, he was hoping that the cause was not that of love.

His glass was empty, and he needed another drink. His imagination was running wild and creating all kinds of details about Quinton and Kat's union. He drew himself up as if a huge burden weighed him down. He walked back to the glass cabinet, picked up the crystal decanter with one hand, and poured a glass of brandy to the rim. He moved his hand slowly and watched the smoky liquid swirl around the glass walls. His senses utterly suspended, lost in his thoughts. A soft sound from the garden pulled him back, and his gaze flickered toward the window. Glass in hand, he took a few big steps and looked out at the manicured lawn, but he didn't see anything outside. He raised his hand and took a long swig. He shut his eyes and relished the smooth liquid as it slid down his throat, giving him the expected satisfaction.

CHAPTER TWO

*H*e needed some information and needed it fast. But how was he going to get it? And from whom? The thought made Patrick wince. He needed a point to start. After that, he would sit down with George, Michael, and Edward and use their abilities to lay out a plan and unearth the truth.

A soft knock snapped him out of his thoughts. "Come," he called as he turned to face the door.

His butler pushed the door open and peeked inside, a cheerful smile on his face. His eyes moved from Patrick to his desk and back. "Are you entertaining the thought of attending any of those events?" he asked. His gaze now fixed at the pile of notes on his desk.

Patrick grinned back at Christian and snorted. "Absolutely not," he said firmly. He walked back to his desk, set the glass down, and shoved the tray with the paper pile aside. "There is no way I will waste my time with silly giggling girls and matchmaking mothers looking for the poor soul who will fall for that type of thing." With an inward frowning, he made a dismissal move with his hands.

"All right then, I can't say that I blame you, so I'll let you go back to whatever you were doing." With a soft chuckle, he started to pull the door shut.

Patrick watched him, and suddenly, he was startled by the idea that ripped through his mind like a tornado. He took a quick intake of breath and called out. "Wait...wait... Christian, please come back in, I need to have a word with you."

Christian's eyebrows rose quizzically, and quickly he stepped inside. Patrick waved his hand in a motion for him to shut the door behind him.

"Come...come...please take a seat," Patrick said, pointing at one of the two cushioned chairs arranged in front of his desk.

Christian strode toward the desk, his eyes on Patrick. "What is it?" he asked with wide eyes.

"Sit...sit..." Patrick's voice trailed. He was shocked by the thought that abruptly entered his mind. Nobody knew more about the happenings in the residences than the servants. He was sure that the idea was God sent. The servants of each home in the ton had formed friendships, and some were even related. The gossip was paramount. All the news and secrets, good or bad, traveled like lightning from one place to the next.

After several moments of silence, Christian coughed politely and tugged Patrick out of his haze. He turned to look at his butler. Christian had taken a seat, trying to read Patrick's thoughts.

"Sorry," Patrick muttered, becoming aware that he had been silent for a prolonged stretch of time. His face was now dark, and his hands trembled slightly but quite visibly to a man who had raised him since he was in short coats.

"What is it, Patrick? You seem upset, my boy."

Patrick clasped his hands behind his back and started to pace across the carpeted floor. After a long and deafening silence once again, he stopped. He breathed in swiftly and immediately regained his composure.

"Tell me what you know about Katherine Weldon."

Christian's eyebrows shot up. "You mean Lady Bennett?"

Patrick winced at the sound of her married name. He pressed his lips in a straight line and continued. "Christian, I know that you don't wish to upset me since you know how I feel about Katherine. But I want to know all the details that led to her marriage just as you heard them through the servant's words. I know that the servants know the raw truth, which does not reach the ballrooms."

Christian was regarding him now with a sympathetic smile and clenched hands over his knees. The sadness in Patricks' voice was overwhelming.

"Well?" Patrick pressed on.

Christian reluctantly swallowed and dropped his gaze to the floor. The words came out slow and precise. "It is said to be a very unhappy agreement."

"Agreement?" Patrick exclaimed, staring at Christian unblinkingly.

"Yes...Lady Bennett involuntarily married Lord Quinton for some unknown matter between Weldon and Bennett."

"Ridiculous! What possible matter would make Weldon give his precious daughter to a rogue like Quinton?" Patrick pressed his hands against his temples thoughtfully. "That is very strange. Why would Weldon have any dealings with Bennett? Their families have been unfriendly for years."

"Maybe the issue that created the distance between the two families has everything to do with this agreement," Christian said evenly.

Patrick paused for a moment and considered Christian's words long and hard. He hmphed out loud "It would have to be something significant to force a marriage between Quinton and Katherine. He is a rogue not a gentleman. He would not hesitate to destroy everyone and everything around him, including Katherine. I'm not going to allow that." Patrick cursed under his breath as he walked back to his desk and slumped down in his chair. "What in heaven's name would make a father do something like that?" He shook his head in wonder.

Christian started to say something but changed his mind and remained silent. But of course, Patrick noticed.

"Christian, you look like you were about to say something. Spit it out, what is it? You do know something about this agreement, don't you?"

"No, not really, but I did hear that there were intense disagreements in the Duke's household before the wedding. The Duchess told Lady Katherine that she had to go through with the marriage to save face for her father."

His words were very near to a whisper, but, somehow, Patrick heard them bouncing off the walls. His lips twisted incredulously, and his body stiffened. His long, lean body of solid muscle shivered at the dark thoughts that entered his mind.

"How did you hear this?"

"Lady Katherine's companion Caroline Millwood was in her chamber during the discussion with the Duchess. She and our cook's daughter Samantha have been friends for years."

Patrick could not shake the sense that there had to be a profound secret buried in the past. "So, Alexander Bennett threatened to destroy Weldon's reputation if he did not agree to the marriage between his son Quinton and Katherine?" Patrick asked.

"Yes," Christian replied firmly.

"I am sure that this union took a sizeable chunk out of Weldon's fortune."

"I scarcely think that any of it matters at this point. What is done is done," Christian said.

Patrick closed his eyes on a long groan. "There had to be an undisputed motive, Christian. Weldon had to have some reason to make such a terrible decision." He turned and met his gaze. He then hit his hand on his desk in sheer anger. "William told me that his father's weakness was Katherine. He would have given his life for her." Pressing his elbows against the armrests, he pushed himself up and strolled to the window. He stood there and stared aimlessly out in the garden. Drawing a slow deep breath, he turned to face his butler. "Tell me that I'm not crazy. The concept of this marriage is illogical, and it just doesn't make any sense at all," he said. "Are the rumors still circulating after all this time?"

"Over the past six years, the rumors should have slowed down a bit. I truly believe they would have completely died down, but Lord Quinton's highly inappropriate activities kept bringing the subject back into the conversations around the ballrooms, soirées, and gatherings. He kept fueling the ton's hunger for gossip continually."

Patrick's discomfort grew and, with it, the need to solve the puzzle. His irritation weighed upon each lungful of air he took. He had no idea how he would handle the situation, but he was determined to start something first thing in the morning. He was now totally obsessed with the idea.

"I will have to speak with Quinton," he muttered, his voice barely a whisper.

Patrick's words dumbfounded Christian. "Are you mad, my boy?" he exclaimed. "You can't possibly believe in good conscience that this is a good idea. I know you are angry, but please understand, this is not your affair any longer."

"I made a promise to William on his burial ground that I would actively look into the reasons for this crazy union, and I aim to keep my word."

Christian regarded Patrick for a long moment. His lips were tight; his eyes were dark, and his expression that of a suffering man.

"Do you want to know a few more details about this marriage?" he asked reluctantly.

"You know more?" Patrick exclaimed.

Christian hmphed. "Well, there is one more thing."

Patrick expected that his butler would be eager to speak up, but soon he realized that he was quite reluctant to continue.

"What is it? What is the one thing? Spit it out, man! I need to know all that you know about this whole insoluble problem."

Christian scowled, and his lips tightened, reluctant to come out with his next statement. The words came out slowly and cautiously. "It is said that Lady Bennett has not accepted her husband in her bed since the night they wed."

Patrick's stunned shock brought a long silence into the room that stretched into what seemed centuries. His jaw clenched, and his body stiffened. He tried to refocus while searching for the right words to say something. Although Christian kept his expression impassive, he noticed Patrick's reaction in his eyes, in his appearance, in his body language. He remained quiet and let the silence provide the time Patrick needed to understand his last statement's significance.

Patrick stifled a groan and, drawing a deep breath, he asked, "How did Quinton react to that rejection?" His tone made it clear that he found the concept incredible. He could not understand why Quinton did not force her to submission by using his right under the law as her husband. He moved slowly to take a seat behind his desk. His head pounded, and his stomach stirred.

"He does not seem to be concerned," Christian said with a curled lip. "He acts as if all is well at home. He has several married women he visits quite often and a steady mistress. His activities are evident, and he's not hiding any part of it to everyone's amazement. He is oblivious that most people already know his marriage has not been consummated. But to those who know him well, they can see that his wife's rejection has angered him to the point that he will try to embarrass her in the world's eyes." Silence ensued.

He remained silent, carefully thinking over his next statement. "Do you know the whereabouts of Katherine?"

"She spends most of her time at the country estate, close to her family's mansion, away from London. Jennifer, the cook, is a good friend with Lady Bennett's companion. She says that she spends her days alone walking the gardens, reading, and sewing. Her governess believes that she knows her father's secret."

A harsh oath escaped Patricks' lips, and his dark blue eyes flashed from sheer anger. "That bloody son of a bitch," he exclaimed in an ice-cold raspy voice. He placed his elbows on the desk and dropped his face into his hands in stunned silence. No doubts remained in his mind that this marriage was the result of a deep-rooted secret. Katherine's feelings were real and had high enough priority now in his life to protect her at all costs.

Patrick seemed severely heartbroken. Christian's eyes scanned his face, startled by his reaction. He stood up and made his way to the liquor table. He refilled Patrick's glass and set it in front of him. Patrick stared at the liquid absentmindedly.

Christian took his seat and pressed on. "What is it, Patrick? Are you still in love with her?"

He lifted his head to meet Christian's gaze without replying. His chin quivered as he swallowed hard. Suddenly, he stood up, glass in hand, and walked away from his desk. The steps to the window seemed to be endless. He leaned against the wall and groaned. He didn't handle well-frustrated desire. He placed the rim to his lips, and without any reluctance, he drained the glass. He found an unexpected urge to speak out. "I have been in love with her ever since we were children. I didn't feel this crippling ache until I arrived home. While in France, the assignments were dangerous and required for my mind to be alert and clear of any interfering thoughts. But now that I am home, it is back, stronger, and more painful than ever."

Christian looked across the room, a sense of compassion for the man he raised from a little boy. He truly loved Patrick as his own. "I always thought that you would offer for her before you left," he said kindly.

Patrick smiled thoughtfully. "Believe me when I say that I will regret that mistake for as long as I live," he replied in sheer exasperation. "I wanted to ask for her hand, but I was afraid that I might not come back. I did not want her to go through the pain. I wanted her to move on with her life and be happy. But things have changed. I am here now, and she is unhappy. I need to do something."

Christian sighed deeply. "But Patrick, the bottom line is that she's married. Good or bad, she belongs to another man."

A tidal wave of emotions poured through him and took his breath away. He drew a deep breath, and through clenched teeth, he growled. "But this marriage is a joke. She's unhappy and does not belong to Quinton."

"Naught to be concerned with Lady Bennett," Christian reiterated.

Patrick picked up the brandy decanter, filled the glass to the rim this time, and eyed the liquid before taking a large swig. He then bored through Christian's eyes, his expression deceptively composed, "Not my concern?"

Christian stared at Patrick long and hard. "Yes, that is what I said. That's not your affair any longer." His voice was steady and firm.

"But it is. It is my affair. It's been five long years since this ridiculous union, and the marriage is still not consummated. That means Kat doesn't want to be with Quinton, and I hate the man. I've always hated him and what he stood for. William was utterly offended when he found out that Katherine was to be married to the rogue. He and I had long talks about this subject, and he told me that he would deal with Quinton when we completed our mission and returned home. And if he didn't make it back and I did, he made me promise to handle the matter to the best of my ability. So, I know he would want me to honor that promise."

"I suggest that you think about this, Patrick. It is a serious business to interfere with someone else's home."

Patrick pondered Christian's words for a very long moment. Christian interpreted the startling silence as a possible agreement, but he was wrong.

"Oh, the devil with all that. Where is Quinton? Do you know?"

"He's in London living it up with every woman that willingly will share his bed every night. He spends most days at the hellholes gambling and drinking his miserable life away. On the other hand, Katherine stays away from London and does not accept visitors but for her family and her best friend, Marisa Thornwell."

"Marisa Thornwell?" Patrick muttered. Marisa was the daughter of a viscount and close friend to Patrick's father, Henry Wingham. "I have always liked Marisa. She was a wonderful girl and quite smart if I remember well. Is she married?"

"No, she is quite picky about the man who will share her dreams. She does not put much stock on the rogues who patronize the ballrooms during the busy season."

Patrick sighed. "Good for her."

"It is said that this year will be the busiest season London has ever had. The invitations already have been sent for all the ballroom dances and dinners on the schedule for this year." His eyes moved over to the pile of envelopes on Patricks' desk. "I am sure your invitations are here. Your success in his Highness services and your rank has already made the circle in every household with an available young lady," Christian said, and his gaze swept over Patrick.

He waited quietly, his words still lingering in the air.

Patricks' eyes narrowed, letting displeasure flash across his face. Being paraded in front of matchmaking mothers eager to ensnare a suitable male for their silly giggling daughters made his stomach turn. He moved the glass up to his lips and sipped the remaining brandy slowly.

His deeply buried desire for Katherine, his Kat, raised

SHROUD OF BETRAYAL

its head. Slowly, he rose to his feet, straightened to his full height, and looked at Christian. His features hardened, and his voice turned harsh. "I will walk through the gates of hell to get to the bottom of this, and you better bloody believe it."

Silence returned. Patrick's expression was that of a determined man.

Christian drew a deep breath, rose to his feet, tugged his uniform coat into place, and quietly exited the room shutting the door behind him.

Patrick's fatigue-dulled senses brought out unreasonable anger. Somehow it enveloped him and settled deep into his bones. He was thinking of hurting Quinton. He had no idea how long he paced aimlessly across the floor, never realizing that Christian was gone.

A knock on the door startled him out of his thoughts.

"Come in."

The handle turned, and a young servant stood in the opening. "Dinner is served, my Lord."

Patrick's brows rose quizzically when his eyes fell on the young man. He thought he was familiar with all the people in his staff, but he couldn't place this young man's face. His fingers stroked his chin thoughtfully, trying to recall, but nothing came to him.

"Thank you, er… what is your name, young man?"

"Mathew, my Lord."

"How long have you been working here?"

"A year, my Lord. My father has been in your

employment for what seems centuries," he said with a soft chuckle.

"Oh! Who is your father, Mathew?"

"Christian Walsh, my Lord."

Patrick fell speechless. He bit back the words that rushed to his lips and stared at the young man in astonishment. In all the years he had known Christian, he never knew that he had been married or had children. Pretending to ignore the revelation, he smiled kindly. "Wonderful," he muttered. "Thank you, Mathew; I'll be right down."

When the door closed, Patrick walked over to the settee and picked up his coat. Does Christian have a son? *Why would he ever keep that from me?* Stepping out in the hallway, he shut the door behind him. *How about that? I'll be damned.* Collecting his thoughts away from the last shocking revelation, he descended the main staircase toward the breakfast room.

Christian was standing by the sideboard, Mathew, on his right. Patrick inclined his head and headed in their direction graciously. Nowhere on his face could Christian see any sign of curiosity. At the sideboard, Patrick smiled, a slow, curious smile but did not speak. It was not the right time to discuss Mathew's details, and to his relief, Christian made no effort to address this any further.

Patrick picked up a plate and helped himself, choosing from the rich verity of foods prepared by the cook in his honor. He took a seat and applied himself to his meal, trying to concentrate on Katherine's issue.

Back in his office, he went through his mail and

discarded almost all the invitations that had arrived. He was in no mood for ballrooms and silly chit chat with women of no interest to him.

The afternoon sunlight surged through the open windows and bathed the room in a golden mist of colors; it reflected off the luxurious brocade curtains, the stunning carved giltwood furniture, and the gorgeous French flat-woven 16th century carpet. Patrick finished writing a note to his friends in the Viper group, inviting them to meet at White's after he returned from visiting his parents. With a small frown on his face, his thoughts went back to the secret that Katherine may hold in keeping her father's honor intact. He was sure that he would need their input to solve the mystery, but he was ready for the challenge. He tugged the bell pull by the door and waited for Christian to appear. He handed him the notes and asked to have them delivered. He then went up to his room to get ready for his visit to the solicitor's office.

CHAPTER THREE

$\mathcal{T}$he private hackney with the family crest on the side was waiting at the door. As soon as the door shut, the horses moved forward at a trot. His gaze was fixed unseeingly in front of him. He was thinking of the unexpected turn of events where Katherine was concerned.

Jonathan greeted Patrick joyfully. As his solicitor and friend, he was happy to see Patrick home safe and sound. He appreciated the complete trust that Patrick had bestowed on him for the past six years. After a long warm handshake, a quick hug, and a few lengthy comments about the war and returning home, they settled down to discuss business.

Patrick was pleased to discover that Jonathan had handled his investments wisely. He couldn't stop a joyful smile from spreading across his beautiful face while looking over the investments and returns documentation. Yes, the numbers looked fantastic. Patrick was a very wealthy man. For a moment, words completely escaped him. Finally, he looked up at Jonathan in utter shock. "How did you do this? These are some big numbers."

Jonathan smiled kindly. "Just lucky, I guess, my Lord. I am sorry that I didn't inform you in advance of the big property investments, but I had limited time to accept if I was to move on with the purchase," he continued softly.

"Jonathan!" Patrick exclaimed. "My God, man, you did a fantastic job and, I am extremely pleased."

"You trusted me with your money, and I didn't do anything more than you would have done if you were home."

Patrick's, excitement was palpable. He was going to reward Jonathan generously, but for the moment, he wanted to get into the details and understand all that he owned and all that he had accumulated.

"Oh, by the way," Jonathan said with a smile, "you are now the owner of all the land that borders your parents' and Weldon's estates, my Lord."

Patrick's eyebrows shot up in startled shock. He didn't need Jonathan to elaborate. He was very familiar with the land he was discussing. He finally let out a hearty laugh. "But how did you arrange that?" It was a great deal more he ever expected to find out.

"The man who owned the land decided to give up those meadows and move to Australia. I heard the discussion one evening at White's, and I thought that would be a great opportunity for you to expand your businesses and build a huge manor for your new bride," he added with a chuckle. By business, he meant Patrick's love for horses. He already owned several prizewinners.

"Good God," he heard Patrick saying with a deep chuckle, still staring at the documents. "I'm lost for words, Jonathan." He finally lifted his head and glanced at his solicitor. "You did a fine job, yes, I must say a very wonderful job."

"Have you talked to your parents yet?"

"I sent a message that I will be heading north in a couple of days."

"Will you be paying a visit to William's mother?"

Patrick frowned. "Yes, I plan to send a message once I arrive at Scunthbury."

"That will be wonderful. I am sure there will be many questions for you."

"Yes, that's what I am afraid will happen. Revisiting William's death will be an awful ordeal." The remembrance held him motionless for a short moment.

"I do understand; however, some of the details might provide closure for the family."

Patrick nodded in agreement.

"Well, this visit might allow you to learn more about the properties you now own. I think the land bordering the Quinton Bennett estate is magnificent." At the sound of the name Bennett, tension gripped him, and his gaze met Jonathan's in an awkward stare. The sudden dreadful look in Patrick's eyes shocked the solicitor.

"What is it, my Lord?"

Patrick tried to compose himself. It was the perfect time to discuss the issue with Quinton Bennett. Jonathan was a very well-known and a very well thought of solicitor with great contacts. He might be able to get information that would help him unearth Katherine's secret about her father. The secret that was so vital to her father's honor, the secret that Duke Weldon took to his grave.

He pursed his lips while searching for the right words to begin what he thought might be a strange discussion.

"What is it, my Lord?" Jonathan asked again with great concern and an emphatic tone.

The firm sound of his voice jerked Patrick's thoughts free and glancing up, he found Jonathan studying him quietly, his hands folded over the folders on his desk. He felt like a child caught in a forbidden act.

"I need a favor." He started to talk in an almost monotonous sound. For the next hour, he spoke without stopping, and when finished, he steeled himself. Jonathan was sitting in stunned silence, listening without interrupting.

Patrick cleared his throat. "Well, now, you know everything that I know, and all that William shared with me."

Jonathan's gaze was on Patrick's face. For a very long moment, both men sat looking at each other in absolute silence.

Finally, Jonathan shook his head, sat back on his seat, pulled a handkerchief out of his pant pocket, and removing the spectacles; he blew hot air on each lens slowly. He seemed lost in thought. He then wiped them in the same slow manner and finally placed them back onto his nose.

"I never knew that you were in love with Katherine Weldon, my Lord. Did she know?" his voice was coated with astonishment.

Patrick shifted uncomfortably, all color leaving his face. Did he say that out loud? "Well, don't feel bad. Nobody knew but William and my butler, and I never had the chance to tell Katherine how I felt. But I promised William that if I made it home and he didn't, I would find out why his father approved such a horrid union. I have no intention of going back on my promise."

"What is it that you need from me?"

"I have a suspicion that something happened during Bennett's young friendship days with Weldon that became a secret detriment to Weldon's reputation. It is preposterous that Weldon would approve a union between his one and only daughter to a daft like Quinton. I know that you have many close friends on both sides of the family. Try to find out if, while signing the marriage agreement, something was said in passing. Someone must know the facts, and anything you can uncover will be helpful." Patrick looked distressed. "I will reward you for your time."

"There is no need for that, my Lord. I will look into it." Jonathan agreed to do a little digging and report back. Patrick stood, bringing the meeting to a close.

Upon his return home, he entered the study. On his desk, he set an armful of folders that Jonathan had handed him and headed directly toward the glass cabinet with the visible decanters. He needed to be alone, to think, and most of all, he needed a drink. Reaching for the brandy, he poured a glass. Sipping slowly, he thought back over the day's events. The day had gone just as he had planned, and he was pleased.

Edgy and uneasy, he approached his desk and set his drink aside. He stared down at the new pile of notes with emotionless eyes and grimaced. "Do they ever stop sending these annoying invitations?" he said out loud. "Does anyone ever work, or do they spend every single moment in the ballrooms and soirees?" His thoughts drifted, and he groaned with disdain. War had changed him. He now thought about the less affluent areas and the dark side that existed in London outside the beauty, the money, and prosperity of his peers. Did the ton think the same way? Of course not, they were the privileged ones with only one thought. Spend their lives worried only about jewels, fashion, matchmaking, and ballrooms. They lived in London for the season, and when that was over, and after they had taken what they wanted, they retreated to their numerous country estates to hibernate until the next season.

He reached again for his glass, and taking a sip, he rolled the brandy on his tongue and moaned with appreciation. He had difficulty thinking that he would be able to acclimate to the old kind of London life.

He decided to go through Jonathan's documentation and get himself back into running his businesses. After several hours, he had read every piece of paper and filed it properly in the right place. He wrote notes to his business associates, letting everyone know of his return. He set various times to meet with each one of them. He summoned his head foreman and his accountant to meet with him first thing in the morning. He glanced at the clock on the mantel. Three hours of work. Not bad. His finger rubbed across his lower lip, and satisfaction painted his eyes; he had accomplished more than he expected. Rising to his feet, he pushed the chair back. A long lazy stretch of his legs gave his muscles what they needed. He reached toward the door and pulled the bell cord. Shortly after, Mathew appeared.

"Can I help you, my Lord?"

Patrick handed him the notes. "Please hand these to a footman and have them delivered as soon as possible."

Mathew nodded politely. "Yes, my Lord. Is there anything else?"

"Yes, please have my bath drawn, I should be upstairs shortly."

He thumbed through the new invitations back at his desk and did not find one that held his attention. He pushed the pile off his desk and into the waste bucket with his arm's swift sweep. He carried his glass to his room.

In his chamber, he shrunk out of his jacket and threw it on a chair. After stripping his shirt off, he glanced in the mirror. His body bore the scars of years served behind enemy lines. He sighed, lifted his drink from the side table, and drained the glass.

He sat on the side of the bed and pulled his boots off. His breeches followed with a soft thud on the floor. His bath was ready, and stripped to his skin, he got into the tub. He sunk into the warm water up to his chin, and an enjoyable sound escaped his lips. Heat settled deep into every muscle in his body, and a delightful sensation seized every thought in his mind. His eyes closed in pure satisfaction as he soaked consumed in pure joy. Nearly falling asleep from contentment, he decided to stand and step out from the tub.

Approaching the mirror, he stared at the handsome face with the solid god-like muscled body looking back at him, while he patted himself dry with a fresh towel. He had spent the past six years in the service of His Majesty's government as a secret agent, and he was happy to be home alive. He fell into bed, anxious to get a couple of hours of sleep before dinner. Kat's vision came rushing in, leaving him unnerved. He couldn't stop thinking of her. What did she look like now? Did she ever think of him? Did she even care about him at all? So many questions, so few answers. Hopelessness hung like a weight on his shoulders.

He finally started to relax, and just as he reached the cusp of sleep, he was shaken awake by a sudden and strange thought. He sat up in bed, running his hands through his hair, looking distressed. How is it possible that Quinton did not force himself on Kat in the five years of marriage? He had every right as a husband to consummate their union with or without her consent.

An anguished groan escaped him. He was now completely awake. It was becoming a very complicated puzzle, with most of the pieces missing. Katherine must have been holding something above Quinton's head that he did not want exposed. What in the hell was that? So many secrets!

He dressed and went back to his study to review a

couple of documents from Jonathan before dinner. Sleep was now out of the question.

At the dining-room door, he hesitated. Still reeling with incredibly disturbing emotions, he was not hungry, but he needed to eat something. As usual, he found Christian and Mathew waiting. He smiled, inclined his head politely, and after heaping his plate at the sideboard, he sat down. "Anything new?" he asked Christian without looking up.

The butler knew just what he was referring to, but he did not show it. "What are you referring to, my Lord?" Christian chose to address him as my Lord while other servants were present.

Patrick took a bite while a footman filled his glass with wine and looked up, meeting Christian's gaze. Both men stared at each other, neither of them speaking. Strangely enough, Mathew witnessed a silent exchange between his father and Patrick. He was surprised to hear his father answering, "No, I'm sorry, my lord, there's nothing new." What did his father mean by that?

Patrick nodded and continued eating. After clearing his plate and draining his wine glass, he stood. "I'm going to the library to read for a while before bed. Please have someone bring me tea." He couldn't wait for the night to be over. The next day, he would dive right into the business matters and forget about Kat. Walking down the hallway, he laughed out loud at the thought.

CHAPTER FOUR

*B*efore dawn the next morning, he met with his head foreman Jason Bates as planned. Together, they rode out to one of his estates north of London where he kept his prize thoroughbreds. The vast land lay in a beautiful, lush location, across the bridge of a broad river, with endless green pastures racing to meet the sky as far as the eye could see. The view of the meadow caught his breath. He had almost forgotten the beauty and the tranquility of the place. His eyes wandered, amazed by the sights in this limitless space.

Jason's voice brought him back to reality. "Beautiful, isn't it, my Lord?"

"Yes, I almost forgot the beauty of it."

"Six years is a long time, my Lord."

Patrick nodded in agreement as he turned the curricle toward the stables. He wanted to see his thoroughbreds and particularly, his own grey Pegasus. When left in Jason's capable hands, Pegasus was ten years old, and Patrick was curious about how time had changed him. He loved his horse more than any other possession, but he prepared himself that he wouldn't be able to ride him as hard as he had six years earlier.

The stables, set in the shape of a horseshoe with a large barn in the center for hay storage, were well-kept. The large courtyard buzzed with activity. Young hands moved swiftly between the barn and the various stables carrying hay, while others mounted horses to ride for their daily exercise. The beautiful animals were led out of the yard in a slow trot, and soon they were in a full gallop heading away from Patrick and Jason and across the green meadows. What a fabulous sigh that had never seemed more appealing to Patrick than it was today.

Stepping down from the curricle, he threw the reins to an apprentice and headed toward the main stable with Jason by his side. Several stable lads were dismounting and guiding their charges back to their stalls. Patrick smiled, pleased with the way things were running. When he entered, he headed straight for a particular part of the stable. He paused to watch a young apprentice struggling to hold a horse's hoof so he could pick the dirt manure and stones from the frog's side. He succeeded but not without great difficulty. Patrick chuckled inwardly and resumed his walk until he reached a beautiful box stall. There waited one of the most amazing greys. Patrick smiled wide in utter pleasure.

Pegasus did not look a day older, sending Patrick's heart racing. Entering the stall, he called for his horse eagerly. "Hey, Pegasus! I hope you didn't forget me." The heavily muscled stallion reacted immediately to the familiarity of his voice in the most affectionate way. He gently brought his head close and tried to bury his nose under Patrick's arm as a low soft nickering sound escaped him. Patrick put his arms around his head and hugged him. He then patted him softly, ran his right palm across his side with reassuring strokes, while leaning gently into him; he fed him a big carrot that he was carrying in his left hand.

Man and horse shared a strong bond. Before Patrick left for France, he had ridden him across the lush meadows of his estate. He was hoping to mount him today and ride him hard to bring back the enormous pleasure he vividly recalled.

Jason was standing at the stable door, hands on his hips, giving Patrick time to enjoy his reunion with Pegasus. He finally gave the horse a fond pat and called for Jason to have a man get him ready for a ride around the property. Stepping out of the stall, he heard a loud nickering sound coming from a booth behind him. He swung around, and his mouth dropped, his heart skipped a beat. It can't be, but he was darn sure that he was looking at the eyes of a young horse that he had purchased three months before he left for France. There was a birthmark right below his right eye, an unmistakable mark.

A stable lad stood by his side, stroking his long neck, preparing him for his daily exercise. Patrick watched him, never taking his eyes off the horse. The boy put the saddle pad on and gently set the saddle on the horse's back. He fastened the strap on both sides. He put the girth on safely and made sure the saddle was secure. While Jason led Pegasus out of the stall, Patrick strode forward and approached the stallion. He was a large thoroughbred from Arabian ancestors, just like Pegasus. He remembered giving him the name Scout. He chuckled out loud, thinking that Scout had tried to get his attention. Did he remember him? Maybe his voice, but the fact was that the horse had tried to get his attention.

With his head raised, his ears pricked forward, Scout kept making low nickering noses. The boy moved to the side; Scout gently lowered his head and touched Patrick's shoulder. Patrick reached around and stroked his silky neck several times and then petted his head and nose. Reaching into this pocket, he pulled another carrot. Scout let out a soft nicker of pleasure and started to chew on it. When finished, he buried his head under Patrick's arm with a louder nicker. Patrick chuckled out loud. "You remember me, Scout, you remember me..." The boy watched with wide eyes, He did not know who the gentleman was and or the connection between him and the horse.

He patted Scout on the side and let the boy take him out. At the door, Jason was waiting with Pegasus, all ready to go.

"Do you want me to ride along?"

"No, I think I'll do this alone." Patrick wanted this ride to be the old connection between him and his horse and find the companion and solace they once had. Grasping the girth, he vaulted onto the saddle. He trotted out of the

54

courtyard and moved into a canter. Once he cleared the working area, he dug in his heels, and Pegasus took off like thunder. Gliding through breathtaking scenery, he had a complete sense of freedom and total control of his own life. Pegasus was just as strong as he was six years earlier and did not show any signs of fatigue.

Patrick felt the horse's power while ripping through the fields at high speed with nothing in his mind but the sound of Pegasus' mighty hoofs hitting the ground. Even at that speed, his visual perception of space around him was acute. The beautiful, lush meadows dotted with wildflowers, and his lips kicked up with pleasure. Taken by the beauty of the place and the incredible feeling of joy that engulfed every inch of his body, he lost track of time. Suddenly, in the distant recess of his mind, the memory of a beautiful face stirred, too significant not to catch and hold. His heartbeat increased and plunged him into a ridiculous fluster. Jaw clenched, and eyes narrowed at Katherine's intrusion into his thoughts, with her unfathomable situation made him decide to go back. His mount thundered across the meadows. The air rushed fresh and clear to brush his young face, and he urged Pegasus to go faster.

A couple of hundred yards before he reached the buildings, he let Pegasus have the last prance before settling and guiding him into the stable yard. Bending down, he patted the silky neck and whispered soft words of praise. He jumped off the horse with ease and grabbing the reins, he handed them off to the lad who waited. Looking for Jason, he turned toward the other side of the buildings and blinked against the bright sunshine. Jason was leaning against the west wall, waiting patiently for his boss. Patrick walked toward him exchanging no more than brief nods and a few words with the other lads walking their stalls' charges. He recognized most of them, but not all. Jason had done a fantastic job with the place. New hands had been hired while he was in France. He was delighted.

"How was the ride?" Jason called out with a chuckle.

"Better than I expected," Patrick said with uncontrollable enthusiasm.

"Are you ready to head back, my Lord?"

"Yes, I need to check on a few things and prepare to visit my parents."

"Do they know that you are home?"

"Yes, I sent a note with a messenger, and mother is anxious to see me."

"Well, I know that the whole family has missed you."

Patrick hmphed with a soft smile.

"It will be a great reunion." Jason followed up his first statement in a soft voice.

"Yes, I expect it to be grand, as both my brothers will be home from school. I have missed them all so very much, and to tell you the truth, I thought, I would never make it home alive."

On the way to the curricle, he raised his arms toward the sky and gave a silent thank you for arriving home safely.

"You will find that Scunthbury has not changed in the last six years," Jason stated.

"I was praying for that, as I am not happy with the changes I have found."

"Are you speaking of Lady Bennett?"

"Please do not use that name when you address Katherine." Patrick's voice was stern.

Jason nodded and fell quiet. He realized that Lady Bennett was a sore subject of discussion for Patrick and could not shake the impression that the worst was to come.

The ride back was business talk and heartfelt laughter at Jason's stories. By the time they reached home, Patrick was sure that he had not missed a single thing in the six years that he had been gone. The curricle slowed as they entered the large gate of the estate.

"Is there anything else I can do for you before I go?" Jason asked.

"Yes, please make sure that you bring Pegasus and Scout to the stables here. I want to make sure that I ride them often." Jason nodded.

He withdrew to his office after a warm bath and late dinner. He planned to look over the estate's papers, including the bills paid and the ones due. His solicitor and foreman had both done a fantastic job keeping his property and financial affairs in a perfect state. Silence reigned heavy around him, and uneasiness settled deep in his bones at the thought of meeting Kat.

He shook his head and picked up the daily post that

Christian had left on his desk with all the ton's updates. He stared at the page, but he didn't see a single word; his mind was already far from that room.

He relaxed back in his large leather chair, let the post drop to his lap, and closed his eyes. A sudden chill surged at the thought of his upcoming confrontation with Quinton, and his reflections stuttered to a stop. Then they moved and changed into a new direction. It was tempting to end Quinton's life in some way, but how? He was sure that it was unwise to jump to such a drastic conclusion and lose his perspective, but he would have to resolve it. He was not sure when exactly that would take place, but it was a must. He was fulfilling a promise to his late best friend. The next time he opened his eyes, moonlight was washing in through the windows. He stood up and lit a lamp and proceeded to pace back and forth across the room, trying to figure out how to end Kat's marriage. Beneath his breath, he cursed. He needed to learn all the arranged marriage details and the secret held by both Weldon and Bennett.

A tap at the door brought him to the present. "Come," he called out.

Christian walked in. "Are you all right, my boy?"

Patrick nodded. "I'm all right."

"Will you stay up much longer, or should I have them prepare your chambers?

"I will be going to bed shortly," he replied and walked back to his desk and let his fingers wrap around a small leather-covered book. He stared at the title, The Sorrows of Young Werther by Johann Wolfgang Von Goethe. He had started to read the book in France but never finished it. He brought it home, and he was now determined to see it to its completion.

In his chamber with a glass of brandy in hand, he paced before the fireplace. The house was utterly silent; everyone had retired. He was sure that if he had laid down, sleep was out of the question; he was so apprehensive about his thoughts. He could not get Kat out of his mind; it was as if she was commanding his thoughts to exclude everything else around him. He was trying to make sense of his unrest. How was he going to behave sensibly in her presence? Brows furrowed, jaw tightening, he kept pacing on, verbalizing in a low voice what he would say when they were face to face. Taking a sip of brandy, he stared out into the night. After a short quiet moment, he moved to the center of the room.

Finally, he lay in bed, hands behind his head, covers to his waist, and let his gaze travel toward the window. With the curtains pulled wide open, the moonlight bathed the room with a silver glow. He was sure that the earth would be a dismal place without its bright light as the night moved on invisibly across the sky. Each day was a different version of itself. His eyes moved back inside the room and stared at the various shapes created on the ceiling. The corners of his mouth kicked up. He was content being home. Ignoring the facts of Kat's situation. Eventually, his focus shifted from Kat back on the book resting on the nightstand. He reached for it, opened to the page with the corner folded back, and started to read in the lamp's dim light. Somewhere in the middle of those pages, he fell asleep.

The bedroom door was shut. Christian, his butler, knocked several times, but there was no answer. He held an important message in his hands, and he needed to get it to Patrick as soon as possible. It was of extreme importance the messenger had said then left without saying anything further. Christian waited a few more minutes behind the closed chamber door, and finally, he decided to turn the knob and enter quietly. The room was full of sunshine as the curtains were still wide open. Patrick was fast asleep on the huge bed; the open book resting on his chest. He approached with fast strides, but Patrick did not move a muscle. Leaning over him, he put his hand on his shoulder and shook him lightly and then more stridently. Patrick woke with a start. He turned, and his eyes met Christian's impassive look.

"What's wrong?" he asked sheepishly.

"It is a message for you, my boy; it is of great importance. You must read it right away."

"Well, go ahead and open it. You know I do not hide anything from you."

"Christian opened the envelope and took out a small piece of paper. He read it and frowned.

"Well?"

"It is your father."

"My father?"

"Yes, he has taken gravely ill, and your mother has

called for you." Patrick moved quickly, threw the covers away from his body, and stood up. He looked lost for a very long moment, and finally, he spoke slowly.

"I was planning on leaving tomorrow. I will be on my way shortly."

Christian reached over and patted him on the back. "Stay strong my boy."

Patrick shook his head without turning. "Please tell Jason to get Pegasus ready to go as soon as possible," he said again in a low voice.

When the door closed, he sat back down and dropped his head onto his hands in despair. He wished that his mother had mentioned that his father was ill. His father was the cornerstone of their home and his hero. His love shaped who Patrick was as a person. He could not bear the thought of losing him. A sudden thought made him groan inwardly. At the age of twenty-nine, he knew his responsibilities to his title better than anyone, but the mere idea of replacing his father made him utterly sick. "No!" he screamed. "Father has to get better."

It was still early in the morning when he walked out the door. Pegasus was waiting in the front courtyard. The fog was dense, and a light wind blew a cold mist across his face. He shivered and tugged his coat tightly about him. His boots reverberated on the cobblestones; he reached Pegasus at a fast pace. He looked up at his beloved horse and ran his hand firmly across his neck in a reassuring and warm pace. He spoke quietly to the horse. "Good morning, old friend, are you ready to go?" As if Pegasus knew what Patrick had said, he moved his head up and down and let out a soft nicker showing his affection. Patrick vaulted to the saddle with ease, and once outside the estate gate, he cued Pegasus. Soon they were moving in a full gallop. The ground shook below his hoofs as he stretched out into an intense run. As an excellent rider, he nudged his horse to move on even faster.

Patrick's thoughts were overwhelming, but it was hard not to notice that the fog was breaking, and a magical sunrise was coming through, brightening the long road with the steep hills that made it for a beautiful ride. He tried to avoid the midday heat by using some shaded trails, making it easy for Pegasus and himself. They rode through wooded areas and splendid white riverbeds. The scenery was spectacular.

CHAPTER FIVE

*I*t was still daytime when he drew to a halt on the cobblestones in front of the elegant mansion in Scunthbury. He took in his surroundings in one glance. The front door flung open, and a man hurried down the stairs. "Welcome home, my boy," he called out, his voice a mixture of pleasure and sadness." Patrick's gaze roamed his old home's walls and came to rest on Jacob's grim face, his parents' butler. The man who along, with Christian, raised him from the time he was in short pants. Patrick held his impossibly sad gaze for a moment and taking a deep breath; he smiled grimly.

"Hello, Jacob." He kicked free of the stirrups and dismounted.

"When did this come about?"

"He fell ill two days ago, and he has been bedridden since then."

"Are the twins home?"

"Yes, they arrived yesterday and are taking care of the house affairs so your mother can be with your father." Patrick nodded and remained silent.

"You did not bring any luggage," Jacob said with surprise.

"A footman is bringing all that I need later this evening. I wanted to ride Pegasus for a while," he said and patted the horse lovingly.

Jacob grabbed the reins and led Pegasus towards the stables where he motioned for a stable lad.

When Jacob turned back, Patrick still stood outside the house, staring at the grey walls as if he was experiencing some type of exchange between the grey stone and himself. "Patrick," Jacob's voice shook him out of his thoughts. "I am so happy to see you back home, boy."

"I am glad to be home," he replied and took Jacob in a warm hug. "How is father today?"

"No change."

"Patrick!!!" He turned toward the sound and noticed two tall figures running toward him. He smiled wide and opened his arms to take both of his brothers in a warm hug. After a long and quiet moment, he pulled back and ran his gaze over the handsome faces watching him with so much love and warmth. "I am so happy that you both are here," he said, "and mother has your support."

"We would not have it any other way," Anthony said. They climbed the front steps and walked arm and arm toward the open door.

He was hailed by his mother's voice as soon as he crossed the threshold. "Patrick!" A small-framed beautiful woman dressed in a blue muslin gown ran across the large foyer and fell into her son's open arms. Patrick held her tightly, overwhelmed by the love he held for his mother. He had missed her more than life itself over the past six years. While in France, Patrick became a firm believer that this moment was never going to happen. He put his finger under her chin and raised her face to his. His smile faded at the sadness that held her blue eyes, and that shocked him deeply. He had looked into these eyes for as long as he could remember and always saw love, warmth, and kindness that assured him safety and contentment. Her eyes were the mirror of his soul and helped see who he was becoming as he was growing up. Helped him understand his place in the world and his purpose in life. Now, staring at the pure sadness in them, he felt lost and unable to comprehend.

She was sad over the man who stood firm and unbending by her side, her best friend and the love of her life. She turned aside to hide the pain upon her face, and her arms tightened around her son, needing his support. His soul shuddered, unable to accept the pain she was going through. "He is not doing well," she said in a soft broken voice, and her eyes flickered the fear of losing the man who stood firm and unbending by her side for thirty-three glorious years.

Slowly, they walked toward the main staircase. Climbing each step at a snail pace.

When in his parents' chambers, he looked around. Nothing was changed. The room was plush with exquisite artwork on the walls. Eloquent dark furnishings filled the empty spaces with heavy draperies floor to ceiling over the large windows. The drapes pulled wide open, let the daylight bathe the room and give it a brighter look. He helped his mother to a chair next to the bed and approached. The face he saw did not reflect the picture he held in his head. The apparent effects of age struck him. His father looked a lot older than his age, and the pale color of his cheeks made him look even older. He was breathing slowly, in an irregular way that might signal that the end is near. Patrick felt weak on his feet and grasped for support of one of the bed columns and gave a low cry. "Father!"

His eyes opened and stared at his son, impassively. Suddenly he smiled. Perhaps it was a hallucination that caused it; maybe it was a flicker of awareness like lightning in a dim sky. His lips moved, but there was no sound. Patrick knew that he recognized him and smiled back.

"Hello Father, I'm home." He neither stirred nor spoke. Within a few seconds, his features seemed to have collapsed into further blankness.

Patrick's heart filled with terror of emptiness. Memories of his father that crossed his mind gave him a painful jab of sensation, but he quickly shoved it aside. For a moment, he stood still, pressing his fists against his temples. He pulled a chair up next to his father's side and turned toward his mother. He cleared his throat. "Has doctor Hamilton been here?"

"Yes, he left about two hours ago."

"What did he say?"

"He said that your father is suffering from influenza. His cough was bad for the first two days, but today is a lot better. However, the fever comes and goes creating confusion and delirium."

"What else did he say? Is he going to recover?"

"We need to watch and wait. Some forms of this influenza can be hazardous, he could not give me any good or bad news. So, I'm still hopeful, but I hate to see your father suffer this way. Patrick, I do not want to lose him," she murmured and started to sob quietly. He ran a hand through his hair, and a flash of frustration crossed his face. He stared at the small wrinkles around her mouth, and something shook deep inside of him. Her face was ashen, almost grey. She turned her blue eyes toward the open window and stared at the blue sky as if in prayer, then at him. "I did not want anything to interfere with your homecoming. This union should have been a joyous one and not this…" she mumbled and turned to look at her husband who was now sleeping peacefully and showing no discomfort.

Patrick smiled, "Don't worry, Mother, there will be plenty of time for celebrations." The next few moments were utterly silent.

He remained next to his father for a couple of hours but very little was said. The room environment, the air in the house, the somberness, the loss of his father's powerful and lively presence seemed to alarm him, but he said nothing.

"Patrick," his mother shook him out of his deep thoughts. Silence followed her word, and his eyebrows arched just a fraction. The words spun around her for a moment as she tried to stand up. He looked at his mother and noticed her searching for something to support her.

Small black spots started to creep over her vision. Sinking back down to her chair, she looked weak and lost. Patrick sprung to his feet and grabbed her hand.

"Mother, what's wrong?"

"I am not sure, I just felt dizzy for a moment."

"Please let us go downstairs and have something to eat. When was the last time you ate?" She shook her head unable to remember and so remained silent. Patrick helped her out of the chair, his arm around her waist for support; he guided her toward the second-floor landing corridor.

"Father will be fine," he reassured her. "You need your strength." His mother nodded in agreement.

Patrick called for Sabrina, his mother's chambermaid, and asked her to sit with his father while taking his mother to the dinning-room.

When downstairs, he guided her into the dining room. At the table, he took a seat across from her and smiled softly. "It will be fine, Mother," He said reassuringly and watched her pick downward at her plate. It was but a few moments later, and his brothers walked in, taking their places at the table.

"Where have you been?" he asked, observing them.

The twins looked at each other, and as if they had their way of communicating, Christopher spoke up. "Anthony and I have been taking care of the house affairs while he is bedridden."

Patrick smiled wide, letting them know that he was pleased for their actions.

"I find that commendable. How is school coming along?"

"We are almost done," Anthony chimed in. There was one semester left.

"That is fantastic!" Patrick exclaimed. "I am so very proud of you both."

"We would like to hear some of your stories from the war when you get a moment," Christopher said.

Patrick nodded in agreement.

Through the various courses served, the conversation drifted between multiple topics. They all kept the talk away from their father's issue, and by the end of the meal, their mother seemed to be a bit more relaxed. A half an hour later, they were standing in the drawing room with a cup of tea.

Cup and saucer in hand, their mother moved toward the open window. It was getting darker, but there was still plenty of daylight left. She was leaning against the window frame, and her eyes roamed the beautiful gardens. Somehow without her husband next to her, they did not seem as picturesque. She felt her boys' gaze on her, and she turned to face them.

"I am so happy that you came home alive," his mother said, taking a sip, her eyes on Patrick. "Your father, brothers, and I were so worried about you, especially after receiving the news about William." At the mention of William's name, Patrick frowned, something clutched his chest, and he denied the impulse to clear his throat. Three pairs of eyes on him caught the change on his face, and they studied him for a long moment. Patrick wanted to discuss his concerns about Kat's marriage more than the war, but he realized this was the wrong moment and remained silent after a brief hesitation. By the time they returned to his parents' chambers, his mother was renewed and lively.

Later, he found himself standing in the middle of his chambers and stared in awe. It looked the same as he left it six years earlier. Not a single thing was out of place. His mother made sure that nothing changed in the room while he was away. His lips kicked up at his mother's thoughtfulness, and his eyes traveled around the familiar furnishings. He notices his luggage had arrived. He sat on the bed and took his boots off, letting his feet sink into the thick carpet's softness sprawled on the floor. Jacob had drawn his bath, so after stripping his clothes off, he sank into the hot water tub and, leaning back, closed his eyes appreciatively.

He had no idea how long he had been in the tub, and it had been as if time was nonexistent. He sat upright for a short moment and pushed himself to his feet, stepping out of the tub and onto the floor. He felt rested and renewed. He threw the towel over his body and walked back into the bedroom. He stood in front of the large mirror; the man looking back was handsome with slightly grey hair on either side of his temples.

He smiled, knowing that he was home. Letting the

towel drop to the floor, he flapped onto the bed and stifled a frustrating gasp. He felt tired and overwhelmed with pain tagging at his heart. "No!" he said out loud, and his voice startled him. "He has to get better; he must get better." He ran his hands through his hair and frowned unintentionally. Even though out of his hands, his father's health would have to be now his only concern.

He lay unmoved on the soft bed, wondering what he could do to make the situation better. It was hard to face the reality that the man who stood virtually indestructible for as long as he could remember was lying helpless. He let his tired head fall back on the pillow and closed his eyes.

The majority of that night, he lay awake, his head filled with a plethora of concerns. The next thought was that of Kat, and as painful as it felt, it would have to take a back seat until his home was back to normal. Normal? What was normal? He tried to analyze the word and concluded that "normal" was his father well and in charge of this home again. This type of outcome was out of his hands; however, he felt positive that things would work out. Somewhere in the midst of all these thoughts, he fell asleep.

He woke the next morning with renewed enthusiasm that this was to be a better day than yesterday. The curtains had been pulled aside, and the room was bathed in sunshine. The weather seemed to remain gloriously beautiful. He was ready to accept things as they came and stay calm and supportive. Over breakfast, he found out that the doctor was on his way, and he looked forward to their meeting.

To his pleasant surprise, the doctor found his father

slightly better but not out of the woods. He returned later in the afternoon and followed up with the shots and the treatment he provided.

It was a routine that kept up for the next two weeks. Soon, Patrick was able to sit by his father's bed and carry on small conversations. He was getting better with each day that passed, and that made him very happy. He would stay for as long as it took to support his mother and see his father back on his feet fully well.

It had been thirty days since he arrived in his childhood home. His father was back to his old self. It was the first time that the whole family sat at the dinning-room table and held a lively conversation. The footmen brought dishes domed in silver filled with venison, roasted fowl, and various vegetables. They served portions to each plate and retreated, their footsteps fading in the thick carpet.

"You are nine and twenty now, Patrick, have you thought of marriage?" Patrick tensed at the sound of his father's words.

"I am sure many mothers out there would like their giggly daughters to have a crack at you." The twins barked a startled laugh, and their eyes turned on Patrick, but he remained silent for a long moment and thankful that his father said no more on that subject.

"So, my boy, will you be staying with us for a while, or are you going back to London?" His father changed the subject.

"I thought I'd stay for a few more days; I need to do things before I go. "

"Things such as what?" His father's voice coated by curiosity.

Patrick could barely contain his desire to talk about Kat. For a moment, his eyes searched his father's. He strummed his fingertips across the tabletop, and suddenly, he stood up. He paced the dining-room and revealed how tense he felt, and perhaps looked. Concealing his emotions had always been his strength, so why was he unable to do it now.

"What is it? Something bothering you?"

"I am sorry, Father; I do not know how to start; it is a serious topic," he muttered, casting his eyes to the ceiling and inhaling sharply. In the silence that followed, they could all hear the clock over the fireplace ticking away minutes.

"Start at the beginning, and let's find out what is so bothersome," his father finally replied to his bold statement. "Can we talk privately in your study?"

"Oh, that serious." His eyes turned to his lovely wife and smiled in adoration. "Olivia, please leave us," he said. She returned his smile and pushed her chair graciously, away from the table. "You too," his father continued turning his gaze toward the twins. They both frowned and opened their mouths to say something, but their father continued quickly. "I know that you have a lot to do." Without a word, they stood up and followed their mother out of the dining-room.

"Will this do?" his father asked watching Patrick carefully.

"No, I would rather hold this discussion in private," he raked his fingers through his hair, and his glace traveled around the room from one helping hand to another as they buzzed around them, moving plates, left-over food, and dinner articles. His father followed his gaze and nodded in agreement.

They walked down the hall and into his father's library. The room was rich in French furnishings, thick carpeting, and draped in upholstery with various burgundy shades, dark blue, and gold. High cherry wood shelves stretched up to the vaulted ceilings filled with books. A beautiful fireplace sat along the back wall with two chairs placed before it with a table in between. A large floor-to-ceiling window adorned the north wall to allow plenty of light to bathe the room but the curtains were closed. Finally, an elegant window seat covered in luxurious burgundy fabric completed the décor. He inclined his head slightly, remembering that the library always gave him a sense of solace and peace as a young man. He shook off the recollections of his childhood with an affectionate smile. He glared at the clock on the mantel across the room. It was still early evening. Before he moved, he threw the door shut behind them. He crossed the floor in large strides and pulled the curtains wide open.

"Would you like a drink?"

He didn't move from his place before the window at his father's voice. Instead he stared out at the planet's miracle. The sun had dipped below the horizon turning the sky grey.

The moon appeared a bald silver saucer half-lit by the dipping sun, and it was now moving slowly across the sky, bathing the back lawn in a dreamlike radiance. His father clapped a hand on his shoulder as he joined him and followed his gaze. "Would you like a drink?" he repeated.

"Yes, please," he replied appreciatively.

A few minutes later, his father handed him a glass of bourbon. "All right, Patrick, we are alone, do you want to tell me what is going on in that head of yours?"

CHAPTER SIX

"*F*ather, I promised William that if he did not make it back home, I would have to resolve a significant secret."

"What kind of secret?"

"I must find out the reasons behind the decision made by his father to give his sister away to a man like Quinton. He felt that she was a sacrificial lamb for something his father was trying to hide. And that something had to be a horrible secret. Would you know that secret?" Patrick turned away from the window and faced his father.

"I'm not sure I understand your question."

"Let me ask you another way. I know that you and Duke Weldon were best friends from your early years and through university. You two built a strong brotherhood that would be very hard to destroy. I also know that Quinton's father was very close to both of you. What happened between you three? There are plenty of rumors out there, but I want you to hear it from you. There has to be a reasonable explanation."

Patrick stared at him as his father turned away, but not before the son saw a flash of uneasiness. He pursed his lips, swallowing uncomfortably, and turned back to face his son. His gaze had sharpened, and his jaw clenched. He held in a deep breath and took a step back. "What is the purpose of your question? How could my broken friendship with Alexander Bennett answer your concern about Katherine's marriage?"

"Father, you have to admit that it is strange for Duke Weldon to agree to such a horrible union between his only precious daughter and a rake like Quinton. He is not fit to marry a lady. He is not fit to marry any decent woman. Something is amiss." "And I am asking you again, how do you relate this to my broken friendship with Bennett?"

"The rumor is that a deep secret exists between you, Weldon, and Alexander Bennett. That secret forced Weldon to succumb to this unreasonable request by Alexander to have Kat marry his son Quinton."

"Kat?" his father's voice was that of surprise.

His reaction to the sound of her name was instantaneous. The rush of blood, the sudden pounding of his heart, and tensing of his muscles were apparent. He gritted his teeth against the nervousness that coursed down his spine. "Yes, Kat," Patrick added, deeply annoyed by the question. "Kat Weldon, the girl I have been in love with for as long as I can remember."

Duke Wingham's eyes widened as he was struck by the

force of Patrick's words. His voice rang with surprise. "You were in love with Katherine Weldon?"

In intense frustration, he scowled at his father. "She was the love of my life, Father. She was the woman I wanted to spend the rest of my life with, the woman I wanted to bear my children."

Duke Wingham could feel anxiety-emanating from Patrick's eyes. His profound words reverberated through him. He narrowed his eyes and searched his son's face. "Why did you not say anything for God's sake, why did you not ask for her hand before you left for France?"

Patrick hauled in a deep breath, and his jaw firmed. His gaze seemed distant, fixed in the past. He turned away from his father and stood still in front of the window and looked out in silence.

Duke Wingham lifted his glass and peered into its depths as if he could read his son's answer. It suddenly occurred to him that he might be assuming too much, so he asked again. "Patrick, why did you not ask for her hand before you left for France?"

Turning, he met his father's gaze levelly. "Because I was sure that I would never see England again. We all knew the odds when we joined. I did not want Kat to become a widow at such a young age."

Resisting the temptation to agree unequivocally with his son, the duke continued. "Based on your decision, my boy, she was free to marry whomever she chose. You do not have the right to interfere with another man's wife."

"Father, you know this as well as any man in the ton. Quinton is a rake and a womanizer concealed beneath his sophisticated exterior. Everyone down to the help has recollections of outrageous exploits. His reputation was sufficiently enshrined in the ton's matchmakers to render him ineligible as a candidate for any available female. So how can he land a lady such as Katherine as his wife? This marriage is a joke."

Duke Wingham's brows rose, his expression stern. "Yes, I have heard it all. But your mother and I chose to stay out of Weldon's business. Katherine is a married woman now, Patrick, and you have no right to interfere in their life whether you and William agreed with that decision or not."

Dropping into an armchair, Patrick drew a deep breath and closed his eyes in sheer frustration. Faced with his son's exasperation, the Duke remained silent.

"I made a promise to William," he said, opening his eyes and waving his hand in the air, "and I am going to see it through. My issue with this marriage concerns a hidden secret. I am sure that this secret was scandalous and would have devastated her father's life if he had not gone along with this ridiculous marriage." His father sighed and looked away. Minutes ticked past. Finally, with a long-suffering groan, Patrick rose and took a few steps to stand directly before his father. "I came to you because Duke Weldon is not with us any longer. I know that he was your best friend. I also know that something terrible happened that broke that brotherly bond with Alexander Bennett. If you do not give me any answers, I will have to rely on my war brothers. Our experience will provide the answers I need to get to the bottom of this."

The moment stretched, and Duke Wingham's face

planes shifted. His expression held a certain uneasiness. He made his way over to the liquor cabinet, picked up the decanter, and filled up his glass. He stared at the liquid for a very long time before taking a sip and stood there in quiet contemplation. "Fair enough," he finally muttered as he swirled his drink around. He took a seat behind his desk and motioned for Patrick to take the chair across from him. Patrick eyed him carefully. The Duke simply looked across the room, drew breath, and started to speak, recalling the facts as they took place.

"It was a long time ago. Gregory Weldon, Alexander Bennett, and I lived together while in college. We were of the same age and best friends. We had created a bond between us that would last until the end of time. So we thought. We spent most of our time at the library studying for tests and raising hell at James Street. White's was the place to eat, drink, and gamble, not much different than today. On one of those nights, Gregory and I were gambling when a footman approached with a note. I must say that at first, we did not pay much attention. He set the letter on the table in front of us and walked away. We just stared at it for a very long moment without opening it. But as the minutes ticked by, I noticed Gregory's eyes pinned on the small piece of paper.

"'What do you suppose this is all about?' he asked, curiosity coating his voice. "I shook my head and just shrugged my shoulders. We went back to gambling, and another hour passed. I guess by then that note had pricked our curiosity. I finally picked it up and turned it back and forth to see a name, but it was anonymous. I flipped it open and saw an address where we were to meet someone who held information. At first, we decided to ignore the note, and we continued with our game. Suddenly, thunder boomed over the noise bringing a short silence to the room and our attention back to the letter. I am not sure why, but a strange chill snaked down my spine. Gregory and I looked at each other as several more thunder booms followed, and it sounded like the doors of hell were about to let loose."

The Duke paused as if gathering his facts, putting his thoughts in order. "The meeting was to take place at midnight, and we decided to go. We summoned a carriage and gave him the designated location. We arrived as the storm unleashed its wrath. When the carriage rocked to a halt, we pushed aside the curtain covering the window; we peered out and noticed that the house looked dark and unoccupied. We found that strange, but our curiosity was already at an all-time high. Just as we stepped down, lightning flashed across the sky, lighting up the darkness around us. I leaned into the door and told the driver to wait for us as lighting flashed once again, and we noticed a man standing by the gate under a cover. It was dark, and we could not make out the face. Lengthening his stride, he closed the distance between us, and we stiffened with surprise if not shock. The man was Alexander.

"'What the hell are you doing here?' I heard Gregory's voice next to me.

"'I received a note saying that I am to meet someone at

this house because they have important information for me. What are you doing here? He repeated.'

"'We received the same letter,' I replied." Patrick noticed that his father's expression had grown grimmer.

"The three of us walked through the gate, ignoring the rain that had started to pick up strength. Our eyes swept over the darkness, trying to penetrate the shadows. Quickly, we climbed the steps and knocked at the door. We waited for a very long moment as the wind suddenly rose in force, filling the night with a terrifying sound. Soon we heard footsteps approaching. A young man opened the door and stepping aside; he motioned for us to enter. We followed him through a very poorly lit foyer and up a staircase. The stairs were narrow and turned at a left angle to the top floor. We walked down a long hallway that gradually led to a large study. The light in that room was much better, and when the man reached a desk, he turned around and raised his head. He could not have been more than nineteen, if that old. Our eyes locked on him as he took a step back and moved behind the desk. He was quivering with what seemed an effort to remain in control. The storm suddenly subsided, we could not hear thunder any longer, and the wind had ceased to blow. The night became still, and the room eerily silent. Unexpectedly, Gregory called out.

"'Well, we are here. What do you want?'

"The young man did not draw his gaze from the three of us. He reached into his coat and pulled out a pile of notes. We stared at the papers inquisitively.

"'What the hell are those?' Gregory snapped, pointing at the papers. The young man's eyes darkened. His voice came out colder than a bitter chill. There was steel beneath his words.

"'I know that the three of you have been selling betting notes for innocuous men and manipulating the results and the monies to your favor,' he said coolly.

"I looked at the others and saw the shock mirrored on their faces. My breath seized, my lips tightened, my heart sped up, and I am sure Gregory and Alex felt the same way. The young man's voice was now louder, and his anger palpable.

"'You were the only ones collecting the gains,' he shouted with rage. An instant of silence followed as we stared in shocked surprise. 'You destroyed lives, and you do not seem to care,' he added with disgust."

Patrick's mouth dropped open in sheer shock, and his eyes went wide. Visibly shaken. "My God, Father, did you do that?" The Duke lowered his head so that his son could not see the shame in his eyes.

"We did place bets, but Gregory and I never knew that we destroyed anyone's life. We always paid their gains but not in full. We kept a big chunk for us. Alexander was the bookkeeper, and he had assured us that everything was working perfectly well. Later, we realized that he increased the size of the debt

for many but never said a word to either one of us." Patrick was confused. He understood what his father had just admitted and tried to understand this horrible behavior on his father's part that did not fit his character and or the family's honor. He waited in silence as the Duke tried to get his composure back and continue.

"We stared at the notes in his hands. He quickly shuffled through them.

"'Why is this any of your business? What do you want?' That was Alexander now stepping forward.

"Grim-faced he met our gazes. 'These are notes with people's names that you have wronged by stealing their money and not providing the promised services. One of those names is my father's.' Gregory opened his mouth to rebut, then closed it as the young man continued. 'You have ruined his life, his marriage, and everything he had accomplished. I am sure you do not know anything about my father or care about him or any other people you have destroyed. However, my father killed himself last week from humiliation.' His voice cracked. Patently evident that he was upset. 'I promised him that I would punish you for your actions,' he added.

"We knew there was no use to fight this since we were guilty of all he said. 'And how do you propose to do this?' I asked quietly.

"His eyes were filled with disgust. He stretched the hand, holding the documents toward us and shook it with extreme anger. 'I have spend countless days and hours to collect all the proof I need. I will turn these documents to the authorities and let them deal with you. Everything they need is on these papers.'

"For a few breathless seconds, we just stared at each other. Then in unison, we moved forward, and he stepped back, shoving the papers back into his pocket. With one finger pointing at us, he stated. 'You will all pay. My father has lost everything, including his life, and it is all due to your actions.' The Duke fell silent.

"So, what happened?" Patrick asked.

"Well, here is where it all becomes unclear."

"What do you mean?"

"It all happened so fast, and for my life, I cannot recall a single thing until I came to."

"I don't understand." Patrick was trying to keep his overpowering curiosity at heel. The Duke looked at him as if he never heard the question; his gaze was distant. After a long moment gathering his thoughts, he continued.

"Right as he finished talking, I felt a pistol's coldness on my head, and all went black."

"What in the devil happened?"

"When conscious again, I saw Gregory trying to stand up, and Alexander already on his feet. I noticed Gregory's pistol in his hand, and mine strangely on the floor next to me. I did not remember drawing my pistol. I was confused. Alexander's face was unreadable, but he pointed to our right and turning, we saw a man's slumped form. Shocked surprise followed by pure panic shot through us when we realized that the body belonged to the young man. He was now lying on the floor unmoved. We approached slowly. My hands and feet were not tied up, but I could barely muster enough strength to think. We finally realized that the man had been shot and wasn't breathing. My head throbbed, and my stomach dropped.

"'Is he dead?' I mumbled.

"'Yes,' I heard Alexander's voice.

"'Who killed him?' I asked.

"'I do not know whose pistol went off, but it seems that it was Gregory's,' Alexander replied, pointing at the pistol in Gregory's hand. 'I did not bring mine,' he added.

"Gregory and I stared at each other in shock. Neither one of us remembered drawing a pistol. I vaguely remembered the coldness of steel in the back of my head. But now I am not sure if that was real. Why could we not recall a single thing that took place?

"'Firing my pistol should have been something I should be able to recall,' Gregory said with a shaken voice. So the question was left as to who killed him?"

The Duke paused, took a sip out of his drink, and continued. "Alexander bent over the body and took the papers from the kid's pocket. 'Let's go,' he said. 'We need to be out of here before they find the body. Did you tell anyone that you were coming?'

"'No,' Gregory said.

"'What about the carriage driver who is still out there waiting for us to return?' I asked in extreme concern.

"'It is way too dark, and he never saw your faces,' Alexander noted. 'I will go out, pay him, and send him off. You two get yourselves together. I will meet you outside.' He was gone before we had a chance to utter another word. We looked down at the young man, and I must say we both felt sick. Something was amiss.

"'I should remember killing a man,' Gregory said firmly, and I agreed. The whole thing was very unusual. We had to move and move fast. If the authorities were alerted, we would have been arrested for murder, gone to jail and put to death for murder. There would have been a lengthy trial and a huge embarrassment in the ton for our families. We walked for a long time through the dark streets, and when we were safely away from the house, we hailed a carriage. Heads back against the squabs, we closed our eyes and took big breaths. The truth was that we had just escaped a terrible situation for the stupid games we played. We did not think that we would be bringing devastation since most of those men were some of the ton's wealthiest men with very dark secrets of their own. The carriage rumbled on down the dark streets. We tensed as the pavement leading to White's rang beneath the horse's hooves. When it drew up outside White's, we stepped down and moved quickly toward the entrance.

"The place was still buzzing with people, and not a single person had missed our absence. We took a corner table and ordered drinks. I turned to look at Alexander and saw an intent expression in his eyes sharpening the soft green. A man approached him, drawing his attention away from me, and they started a frivolous conversation. I seized the moment to study his face. Call it intuition, but something about Alexander did not sit well with me. I looked at Gregory, lost in his thoughts. It had been a strange night of events with many unanswered questions, but we remained quiet and swore not to bring the subject in light.

After that night, we went back to our lives. While in school, spending time at Whites and when in London, attending balls, soirees, parties, and dinners. Gregory, Alexander, and I spent a lot of time together but never discussed the horrible night events."

The Duke stopped talking and raising his glass; he took a long sip. He glanced at Patrick and confirmed that he was listening intently, and he grimaced. Patrick read his father's thoughts, sighed, and rose to his feet. After several moments of pacing, he stopped in front of him with his hands behind his back.

"That is a terrible story and utterly inexcusable, but what does it have to do with Katherine's marriage?"

With a muttered curse, the Duke rose to his feet and faced his son. "It has everything to do with the fact that Gregory gave his precious daughter to a scamp of a man like Quinton."

Tension leaped, and silence descended, then Patrick drew a breath. "I was sure that a dreadful secret destroyed the friendship between the three of you.

A tense moment ticked by then, his father slumped against the wall behind him and closed his eyes. "Yes," His expression was distant as if he was trying to recall that conversation's details.

Patrick dropped into an armchair and waited patiently for his father to speak.

The Duke dropped his gaze, unable to bear his son's dreadful expression. Guilt consumed him, settling so deeply into his bones that he thought he might choke from it. However, he knew that now he had no choice but to press forward with the details. "To my surprise, Gregory came to see me right after you boys left for France. I was not sure if it was for advice or guidance until he started to talk. He was heartbroken and could not discuss the issue with anyone else. We were best friends. He told me that

Alexander had visited him and asked for Katherine's hand for Quinton. Gregory was in shock because Quinton's reputation was well known in the ton. He was a womanizer and gambled his father's fortune away. Alexander wanted to get Quinton married to a young lady with a sizable inheritance, and Katherine fit the bill. He told Gregory that he still had the papers taken from the young man that dreadful night. If he disapproved of this marriage, he would tell the authorities that he witnessed the murder. He accused Gregory and me of the murder of Brantford Wesley, a murder case still open and unsolved."

"But, Father, something is amiss." Patrick's frustration mounted, and he could not shake his apprehension. "You thought that you felt the cold steel of a gun against your skin. If you three were standing side-by-side, there had to be someone else in that room."

The Duke nodded his head in agreement. "My memory is not clear about all the details, and I may have been hallucinating, but things did not seem right to me while struggling at the edge of consciousness. Someone had to have hit me from behind. We discussed this particular item when Gregory came to see me after Alexander requested Katherine's hand for his son. He told me that he, too, was hit from behind. When he came to, he saw me still passed out on the floor and Alexander standing over me. That did seem strange to both of us, but we could not come up with a good explanation. We also discussed the papers that Alexander had brought up to Gregory, and I realized that it would directly affect me if those papers reached the authorities. We were both devastated. The terrible feeling of that night started to creep up again. Gregory and I discussed the young man's words, and we became even more confused. As I told you before, we did handle bets for many men, but we never kept all the gains if they won. We held a big chunk per the agreement we had made before taking their bet but never all of it. So, people who gambled always made money, just not as much as they should receive. I am confused with the idea that this would drive any man to suicide.

Something was strange about how things worked out, and Alexander's awful feeling never left us as the years went by, but we never thought he would stoop to that low level."

"So, Alexander handled your bet ledgers?" Patrick asked.

"Yes, he was the finance man."

So, the question was left as to who killed the young man. Patrick felt the moment grow more substantial as he tried to absorb the indisputable facts. Transfixed, he stared, his father in shock. His mind sorted through all the information he had heard. "Father, something is not right about the whole story. I will have to probe into the details a bit more and find out what happened. I have a sick feeling that Alexander set both of you up with other conspirators to make sure that he came out of this mess without a scratch and would hold you both to his debt for as long as he chose to do so."

The Duke huffed and shook his head. He shoved his hands into his pockets, staring at his son. "This has been weighing on me for years," he said.

Patrick could see that his father was agonizing over his thoughts. "Father, I understand now why Duke Weldon agreed to this horrid marriage. His refusal would have destroyed everything he held dear, his family, fortune, and life. Duke Alexander Bennett is a repulsive and vicious man. I am not surprised that Quinton turned out to be just like his father. But I am astonished by your friendship with this dreadful man. "

The Duke stiffened. His son had hit a nerve. His expression took an icy look. Patrick raised his eyebrows. "Patrick, that was a long time ago. Gregory, Alexander, and I worked hard to excel in school. We never realized that the man we knew would turn out to be the same man we are discussing now. "

The night appeared to approach quickly, and both men seemed to have come to an agreeable conclusion. Patrick would contact the Viper group. "Father, I will send for my friends and ask their assistance to uncover this ugly mess. Will you give me your approval to dig into whatever is required?"

With a heavy sigh, Duke Wingham nodded as he filled their glasses and took a seat. The ice in the glass clunk against the crystal as he spun around to face his son. Rage swept the Duke's face. His words came out slow and deliberate. "Alexander cast-off a shroud of betrayal over the details of this murder. He let Gregory and myself believe that we are guilty of murder. But all he cared about was Katherine's fortune. Gregory made Katherine aware of the notes Alexander said that he had in his possession on his deathbed. He explained to his beloved daughter why he had agreed to this dreadful union. He thought he had murdered that young lad. Katherine was devastated, but I know she would never have jeopardized her father or her family's good name. Duke Wingham gazed at Patrick an unhappy light shone in his eyes. Please help me, son." His smile was every bit as unsettling as his frown.

Patrick ran his fingers through his hair in sheer frustration. He was silent as thoughts swirled through his head. Now he was hell-bent on solving what his father and Duke Weldon were unable to do and bring closure to this terrible situation. Strumming his fingers across the armrest and pushing his chair back, he rose to his feet. He cleared his throat, took a deep breath. The tension in his long frame was now gone. "Of course, I will help, Father; this is something I must do for William and both of us."

After exchanging warm smiles, they shook hands and retired to their chambers with the agreement to talk more about a plan the next day.

CHAPTER SEVEN

*I*n his chamber, Patrick closed the door behind him. He shrugged out of his coat and threw it on a chair by the fireplace. He strode to the bed and dropped onto the bedspread as if the strength had left his body. He forced his limbs to work and removed his boots. His feet sank into the thick carpet. He tried to shrug off the uneasiness that clung to him like a cloak. With a satisfied sigh, he walked over to the dresser and reached for the bottle. Taking a glass, he poured the best brandy found in England.

Glass in hand, he moved toward the window. The candle on the table flickered as he passed, and bending down, he snuffed it. He pulled the curtains open and let the moonlight stream in, bathing the room with plenty of light. He reached for the latches, and, pressing down, he pushed the windows wide open. He stared at the beautiful silver circle of the moon, suspended in the dark sky. It was a beautiful night; the light breeze sweeping the green fields' fragrance had the most intoxicating effect stroking his senses. The wind blew softly across his face, and he closed his eyes in complete pleasure. For six years while away from home, he dreamt about this. His thoughts had grown distant but abruptly refocused on the current situation. The revelation of the past seemed to bring such a bitter shame to his father. He inhaled deeply and pulled the windows shut. He left the curtains open and let the moonlight guide him to his bed. He set the glass down, and, exhausted, drifted into a deep sleep.

He woke the next morning, and immediately, his mind went to Kat. How would he accomplish this task with no damage to Kat's reputation and his father's name? He felt rested and ready to take on the day. He raised himself on his elbow, and his gaze turned toward the window and the deep blue sky. The sun sent countless gold streams of light and filled the room with a fabulous bright light. Bathed and shaved and dressed in fresh attire, he left his chamber and headed downstairs. His mind filled with all the questions that were facing him. However, he walked into the breakfast room with a keen sense of calm. He found his family already sitting around the table. There was a spirited conversation going on that immediately stopped when he entered. Four pairs of eyes turned to face him, and warm smiles made him feel welcome. He spooned a small pile of eggs onto his plate, selected a slice of ham, and carried it to the table.

"Sit my boy," his father said, pointing to the chair

across from him. Patrick walked behind his mother, set his hands on her shoulders, and bent down pressing a soft kiss to her cheek.

"Good morning, Mother, how are you feeling this morning?" She patted his hands and looking up, she smiled wide. He knew that smile. It was a happy and content smile. He took his seat and inserted himself into the family conversation that had started before he arrived. He was not going to bring up the private discussion he had held with his father the night before. While his brothers got into a back and forth with their father, Patrick picked up the latest London post from the table and held it before him. He casually scanned the headlines while listening to the conversation around him. He did not find anything of interest, so he put it back down.

"What are your plans for today?" his mother asked.

"I would like to invite the Viper group here for a few days if that is all right with you."

"Oh, that would be fantastic," his brother Christopher chimed in with extreme enthusiasm before their mother had a chance to reply.

"We would love to hear some of the war stories," Anthony said joining in his brother's excitement. Patrick acknowledged their eagerness with his usual charm.

He turned back to his mother and met her sweet, agreeable smile. "Your father and I are happy to welcome and meet such wonderful friends."

"Mother, they are more than friends. They are brothers to me. I owe them my life many times over."

Reaching across the table, she took his hand and

pressed it softly, "As they owe their lives to you, I am sure. That makes it even more of an important reason to make them feel at home."

"Thank you, Mother." His gaze moved slowly to his father; he noticed a flash that crossed his emerald eyes, and his lips quirked downward. The Duke knew the reason for the visit. Patrick thought about the secret his father had held for so many years. Now he was hoping to resolve it once and for all.

After breakfast, Patrick excused himself and strolled out of the room. His boots echoed on the tile floor as he walked toward the main staircase. He reached the second floor scaling the steps two at a time and turned left toward the library. The room was dark; he shut the door behind him, leaning against it. The pleasant silence wrapped around him, giving him a sense of solace. He then walked forward to the window and reaching up, he drew the curtain fold aside. The vast library had windows facing both front and back gardens. It was June, the weather warm and pleasant. His eyes fell on the beautiful green fields that stretched as far as the eye could see. His instantaneous reaction was that of admiration. The gardens below were bursting with plentiful growth and flowers of every kind, creating a sea of color exuding an air of summer. He took a brief look around the room before calling for tea to be brought up to the library.

Sipping his tea, he penned the same invitation for George, Michael, and Edward. The invitation read:

. . .

Dear brother, I have decided that it is wise to seek your assistance with a sensitive matter that requires our expertise. The outcome will have a direct effect on William's family and mine. I will give you all the details once you are here.

Sincerely,
    Patrick

He read the note a couple of times. He was sure that his friends' instincts would know there was a lot more to that note

than the simple words. The fearsome Viper group had spent the past six years or more in His Majesty's government's service as agents throughout France, collecting information on enemy troops, ships, provisions, and strategies. They'd all reported to Paul Landon Webster, the spymaster. The information provided by the spies was held and buried in Whitehall's depths. Paul oversaw all English military agents on foreign soil. Patrick was sure that his friends were experts in tactics and strategy; they weren't about to be tricked by the enemy. If they had any say in it, they would do the tricking. Once satisfied with the content, he rang for Jacob and asked him to send a footman to deliver the messages to the designated addresses.

With a half-empty cup of tea in hand, he let out a sigh

and sank back into the large leather armchair. His thoughts turned to Kat, and he smiled as a warm feeling engulfed him. He was sure that Kat would soon be released from her horrid situation and into his desperate waiting arms. A knock at the door brought him back to reality. "Come," he called out. Christopher and Anthony stood in the doorway.

"Would you like to go riding, brother?" Patrick considered the offer.

"Let us show you the progress we have made while you were gone." Christopher added.

Patrick's eyes widened. "Have you been working with father all these years? I thought that you were attending college."

"We have been coming home between semesters helping father. He is getting older," Anthony stated. Patrick nodded with a soft smile. It was something he never expected to hear. He found himself filled with pride and respect for both of his younger brothers. He was halfway out of his chair when loud hoofbeats approached. They moved to the window and saw two men dismounting in the courtyard. Jacob ran to welcome them. He took the reins and pulled the horses toward the stables. Patrick frowned. He was not expecting company. Soon they heard booted feet making their way up the staircase.

"Who the devil are they? Are you expecting company?"

His brothers moved away from the window and chuckled with pleasure. "Calm down, Patrick; they are Katherine's brothers. Duke Nicholas Weldon and Lord Garret Weldon. They are our best friends. They came home from their military assignments last year, and we have been spending time together, riding and visiting London to attend ballroom dances."

Patrick's brows flew. He could not remember their faces. He stood and shrugged uncomfortably, but he was now happy to see them both. Nicholas, as the oldest brother, had taken his father's title and responsibilities. In the distance, a grandfather clock rang ten echoing thumps. Anthony opened the door, and soon two very handsome, well-dressed men halted in the doorway. Nicholas started forward and met Patrick's gaze. Extending his hand, warmly addressed him.

"Welcome home, Patrick. I am so happy to see you back, chap." In a more sober and solemn voice, he added. "Thank you for taking care of William while away. He often wrote about you and the Viper group. We are all so proud of you and your accomplishments for England." Lips tight at the sound of William's name Patrick nodded, squeezing Nicola's hand warmly.

His gaze moved past Nicholas, and reaching over, he took Garrett's hand. "Hello, Garret, how are you?"

Garrett shook his hand with the same enthusiasm. "I am well, Patrick, thank you. I am also happy to see you home."

Unhurriedly, Patrick moved his eyes on both brothers. "I understand that both of you spent four years behind enemy lines to note the enemy's positions and strength."

"Yes, we did," Nicholas said pride in his voice. "We performed different roles in the acquisition and distribution of intelligence. Making it home alive was a miracle. Mother and Katherine were delighted to see us back. William's death was a massive blow to the family. I am sure that if our father were still alive, he would have been devastated."

Clearing his throat, Patrick said, "I understand the sentiment and am happy to see that you made it back alive. I know that England and everyone around you is proud of your accomplishments as well." Patrick gave them a warm smile.

They turned in the other direction and exchanged warm hugs with Antony and Christopher.

Patrick hesitated before he mentioned Kat. "How is Katherine?" he blurted out. They all turned to face him. There was a short silence, and eventually, Nicholas blew out a breath.

"I am sure you heard the rumors around our sister's horrid wedding to that rake of a man." Anger coated his voice and disgust made his lips twitch.

Patrick felt the same way but did not expect such an intense reaction from her brother, however he understood. "She lives here now with our mother. She is staying away from London and Quinton all together," Garrett Added.

"I am so sorry to hear about the loss of your father," Patrick said. They spent the next hours chatting about their family and Katherine's situation.

"Do you know why your father gave your sister's hand to a man like Quinton in marriage?" Patrick asked in a soft voice.

"Father never said anything to us, but we are sure he talked to Katherine," Nicholas said. "There were many arguments and loud discussions before the wedding between father, mother, and Katherine. I am sure they know the reason but have never shared it with us." Frustration was coating his voice. Slowly he drew in a deep breath, exhaled, and moved toward the window. "We would have loved to help and prevent the union, but whatever the secret was between my father and Alexander Bennett, we were left out."

Patrick moved closer to Nicholas, and reaching over, he clapped his shoulder in support. "I have a plan, and I am hoping to get the issue resolved soon. Hopefully, it will release Katherine from her horrid union and make your family's honor whole again."

"Can you talk about your plans?"

"I summoned the Viper group to discuss the details to conceive a plan that will work. We are going to unearth the secret that has plagued both our families for many years." Undefined warning shaded the words.

"Have you talked to your father about this?"

"Yes, we talked last night, and I am now aware of many details. Alexander Bennett is a huge enigma, but I promised William I would resolve it. It was a promise I made to your brother, and I aim to keep it. Besides," Patrick hesitated for a short moment.

"What?" Garrett asked anxiously.

It took him a few minutes to find the words, but he eventually raised his head and said. "I have loved Katherine ever since we were children. I would have asked for her hand in marriage before William and I left for France, but I did not believe that I would survive the war and did not want Katherine to become a widow at such a young age."

Nicholas and Garrett stood for a long moment in utter

shock. Soon their eyes widened as the truth of his statement sank deep into their bones. Patrick studied their eyes and faces. He was sure that this was the initial reaction to his words. They flashed him a wide grin to his great relief, and the conversation that followed was of warm and enthusiastic content. Both brothers were enormously exultant to hear Patrick's admission of love for their sister and could not help but reach out and take him into a bear hug of enjoyment.

"Will you be visiting Katherine?" Garrett asked.

"Yes, I was planning on it." All the memories came flooding back. "Do you think she will see me?"

His question seemed to surprise her brothers. "Patrick, she has not stopped talking about you ever since she heard that you were back."

Patrick slowly looked at Garret. "Really?" A bolt of pleasure shot through him as if the thought was physical touch.

"Yes," he replied in a firm voice. He then cleared his throat. "This calls for a celebration. Do we drink or ride?"

Laughter followed. They did not have to think for long. He glanced at the clock on the mantelpiece. It was still early. With a smile, Patrick grabbed his coat. Soon the five of them were out the back door heading toward the stables. He called for Pegasus to be saddled while the others did the same for their

favorite horses. He vaulted Pegasus, who was fighting to spring out before he even loosened the reins. His mood was restored to that of a happy-go-lucky, man. The moment they left the stables and reached the lush greens, he let Pegasus have his way. The thoroughbred thundered up and then flew across the beautiful fields. Patrick felt the air rush past his face, felt an excitement he had almost forgotten shooting down every pore of his body, and swore this had to be paradise. They went across the endless greens in record time. He took in all the familiar places engraved in his memory. Each treebank, river, bridge, hill, road turn, and rocky bed was as he recalled. He felt an indescribable connection to the property.

From a distance, he could see the Weldon residence's immense dominant feature that bordered the property his solicitor purchased for him. The land rose steeply at the end of the estate. When they reached the top, he slowed Pegasus to a walk and then to a complete stop. The land fell away in a slight bow to the beautiful mansion. The view was stunning. Far in the distance, he could see the sunlight bathing the sea with a magnificent golden blanket. He drew a slow breath. The sight mesmerized him. He felt the surge of emotions that rose to his throat and nearly choked him. Kat was there, so close yet so far. His heart was there, but was he ready to face her? The indescribable joy of attaining his dream was shadowed by the dark secret that needed to be solved. With the corner of his eyes, he saw the others approach and stop next to him. Their gaze followed his to the Weldon mansion.

"The house has not changed much," Nicholas said.

"It looks just as wonderful, and just as powerful as ever," Patrick replied without looking at them.

"Please come and visit soon."

"Yes, I am planning on that, maybe tomorrow, if you think Katherine would not mind."

"Oh, we are sure that she will be delighted. Please come." Dragging in a breath, he filled his lungs with the fresh air. He set his jaw in a happy smile and sent Pegasus trotting.

Christopher and Anthony took them around the property. Patrick saw firsthand that his brothers had been in charge of cultivating the soil, and the crops—Corn, soybeans, wheat, and cotton—grew in abundance. He knew they had their hands full by mixing crops and livestock. They had done a great job dividing the resources over various activities. There were several locations with a wide range of fruits and vegetables, from apples to cranberries, and so on. They rode by well-kept buildings with livestock. He met the help hands and the foreman who had taken residence in homes built within the property boundaries. They seemed happy and pleased to meet another member of the family. The locations looked tightly controlled, turning out reliable products. The last place they visited was the stud farm located a couple of miles away. He recognized a few horses, but most had been acquired while he was in France. He let out a low sound when he watched an older man approach. It was Nick, one of his favorite trainers and a good friend. Nick approached in giant strides, and Patrick jumped off the horse. "Patrick!" Nick exclaimed in utter pleasure. "I had heard that you came home safe and could not wait to see you again." He shook his hand, wide smile on his face, but Patrick moved closer and took him in a bear hug.

"A handshake will not do." They laughed out loud and spent a few minutes going back and forth about the family and his children. Patrick was so pleased to hear that all was well in Nick's life. His gaze went over the old face, much wind-swept, and green eyes able to evaluate every stride and tell accurately how each horse was fairing. He was irreplaceable. They walked and chatted. "I will come back in a few days to ride around the property with you and talk some more." Nick nodded in agreement. After spending an hour or so, they bid him goodbye and headed home.

His brothers had invited the Weldon boys to have dinner with the family after riding. They strolled into the dining area. The midday sun sent streams of bright light into the room. Duke Wingham and his wife were thrilled to see the Weldon boys. The Duke stood and extended his hand. "Good to see you both," His voice was cheerful. "How is your mother?"

"She is fine," Nicholas assured him. "She stays busy working in the garden. She seems to get pleasure spending time among the flowers." He chuckled softly.

"And how is Katherine?" Olivia asked

"She spends most of her time reading, gardening, and riding her horse. It is hard to tell how she feels as she does not open to any of us." Casting a sidelong glance to Garrett, he pursed his lips and continued. "We tried to make her reply to the many invitations that arrive daily for her, but she ignores them all. I am sure she is afraid that she might run into Quinton. She loathes him with the kind of hate that I never knew existed."

They sensed the tension in his voice, and Patrick's hand

balled into a fist at the sound of Quinton's name. He quickly changed the subject. He clapped Nicholas on the shoulder and gave him a soft shake. "I am so glad that you came with us to visit the properties. It has been six years since I have seen many of the places. It was beautiful to see them again and to share the day with you both.

They took their seats around the table. They consumed a healthy amount of food and wine and then sat back and swapped stories about their morning ride, the properties, issues of the society, and funny stories of the ton. Patrick could not help mentioning the fabulous work his brothers had done.

His father smiled with satisfaction. "They have done an even better job with the books and finances. If not for the boys having to go back and finish the last semester, I would not need a solicitor any longer." His brothers beamed at their father's words.

"The food was delicious," Nicholas said pushed his chair away from the table, "We must be going." Getting to their feet, they exchanged warm greetings.

"We will expect you tomorrow, Patrick," Garrett added. Patrick inclined his head.

Late that evening, he made his way into the library and called for tea. Long rays of shimmering moonlight came through the open curtains and spilled across the darkened room. He sat in the armchair, nursing a cup of tea along with his thoughts. Closing his eyes, he agonized about his emotion, about his predispositions. He tried to will away the persistent pounding in his head. He didn't want to contemplate just how difficult it would be to free Kat from her horrid union, at least not until his friends arrived later in the week. He clenched the cup and downed the remaining contents and stood. He strode to his chambers and closed the door shut. He lit the single candle on his dresser and paced before the fireplace for a long moment. The lighting created a golden hue throughout the entire chamber. He crossed the floor in slow strides to the window, reached for the curtain folds, and pulled them shut. The evening air had turned chilly, and the room was even colder.

He shrunk out of his coat and draped it over the back of the chair near his bed. Relaxed, he let his mind drift. Like a slow, unstoppable wave, the emotions that had swept him earlier returned. He cursed silently. He would unearth the secret that held Kat prisoner to Quinton. He had also set his mind on his style of dark vengeance ever since he returned to England. The silence in the room was deafening except for the crackling of the logs in the fireplace. He sunk back into the leather armchair, stretched his booted feet, and watched how the glass vase on the table caught the light from the fire for a long moment. Lost in thought, He rubbed one hand over his unshaved jaw. He reached for his book as a piece of coal broke and slithered to the hearth, startling him. He fixed his gaze on the flames leaping in the fireplace and focused his thoughts on the hand's objective. Minutes ticked past in that unsettling silence. He let the fire die down and changing his mind; he set the book aside and took to his massive bed.

He felt like getting comfortable and unbuttoned his

shirt. The coolness of the room against his skin felt refreshing. The tie came off next, and he tossed it onto the nightstand. He sat at the edge of the bed and pulled his boots off. He remained quite still for an unknown amount of time before he stripped off the rest of his clothes and slipped under the covers. He leaned back and fell on the soft pillows. It was sometime later when the rain came, and he heard the splattering against the window. A smile coated his face as his eyes closed, and to his surprise, sleep claimed his exhausted body quickly.

CHAPTER EIGHT

*E*arly the next morning, he walked into the breakfast parlor dressed to ride. He grinned; the whole family was already seated at the table carrying on a casual conversation. "Good morning," he called out and walked toward the sideboard. On his way, he paused and planted a quick kiss on his mother's upturned cheek. He then proceeded to fill his plate with eggs, ham, and fruits. Taking his seat across from his father, he reached to lift the coffeepot. His mother started to say something when Jacob reached and took the pot from his hand.

"I will fetch some fresh coffee, my Lord."

"Thank you." The moment Jacob left the room, Patrick turned his gaze to his mother. "Were you going to say something?"

She cast him an easy glance, her next words a whisper. "You seem extremely happy this morning, and I wondered where you were off to." She concealed a ghost smile watching him.

Patrick caught her gaze. He clearly understood what she was thinking. "Going to visit Lady Katherine and the family," he said in a casual tone.

She watched him; her head slanted to one side; her eagerness completely exposed. "Wonderful!" she exclaimed. A chuckle from his brothers made Patrick smile; they were right. He was anxious to see Kat again.

"I know that Duchess Mariam will welcome your visit. She is one of my closest friends and has been very concerned with Katherine's state of mind. I feel so bad for her. She has not been able to get Katherine to reply to any of the invitations that keep pouring in the house requesting her attendance to the ton's ballrooms. People love her and want to let her know that they are supporting her decisions and not Quinton. It is as if she has built this wall around herself, and nobody, including her family, can breakthrough."

Patrick stiffened at the sound of Quinton's name and rubbed his chin with obvious annoyance. He pushed his chair away from the table, stood, and tugged his waistcoat. "I must be going before it gets too late." He left the breakfast table bound for the front door.

Grey skies welcomed Patrick as he stepped outside. He scanned the courtyard; he didn't mind the gloomy weather but did not like to ride in a downpour. He was pleased to find that the rain had stopped, and an uplifting breeze chased the storm clouds across the sky. He smiled wide, looking at the patches of beautiful blue sky coming through the breaking clouds.

James, his parent's foreman, came out of the stables pulling Pegasus toward the courtyard. Patrick smiled wide at his beloved horse's sight with the huge brown eyes now fixed on him. There was an unbroken bond created between them. He nodded graciously to James and took the reins. With the reins gripped in one hand, he ran the other along Pegasus' neck, feeling its muscles quiver under his touch. Pegasus brought his head close and nuzzled Patrick's neck. A deep nickering sound escaped him showing his unwavering affection. Patrick vaulted onto the saddle and rode Pegasus out of the estate. To his surprise, the road to the Weldon's mansion was well graded. Thick greenery and huge trees adorn the path. The rain had left splendid glittery morning dew on the grass and a silver glow on each branch and leaf. The trees thinned as he got closer, and suddenly, they exploded into a picturesque clearing.

A beautiful three-story house built of grey stone had stood for over two centuries. The massive iron gates were wide open, awaiting his arrival. Tension gripped him, locking his breath in his chest. He rode in, Pegasus' hooves beating along the graveled drive. He drew rein before the front steps. Footsteps pattered. Dismounting, handed the reins to Gunther, the stable foreman, leaving him in charge of settling his horse. He paused and looked around him. The view embraced him in its fabulous arms, and he closed his eyes for a short moment and took a deep breath. He did not see many changes. Beautiful gardens still surrounded the house covered in countless varieties of flowers, creating a sea of color. Shrubs filled the empty spots beneath the enormous trees. In the distance, he saw the beautiful lake that brought back sweet memories of his childhood. A feeling of warmth gripped him as he ascended the stairs and pulled the brush handle up, letting it fall against the door with a loud bang. It was not long before the door opened. Henry, the Weldon's butler, stood just inside the door. He nodded politely and waved him in. Patrick stepped into the large foyer.

"Good evening, my Lord. I am so happy to see you back in England."

He pulled his gloves off and shrunk out of his coat, letting it fall into the butler's hands.

"Thank you, Henry."

Patrick moved further into the foyer and paused. Behind him, Henry shut the front door quietly.

Nicholas hurried down the main staircase, followed by Garrett. Patrick gripped the hands offered with real pleasure. They were both dressed in the most elegant style, exhibiting class and elegance.

"Welcome to our home. Did you have a good ride? Mother has been eager to see you again. She was overwhelmed with joy when we told her that you were coming. She is waiting for you in the library." Patrick could not help wondering about Kat. Was she excited to see him again? He smiled with pleasure. He tried hard to hold back, but the words just rolled out of his mouth.

"What about Katherine?"

Nicholas chuckled under his breath. He met Patrick's gaze. "We know her well enough by now, and even though she did not say much, she is overwhelmed with pleasure."

When he entered the library, the fire was burning, giving him a warm feeling. As they crossed the threshold, Patrick saw Duchess Weldon; she was just as he remembered her. A small woman who carried herself with an imperial grace that suggested her roots had been regal. She was alone standing by the fireplace, beautifully dressed in a gown of light blue muslin adorned with vibrant spring flowers. She was an example of aristocratic English grace. Her long, elegant fingers curved around a cup of tea. The moment she saw Patrick, she set it aside and walked toward him with open arms. She held him tightly for a very long moment. Patrick felt his eyes moisten; this hug was for William's arrival home. He returned her embrace and realized that this moment meant everything to him. When he pulled back, tears ran down the Duchess's lovely face. She fixed her gaze on him. "I want to hear all about William." She took his hand and guided him toward the sofa before the hearth.

"Shall I ring for tea?" she said, pressing his hand softly. He accepted though he would instead prefer it was a glass of brandy. She tugged the bell pull, and five minutes later, Mrs. Steward, her maid, walked in. The Duchess asked her to bring a tray of finger sandwiches, scones, and a pot of hot tea.

She then sank into the sofa and asked him to sit next to

her. Nicholas and Garrett took their seats across from them, anxious to hear all about their brother.

Patrick started to talk about the Viper group and their time in France. William was the main person he mentioned most of the time. She gave him approving warm smiles and encouraged him to expand. It was in the midst of his stories when the tea arrived. While she poured, Patrick wondered how long he would talk about his best friend without breaking down. A blast of emotion suddenly roared six years of memories up, making him recoil in memories of war, friendship, brotherhood, laughter, terrifying assignments, successful outcomes, and finally, death. He gave his head a shake and attempted to sort his thoughts before he continued.

She handed him the teacup without a rattle on its saucer. "Cream and sugar?"

"Yes, please."

While they sipped, they exchanged questions and answers. The conversation was easy, sharing the skill of the Viper groups' experiences and the commitment they had to each other. They were willing to die for one another. When finished, a quiet approval of his words glowed through the Duchess's eyes that seemed deep-rooted, vastly definite, and almost tranquil. Patrick planned to discuss Quinton's issue with the Duchess, but he did not think this was the right time. Refocusing, he realized that Katherine had not shown up yet.

What if she had changed her mind and did not want to see him? Raising his cup, he sipped and savored the warmth as it slid down his throat.

Nicholas and Garrett had informed the Duchess of Patrick's feelings toward Katherine, and she didn't miss Patrick's constant stare to the library entrance. His facial expression had changed to that of restlessness. After a fractional hesitation and a soft smile, she came out with it. "Katherine should be here momentarily. She had an important appointment."

Patrick went still; he felt like a schoolboy caught in some sort of mischief. Stretching his long legs on the lush burgundy carpeting toward the hearth, he crossed his ankles and stared at his boots' tip for a short moment. He looked up at the Duchess and then nodded with a smile. In the distance, a grandfather clock rang the hour.

"I can say without reservations that I am happy to see you again and internally thankful for sharing the details about William and his time in France. I only wish my husband was still with us to enjoy the wonderful stories that you shared." Sadness coated the Duchess's voice.

Patrick snapped to his senses, and his body shivered with anticipation as footsteps approached. He heard the door open and quickly rose to his feet. He turned to face his life's long dream. His lips curved, entirely spontaneously. For a short moment, he found himself enveloped in pure desire and lost for words. She was astonishingly, breathtakingly, excruciatingly beautiful.

She wore an outrageously fashionable emerald silk gown that hugged her perfect figure tightly. His eyes drowned in her luscious full lips and moved slowly over her lovely face, the straight, beautiful nose, and those amazing blue eyes that held him captured for all these years. Beauty enveloped over her like a dazzling star. For the life of him, he could not hide his extreme happiness. He was in love. He had dreamed of this vision for more than six years.

Her eyes bore into his as soon as she stepped inside the room. She felt a jolt that made her body quiver, and extreme heat surged through her veins. Patrick caught Katherine's look; her gaze moved slowly and seductively up and down his body. Dressed with unpretentious elegance, he was a sight of title and wealth. From the exquisite cut of his grey coat to his buckskin breeches, every part of him was fabulous, molded to long powerful legs vanishing into glossy black Hessians. Katherine drank in the classic nose and chin, the aristocratic cheekbones, the beautiful dark blue eyes, and the distracting, candidly sensual mouth. She caught her breath, and with a great force of determination, she moved closer. He was the man of her dreams. He had controlled her thoughts and desires ever since she was a young girl. She had been heartbroken when he left for France. Now he stood only a couple of feet away from her. His face was just as beautiful as she remembered. His lips were partly open with that fantastic smile of his, and all she wanted to do was move into his arms and sink into a passionate kiss.

Katherine controlled her emotions as Patrick watched her gracefully advance even closer. She stopped right in front of him, a grin on her face. The top of her head barely reached his chin. She looked magical, just like a dream, a dream he had over and over again. He closed his eyes, but when he opened them, she was still there. His palms ached to cradle her face. Instead, he took her hands in his, and bowing elegantly, smiled down at her. Under his fingers, the softness of her skin sent a tidal wave of desire through his body, waking up every nerve, every muscle. He drew a deep breath and gave himself a mental shake. His gaze rested on her, and the world disappeared. She was unquestionably the woman he was going to marry.

"Hello, Kat."

A glance of pleasure danced in his eyes. It was evident that her presence was the only thing missing from his life all these years.

"Hello Patrick, I am so happy that you are home." After a short silence, she continued. "Thank you for taking care of my brother. He often wrote about your experiences in France. Do you find English society different from Paris?" She looked a bit nervous, trying to make small talk.

For a whole minute, silence held control. The corners of his mouth tipped upward. "We did not socialize much while in France. It was wartime." The silence stretched again as she wracked her brain for something to say. She seemed to be utterly distracted by his presence.

The Duchess's voice broke the silence. "Did you get everything done, my dear?" Gazing over his shoulder, she looked at her mother and wordlessly nodded.

Her fingers were still trapped in Patrick's warm clasp. Letting out the breath she held, she inclined her head and slowly retrieved her hands. She looked across the room at her brothers and veered in their direction. The curve of

Patrick's lips deepened as he watched her walk away. She hugged her brothers and turned toward the fireplace. Stopping to rearrange the beautiful flowers in the vase by the sofa, she took a seat next to her mother, pressing a soft kiss to her cheek. Immediately, they fell into an in-depth discussion. Nicholas and Garrett joined Patrick in the conversation.

It was not long before the Duchess stood up and exchanged a warm glance with Patrick. "Please excuse me; I need to attend to household duties. It will give me extreme pleasure if you will consider joining us later for dinner. In the meantime, I am sure Katherine would be happy to take a stroll with you and show you the gardens and the improvements she made to the greenhouse this season." A chuckle escaped her brothers.

"See you then," they called out as the three of them walked out of the library.

"You might not," she whispered irritably.

"What is all that about?" Patrick said softly, bemused.

"Oh, they have been making jokes about me spending all my time in the garden. They want me to go out and socialize with my friends." There was a silence that followed her words.

"Why don't you?" he asked even though he knew the reason very well. It would be a great time to discuss Quinton.

"Perhaps it is because everyone expects to see me in the ballrooms, ready to create their own, horrible stories and measure my unhappiness to suit their relationships. I refuse to give them fuel to start a fire. I will be the one to suffer the consequences of their lies, and the gossip spread throughout London. You know how the ton works." She lifted her gaze, and her beautiful blue eyes bore into his. He found himself lost; his thoughts scattered utterly captivated by her presence. He stammered, almost forgetting her question and what he meant to say.

"Yes, I do," he finally murmured. "I have been avoiding their invitations like the plague." She chuckled at his words.

She gave him a somewhat uncertain smile and reaching over; she placed her hand on his forearm. "Are you ready to walk with me?"

Patrick inclined his head. "There is nothing that would make me happier than to spend time with you." She stared up at him, and he frowned at the loneliness he found deep in her eyes.

"What is it, Kat?" He tried hard to control his emotions; all he wanted was to take her into his arms and hold her there and keep her safe forever. Katherine shivered at the sound of her name. She found it exhilarating, sexy, and desirable. She did not tolerate anyone else to call her Kat. It was only for him. She inhaled deeply. Looking up at him, she frowned as ugly memories of her marriage rippled through her.

She pressed her fingers on his forearm, and they walked out the door. He fell into step beside her as she led the way down a beautiful path adorned by roses of all colors. He lifted his other hand and cupped hers, giving it a soft squeeze. She gasped inwardly and took a deep breath. She pointed at the pathway down in the distance. "Do you see that?" Patrick followed her finger and noticed a beautiful bench placed between the roses, under a sizeable, picturesque tree, close to a lovely pond's edge. "I had it placed there for a reason. Do you remember the tree?" He sensed rather than saw her excitement. He looked thoughtful for a long moment. He quickly scanned his mind, going back to the part of his brain that held the most significant memories of his life. He probed into his soul into secret places he hadn't known existed. Suddenly, his eyes widened as memories flooded his thoughts.

"Yes, I remember it," he replied, dragging in a shaky breath. His hand came up and caressed her cheek softly. His touch made her quake and burning fire traveled down her spine. He moved closer, and she blinked. A shiver of apprehension ran through her. "That was our tree," he added. "We spent so much time sitting and reading to each other scary stories when we were children. I remember William scaring you to death and me coming to your rescue." They both broke out into a hearty laugh. Patrick took her hand and placed it on his forearm. He looked around as they strolled further down the path covered with flowering rhododendron shrubs filled with white, lavender, and pink blossoms. The large rose bushes provided a blanket of all colors. The aroma of the jasmine filled the air, and the azaleas bloomed profusely. A wide smile spread across his face. He was sure this was Paradise.

They reached the bench and sat close to each other. For a moment, looking at her, his memory flashed back to the little blond girl he chased across the gardens while playing hide-and-go-seek. This girl was all grown up now. She was beautiful, graceful, and lovely. Leaning even closer, every muscle in his body tightened as he breathed in her hair's pleasant fragrance. His eyes fell on the large pond where the reflection of the long grass and the trees surrounding that part of the property shimmered."

Her voice came out soft and measured. "I spend a lot of time here reading. I feel happy, safely surrounded by our memories."

He fought the desire to reach out and run his hand down her face to remind him of her beautiful alabaster skin's softness. The realization that he loved her so profoundly nearly took his breath away. He cocked his head and pinned her with his gaze. "Kat, what happened? How did it come to this? What made your father accept this marriage? I am here to help. I want to end this foolishness. I want to free you from Quinton."

Long minutes passed in silence. Uncertainty burned deep inside.

Could that be possible? She swallowed hard, and her gaze lifted to his. "How? How can you do that?"

He watched her face, registering the quiet sadness behind her eyes, then continued, with a voice of reassurance. "Kat, I have a plan."

"But how? My father assured me that there was no other alternative."

Patrick hesitated. "A few evenings ago, I discussed with my father the secret held between your father, Alexander Bennett, and himself. He told me all that he knew. I find the story full of holes, and I want to hear your side. You are all that matters to me in this whole affair."

Katherine clenched her hands and shifted anxiously. His words were soft with concern, and she wasn't expecting the emotion that crashed through her. She kept her head down as tears sprang to her eyes. He still cared for her. A shiver of pleasant sensation shot through her body. "So, what is your plan?" she asked again.

"I summoned my friends. We specialize in exposing secrets as such. We will get to the bottom of this one quickly. I told my parents that the commitment I made to William I aim to keep. I will ruin Quinton alongside his father. I have vowed revenge, and nothing will stand in my way." He leaned closer and set his lips on her temple. His breath was soft against her cheek. "You are mine, Kat," he whispered. "You have always been mine. I have loved you as long as I can remember. I only pray that you love me, too."

Katherine closed her eyes, shook her head, and her voice came out thick with emotion. "Why did you not ask for my hand before you left for France? I loved you, and I thought that you didn't care for me. You broke my heart. Why?"

He stilled. The question set him on edge. He came to his feet and pulled her up to him. Drawn as if by a magnet, he put his finger under her chin and lifted her face until their eyes met, and she stopped breathing. She lost her balance, and his right arm wrapped around her waist, holding her steady.

"Do you believe that I wanted to hurt you?"

She drew in a breath and shook her head. "No, but you left. There was no other explanation left in my mind." She saw a faint smile of sadness on his face.

"Kat, I was sure that the war would claim our lives. I never thought I would see England again. I loved you deeply, but I did not want to leave you a widow at such a young age. I wanted you to have a chance to fall in love and have a happy life."

The meaning of his words penetrated her mind. She stared into his gorgeous blue eyes and his perfect face, trying to take in every inch of him. She focused on fighting to keep her breath slow and steady even though her heart hammered wildly in her chest. He swept her into his arms in one swift movement, and bending down his head, touched her lips with his momentarily. Quickly, he pulled back as if asking for permission. Her arms came up and wrapped around his neck. She intertwined her fingers in his beautiful hair and pulled him down to the kiss once again. And then between one heartbeat and the next, the kiss deepened to one of unbelievable sweetness. His hands moved slowly down to her hips, making her shiver as the kiss became voracious, and they both moaned with excitement. The shudder that ran through them seemed to jolt them to their senses. Abruptly, the kiss ended, and they released one another. He took her hands and brought them down to rest on his chest.

"I am sorry, Kat. I only meant to…" he whispered but did not finish his sentence.

"You don't have to be sorry. I wanted you to kiss me. I

missed you and have been dreaming of this moment for more than six years now."

He sat back on the bench and pulled her down next to him. "Kat, I need to know what happened between you and your father."

Her eyes were bright and serene one minute and then darkened with anxiousness. Recalling the conversation with her father seemed to make her extremely upset. She looked up with eyes full of unshed tears. She nervously licked her lips and started to talk in a low voice, and for the next hour, Patrick listened to every word she said. The information was no different than what he'd learned from his father a few days earlier.

He pulled her closer and stroked her back, trying to calm her. "Do you remember anything else? Please try to think; every possible detail you have will be essential in resolving this agreement's mystery."

"Patrick, I have thought about this for years now, and nothing new comes to mind. I tried to refuse the offer, but my father insisted." Tears rolled down her beautiful face. "Alexander Bennett showed up one morning utterly unannounced and held a meeting with my parents. My father insisted that I attend this meeting. Bennett said that he had documents that could prove my father killed an unarmed man helped by your father. My mother and I sat quietly horrified by the accusations. He continued by saying that if I accepted to become Quinton's wife, the proof papers would never surface. If I refused, he would turn over everything he had to the authorities. I remember my father telling him that he did not believe him since he was present when this killing took place. Bennett had laughed at his face and spit out with fury. He would tell them that my father and yours had threatened his family with their lives, so he kept quiet for all this time. He added that he was going to destroy both families with a blink of an eye." She dissolved into tears once more.

Patrick swallowed his disgust for Bennett and his son. "I will make sure that we find those documents. I have a feeling that he had conspirators in whatever happened that night long ago. There is one more thing I want to ask you."

She cocked her head to the side, watching him closely. "What is it?"

"Did you sleep with Quinton?"

She stiffened at the question, her gaze boring into his. "What do you think?"

"There is a rumor out there that you did not sleep with him."

She arched an eyebrow at his statement. "Is that what they say?" She smiled and took a deep breath. "How would they know? How would anyone know? I did not talk about it, and I am sure Quinton never did. It would have been a huge embarrassment to him."

"Kat, I love you. I must know. How did you stop him? As your husband, he had the right to consummate the union."

She flashed him a dazzling smile. She squared her shoulders and said, "I have sources who kept me informed about his activities. One of them was the High chief constable's wife."

"Oh!" Patrick exclaimed and stood with his mouth

agape. "But how is it possible that information like this did not reach someone in the ton? Who is your source?"

"Marisa."

Patrick's brows lifted astoundingly. "Marisa? How could she possibly know?"

"Eloise, Lady Bennett's maid, heard Quinton fighting with his mother about many of his disgusting activities along with this very issue. She is faithful to her ladyship, but Marisa is my best friend. I am sure that she would have kept this information to herself, but she and I have a friendship bond that will never break. We talked about my marital situation almost every day. She wanted to help me to keep him away." Her mouth twisted in disgust. "Quinton is a despicable human being, a rogue, a scoundrel. If found out, this information would lead to a duel with one of the best shots in England." She tilted her head to one side and looked at him with bemusement. "I told him that I had several witnesses, and I would not hesitate to turn him in. I am sure that the fear of facing the chief constable in a duel did not sit well with him, so he left me alone."

He had his answer, which made him extremely happy. Kat was his and his alone.

He stood up, cleared his throat, chuckled, and held his hand out to her. "Come, let us go back to join your family. I do not want you to worry about this. I will make everything right." He dropped a kiss on her hair and pulled her closer. Her lush body pressed against his, and he was lost. He lowered his head and pressed his mouth on hers. The taste of her on his tongue was maddening. He wanted to take her right then and there under their tree, but he had to control himself. The heat in her eyes ignited his desires. Clenching his teeth, he let her go and took a step back. "We must go. I know your family is expecting us for dinner." She nodded in agreement. He gently grasped her elbow and led her toward the house. She sensed that grace and elegant manners did not require Patrick's effort; they were all second nature to him.

CHAPTER NINE

*B*road smiles welcomed their entrance to the dining-room as polished silverware clattered against the fine china. Patrick led Katherine to the sideboard heaped with every sort of food and delicacy. He picked up a plate and asked her what she preferred to eat.

She looked up and sent him a sweet smile. "Patrick, I can do this on my own."

He chuckled inwardly. "Yes, I know, Kat, but I want to do this for you. Please let me," he murmured for her ears only. Katherine felt a hot shiver slide down her spine. She felt the touch of his beautiful blue eyes on her cheek. Determined, kept her head down not to let her family notice her state of mind. Closing her eyes, she nodded in agreement. The room was large, with a massive fire roaring in the hearth. At the table, he held a chair for Katherine. He then took a seat across from the Duchess.

"What did you think of the garden?" the Duchess asked Patrick.

"It is simply beautiful. Katherine has done an amazing job. It is such an impressive spot." Patrick did not miss the glow in Katherine's eyes. For the next hour, they slipped into a pleasant conversation about everyday issues. Laughter followed Garrett's updates about all the gossip spread across London's elite for the past six years. He noticed his sister's expression alternating between anxiety and insecurity, so he did make sure to stay away from the subject of Quinton. At the end of the meal, the Duchess rose to her feet. Her gaze met Patrick's. "I hope you have time to take tea with us and talk for a while longer.

"Yes, thank you."

She turned to the butler and requested to bring the tea into the drawing-room. Patrick offered his arm to the Duchess and walked out with Katherine between her two brothers. "You do not have to have tea," the Duchess added with a soft chuckle. "We have some nice French brandy."

"That would be wonderful," Patrick replied.

Entering the drawing-room, he paused just beyond the threshold. It was magnificent. The walls were beautifully paneled, while above them ran complexly ornamented stucco ceilings and artworks in themselves. A stunning carpet covered the floor, and a stone-faced fireplace dominated the north wall of the room.

Ten minutes later, the tea trolley arrived. Patrick poured tea for the ladies. He then walked to the table and picked up the brandy decanter. Nicholas and Garrett already had helped themselves. He poured a full glass for himself and took a seat across from the Duchess.

"Thank you for staying." The Duchess rested her eyes on Patrick. "I would like to discuss the issue with Quinton and Katherine. I am sure that you are familiar with the scandal this horrid union created for the family." His gaze met Katherine's over the rim of his glass as he took a sip. She had finished her tea, but her mouth went parched at the sound of Quinton's name.

The conversation that followed was easy and straightforward. Unrestricted by the usual demands of polite discussion, they openly talked about the issues at hand. After establishing all they knew, they settled on the questions that most needed answers. "Yes, I spoke with my father, Katherine, and I have also heard all the rumors spread among the ton and their servants. I must say William and I were shocked to hear about the union between you and Quinton. As I told my family and now yours, I promised William that I would expose Quinton and his father. I will unearth the secret that forced this union and aim to keep that promise if it is the last thing I do."

Straightening his broad shoulders, he glanced around the room. The Duchess looked startled. Her brows rose and held his gaze steadily. "How are you planning on doing that?"

He took a long sip of his brandy. "I have a plan. I have evaluated all the options and have come to a solution."

Nicholas looked at Patrick. "Do you have to go to London to follow up with your inquiries? If so, you can count on us."

"Thank you, Nicholas. I will be meeting with my Viper friends at my parent's home; I will be staying there for a few days. I will keep your generous offer in mind. Finding out secrets was our specialty for six years, and it worked beautifully for England. I am sure it will work out for this issue, too." He chuckled out loud, and they joined in. Patrick refocused on the Duchess's face. "Please do not worry. You know that I have a personal interest in freeing Katherine from this union."

Hands clasped in her lap, she breathed deeply. "Yes, I know, and I am very thankful." She leaned forward, and reaching out, she took his hands and pressed them softly. They fell silent for a very long moment.

He finally stood up and propped himself against the mantelpiece. He drew a breath and broke the silence. "Is there anything else I need to know before I go?"

"Ah, no," Nicholas muttered, and they all agreed. They had nothing more to add.

Pushing away from the mantelpiece, he strolled toward the Duchess. She held out her hand. His fingers closed about hers as he bowed. "I want to thank you for your gracious welcome and the delicious meal."

She smiled wide. "It was my pleasure. Thank you for coming. Please come back soon."

Patrick's gaze turned thoughtful. His soft voice took on a sad tone. "I am sorry for the loss of Duke Weldon. He was my father's best friend, and he will be greatly missed."

"Thank you, my dear boy; we are still trying to deal with his loss."

"I am happy to see you doing well. I know that

Nicholas and Garrett will take care of business. They are good men." She nodded in agreement.

He shook hands with the brothers and strolled toward Katherine. She left her chair and was standing by the door. His gaze had already fixed on her. She was a vision of beauty adorned in that stylish, elegant emerald gown. He had spent the last six years thinking of little else but Kat.

She dragged in a breath; lifting her chin, she smiled and fixed him with a look made to kill. She then turned to her mother. "May I show Patrick out?" Warm approval shone in the Duchess's eyes.

"Indeed." Katherine could feel his gaze drifting over her, and a slow blush rose to her cheeks. She set her hand on his proffered arm, and a shiver rippled through her body. She glanced up at him and met his broad smile.

"I would like nothing better, my dear," he muttered, and his smile deepened. "Shall we go out?"

The door closed behind them, and together they walked down the long hallway. The lit chandelier with dozens of candles hung at the foyer from the gilded ceiling. The large grandfather clock chimed five o'clock, and he tugged her closer to him before they stepped outside. The few scattered clouds in the sky reflected the sun's bright glow slowly dipping below the horizon, turning the evening skylight grey. His arms gathered her even closer, and all the emotions he kept in check up until this moment burst out. His mouth came down on hers. He traced her bottom lip with the tip of his tongue, and she parted her lips, giving him access to the sweetness of her mouth. He deepened the kiss, filled with eagerness and desire. She was on fire, and he held her with longing. Hunger hammering intense in his veins. He moaned blissfully, and the kiss became more and more passionate. "I love you, Kat," he muttered. "You have always been my girl, and now you are going to be my wife." His words focused her mind. Exhilaration swelled scorching Katherine's chest.

"Oh." Katherine looked deep into his eyes and drew a deep breath. Rising to her tippy toes, she kissed him back. "I love you, too, and I don't want you to go." She murmured against his lips.

Patrick pulled back and glanced down at her. "I think I'd better be going," His smile was every bit sensual as it was erotic. She nodded and inhaled a shaky breath.

Katherine looked up, and he did not miss the sadness in her eyes.

He arched an eyebrow, "What is it?"

She swallowed hard and wrapped her arms tightly around her chest. "Quinton has been trying to come here off and on. I have told him that I do not want to see him, but he seems to ignore my requests. It will be a lot harder now."

"How so?"

"I know that you are here, and that changes everything."

"I don't understand."

"I know that my tolerance has reached the point of no return. I hate Quinton so much. The thought of setting eyes on him makes me physically ill."

He puckered his lips in distaste, and his eyes flashed

with irritation. "I do not want to talk about Quinton right now. I want you to trust me and be patient. I will try to resolve this as fast as I can. I do not want us to make any mistakes that might create additional problems."

She nodded slowly. "Must you leave now?" she whispered.

"Yes, but I will be back.

"I will miss you."

"Indeed!" He smiled, and, leaning back down, he pressed a kiss to her forehead. His gaze intensified, and she almost lost herself in his eyes. "Kat, I will miss every moment away from you. I love you more than you will ever know. I will be back soon, my love."

She clung to him like a drowning person onto a lifeline. Patrick fell back into a kiss, feeling every muscle in his body contract. The pleasure was shattering, and her knees buckled. He wrapped his arm quickly around her waist, holding her steady against him. Even though he wanted to prolong the kiss's pleasure, he stopped and pulled his lips a hairpin away. "I have to go," he breathed against her lips. "I want to stay here with you forever, but… I can hear Pegasus hooves thumping on the courtyard stones." With reins in hand, Gunther the stable foreman appeared around the corner.

As they neared, his gaze slid from Gunther to his mount. A wide smile spread across his face. Pegasus was his pride and joy. He turned back to Kat and found himself drowning in translucent blue eyes darker than his own. His gaze overwhelmingly was drawn to her perfectly shaped lips. He was sinking fast, but he had to resist. Sucking in a breath, he pulled back, inwardly shocked at how easily she could take control of his faculties. Patrick set a quick kiss to her forehead and let her go.

He descended the front steps and chuckled when he heard Pegasus snort and tossed his mane as he approached. Taking the reins from Gunther, he bestowed an affectionate pat on Pegasus's neck and stroked his coat. He vaulted on the saddle and swung around toward Kat, flickering his warm gaze over her. She was now aware of an ache that settled deep in her chest. She brought her fingers to her mouth lightly, touching her lips.

He smiled at the kiss and inclined his head. "I will see you soon!" he called out as he led his horse away from the courtyard. He gently spurred him on, and Pegasus lengthened his stride from trot to canter. Soon he was galloping toward the broad path and the rolling hills that were surrounding the Weldon residence. When he looked back again, the house had grown smaller and smaller, but she was still standing there watching him. He wanted to turn around and hold her in his arms one more time. He frowned at the ache that was building deep inside of him, and with a heavy heart, he headed home.

With a slight frown, Katherine watched Patrick until she could not see him any longer. She buried her face in her hands, and, turning on her heels, she walked through the door and quickly shut it behind her. She walked at a fast

LILIAN ROBERTS

pace until she reached the grand stairway. Climbing the steps two at a time, all she could think about was to be alone. She walked quickly down the corridor and entered her bedchamber, which was decked out in light blue and gold velvet of luxurious texture. Her eyes roamed the room that had always provided a serene and tranquil feeling. The domed ceiling held a massive chandelier in the center of it. A four-poster gorgeous canopy-style bed adorned the center of the room. The wall was covered with magnificent leaves and branches that matched the blue and gold color of the headboard. The room filled with dark wood exuded a sense of elegance. The furniture was distinguished with intricate carvings and original images of leaves, flowers, and carved lines. She shut the door and leaned against it, letting out a deep sigh.

Her thoughts were full of Patrick. He was stunningly impressive, and now she had been assured that he was in love with her. Excitement and anticipation surged through her. She went over every word he had said. She could hear his voice and felt the warmth of his eyes. She had fallen profoundly and irrevocably in love with him when they were children. She had always been sure that he was the man that fit the image etched in her very soul, captivated by his mere existence. She pulled the bell cord and summoned for hot water. A few minutes later, the chambermaid came in and drew a warm bath. Dropping her gown at her feet, she walked through the bedroom and entered the washroom. She slipped under the fragrant water with a delicious moan. She closed her eyes and rested her head

136

against the bath's edge. She was sure that the next chapter of her life was about to begin.

Patrick flicked the reins. He had waited to see her for so long that he had started to believe it would never happen for him, and now it had. Kat was his. She told him so. She declared her love for him, and he was elated. He would be the most fortunate man to have her for his wife. He wanted children, at least three, and no other woman would do but Kat. A warm feeling enveloped him, and his heart swelled with pride as if he was already a father. He laughed out loud and sent Pegasus further down the road.

Arriving at his parent's home, he went straight to his father's study. Three men were hovering over a desk littered with ledgers and a few piles of unopened letters. "Welcome, my boy," his father called out without looking up. "How was your visit to the Weldons?

"It went quite well. It was nice to see the Duchess and spend time with Nicolas, Garrett, and Katherine." At the sound of her name, all three looked up.

"Well?" Anthony was looking at him with eyes full of concern.

Eyes widened; "Well, what?" A heated rush of emotion swirled low in the pit of his stomach.

His reaction did not escape his father. "Was she happy to see you?" he asked.

"Why ever not? She was a close friend."

"But she is a lot more than that," added Christopher with a soft chuckle. "Shall I dare to uncover your feelings?"

Patrick gritted his teeth. He did not want to discuss his feelings about Kat. "Yes, she is a lot more than that to me, but we did not discuss this at all. We mostly talked about William and the moments we spent together in France over the six years."

"I am sure that Marian was extremely pleased to hear details about her son," his father added, referring to the Duchess. "I can relate to her feelings, as I know your mother, your brothers, and I missed you immensely while you were gone. Not to mention the worry that lingered for all that time." Nods of agreement came from his two brothers.

At his father's words, Patrick's lips quirked into the tiniest of smiles. He walked across the room and helped himself to a splash of brandy from the decanter on the sideboard. "Brandy?" he offered his father and brothers. They all nodded. He poured the glasses generously. He took a healthy swallow and sat across from his father's desk.

"When are your friends arriving?"

"I sent the notes a couple of days ago, so I am hoping soon."

"Do they know why you summoned them?"

"No, but they will surmise it is important to me."

"I guess Quinton will be the first to deal with," Christopher said.

Patrick's face went rigid. His outburst shocked even himself. "It is beyond belief," he hissed, "that one man can deliberately hurt another person the way he hurt Kat. He is selfish, heartless, insensitive, and ruthless. And that includes his father."

Three pairs of eyes stared at Patrick with different degrees of surprise registering on their faces. His anger was palpable, bouncing against the polished wood paneling. He swirled the brandy in his glass and kept his gaze fastened on the dark liquid. When he finally raised his eyes, he met their silence as if they expected him to continue with his rage. Patrick drummed his fingers on the armrest and took another deep swallow of brandy. Then suddenly, he spoke again. "Someone needs to unearth their secret and teach them a lesson that they will never forget, and I aim to do that."

The Duke watched his son intensely, but he remained silent. Patrick could feel his eyes on him. Suddenly he spoke, his voice sharp. "They are both arrogant fools, and their characters are too much to bear. I am so proud of you, my boy, for taking on this task. Let me know if you need my help."

Patrick rose from the chair and inclined his head. He felt a thrill at the sound of his father's words. "Thank you, Father, I do not think it will be necessary, but I will let you know if I need help."

There was a short silence until Anthony spoke. "I am not sure what your plans are at this moment but when your friends arrive and you decide to ride out, Christopher and I would like to go along." His eyes widened. He looked at both his brothers with pride. They were so grown up.

"As I told father, if I need your help, I will let you know."

"Do you promise?"

He cocked an eyebrow at his brother. "Of course, you have my word." He drained his glass and set it on the sideboard.

A tap at the door had them all glancing that way. The door opened, and Jacob stood at the opening. "What is it?" the Duke muttered.

"It is time for supper, your Grace; the Duchess is already in the dining room."

"Thank you, let's head that way. Your mother does not like to wait." The Duke's lips curved, and a soft chuckled escaped him.

They entered the dining room furnished in the same elegance as the rest of the house, the table covered with a beautiful cloth. The meal was not fancy, but it smelled delightful. The Duke approached his wife, who was already seated. He took both of her hands in his and closed his fingers about them, lifting them to his lips. She raised her face and smiled sweetly. "Hello, my dear," he murmured. "I hope we did not make you wait." He pressed a soft kiss to each of her hands and moved to take his seat at the table's head. They all took turns at the sideboard, loading their plates with pieces of roast beef and potatoes. The meal tasted delicious. After supper, Patrick took his leave.

In his chambers, he pulled the bell cord and summoned for a bath. Five minutes later, Jacob and a footman brought hot water. Patrick paced in front of the fireplace for a long moment. He then removed his clothes and made his way naked to the washroom. He eased himself gently into the welcoming water. Grabbing the soap, he lathered his body and hair and sank to rinse off the suds. Closing his eyes and chin-deep in the water, he rested his head against the tub. Kat was the only thing occupying his mind. He remembered the feeling that enveloped him as soon as he had reached the Weldon residence. He could sense her before she even entered the room, drawn to her like a moth to a flame. He doubted that she realized the effect she had on him. Now he was weighing his options for his next move. He spun all the details of the conversation he would have with the Viper group in his mind. He lost track of time, and it was much later when he realized that the water was getting cold. He reached for a large towel, wrapped it around his body, and stepped out of the bath making, his way back to the bedroom.

A fire roared in the hearth. Patrick collapsed onto a large couch right in front of it. He took up the newly filled decanter of brandy on the side table and poured a glass. Settling his shoulders against the sofa's back, he stretched his legs and crossed his ankles. He let the liquor slide down his throat, heat enveloping every pore and every muscle of his body. He watched the orange and red flames dance wildly, in the fireplace, casting shadows across the floor and the walls. He finally moved to the bed and climbed in. He pulled the covers up over his chest and fussed with the pillow before settling his head on it. He closed his eyes, and Kat was his last thought before sleep claimed him.

CHAPTER TEN

*P*atrick woke up early the next morning. Weak light was just starting to sneak through the opened drapes, and from the garden below his window, the divine chirping of a bird was filling his ears with lovely music. He sat up, pushing the covers away, and immediately he was hit by the room's coldness. His gaze turned toward the fireplace and met an empty hearth and a pile of ashes. He sighed and fell back on the bed, pulling the covers up over his ears. He closed his eyes and let himself imagine Kat in his bed. He remembered the feel of her body against his and could vividly see her breathtaking face. Dragging in a breath, he smiled at the sensation that took over his senses. Thinking of the promising passion, lust, and pure desire, he felt his erection becoming more evident.

A soft knock at the door stabbed at his consciousness. He frowned, and grudgingly he opened his eyes. He stared at the ceiling for a short moment. The sole thought of Kat drove his desires to places he had never known. No woman had ever occupied his mind in that way. Finally, he jerked his gaze toward the door. "Come," he called out.

The door opened softly, and Jacob walked in. "Will you have breakfast, my Lord?"

"Yes, thank you. I tried to get up, but this room is too bloody cold." Chuckling, he remained unmoved under the covers.

Jacob laughed out loud. He crossed the room with vast strides, and soon a beautiful fire roared in the hearth. Patrick lifted himself on one elbow. "Thank you. Tell my mother I will be down soon." He knew that his mother had sent Jacob to persuade him to get out of bed. Meals at his parent's home were critical times for family interaction and unique discussions. He flicked the covers aside and swung his legs out of bed and rose to his feet. Fifteen minutes later, washed, shaved, and dressed, he walked out of his chamber, shutting the door behind him. He descended the main staircase moving and stretching his shoulders beneath his morning coat. He strode to the breakfast room that was flooded by the sun's golden rays.

The rest of the family had already approached the sideboard. Pushing through the door, he reached his mother and pressed a warm kiss to her proffered cheek.

"Good morning, Mother."

"Good morning, Patrick. Did you sleep well?"

"Yes, thank you. I meant to tell you that I was a little surprised that you kept my room exactly as I had left it when I moved to London."

The laughter he heard came from his brothers, but neither of them said anything aloud. Patrick's brows furrowed. "Am I missing something?"

They allowed themselves a few minutes of silence before they came out with it. "Nobody was allowed to enter your room." More silence.

Patrick's head turned to stare at his mother. "Why is that?"

Jaw set, she looked up at him and waved the question aside. "There are more than thirty available rooms in this house. I could not see a reason that someone would need to use your chamber."

"Mother, I sense that there was a lot more to your decision."

It took a few minutes before she could force the words out. Her eyes fixed on Patrick's face. "It made me feel that you never left. I used to go in your room, sit by the window and talk to you as if you were here." He could see moisture rise in her eyes.

He held her gaze as a gust of emotions suddenly roared through him. He reached over and took her in his arms. "I missed you, too, Mother." He pressed a soft kiss to her forehead. He then glanced at his father standing by the sideboard, holding a plate full of eggs, bacon, sausages, and a happy smile. His brothers strolled forward and helped themselves to a hardy breakfast without anything further to say. They all finally took their seats around the table. Their cups were filled several times throughout the meal from carafes of coffee and tea set in the table's middle. The conversation was a pleasant one. Patrick realized that he had missed his family more than he ever thought that he would.

They pushed their chairs away from the table while the servants removed the plates, and the Duchess took her leave. "My dears, I must be going, I have matters I must attend to."

"Where are you going, Mother?"

"Countess Nisbet of Edinburgh is holding her monthly gathering to discuss the schedule for the season's balls, soirees, and all the other festivities. The dates are firm for most of them, but there are a few without dates."

Patrick narrowed his eyes. "For heaven's sake, Mother." His voice was layered with irritation.

"What's wrong, dear?" Amusement coated her voice. She knew how Patrick felt about the ton.

The words ballroom and soiree sent a feeling of disdain through his body. The years he had spent with William roaming the balls, up to the moment they had left for the war, taught him one thing for sure. These rooms were always filled with mothers and papas hunting for rich, titled men for their young, innocent daughters. Giggly girls with questionable intelligence would accept any handsome, wealthy nobleman even if they had absolutely nothing in common. He shook his head in disgust. He didn't immediately reply. Eventually he responded. "Here, we are twenty days before the season begins, and they are already out for the chase."

His mother kept her eyes on him. She was trying hard to hold back mirth. "I take it that you did not see the invitations that arrived this morning. I had them sent to your room." Laughter filled the air as his mother turned and walked out.

Patrick's frown deepened; the thought of the feminine chatter, the giggles of silly young girls, and the parents' calculating looks made him cringe.

When Patrick and his brothers left the breakfast room, they strolled down the hallway, halting before their father's study. Patrick crossed the threshold, and his eyes moved around the room. His father's study reflected his personality even more than the rest of the house. The room was vast and dark but brightened by an ornamental plaster ceiling and two huge windows that adorned the beautiful gardens' north wall. There was no question that the study resounded richness, grandeur, and power. The furniture was comfortable, echoing Louis XV style of the previous century. Elegant matching silk fabrics for the curtains and seat covers, only enhanced the beautiful bookshelves and all three oak-paneled walls. Patrick approached the desk along with his brothers and looked at the spread-out ledgers. The plan his father set during breakfast was to work and balance the numbers for all the products. Then spend the day riding out to gather more information and results from the foreman running the estate's various businesses. It was part of a daily task, and he wanted to help while waiting for his friends to arrive. He felt his father's gaze.

"Do you want to give it a go?" his father asked.

Patrick looked at his father and nodded. He had never

gotten involved in his father's business. His parents had always been in total control of the estate, giving the sons room to grow and take over when the time was right.

Suddenly, laughter drew his attention to a side table. With hands in their pockets, Christopher and Anthony stared at the avalanche of letters and invitations that had arrived. His eyes opened wide, and he mentally paused, wondering why there were so many gatherings during one season. He smiled and, moving to the side table that held the brandy, poured a glass, taking a seat behind the desk. He fixed his gaze on the amber liquid inside the glass, and finally, he looked up and focused his gaze on his brothers.

He pointed to the letters. "You know what this means, don't you?"

"What?"

"You both are marked as wealthy, titled, unmarried, and eligible young men. Now the ton's mamas are seeking you out as candidates for their unmarried daughters."

Their eyes widened in disbelief. "You couldn't possibly believe that we will fall for that," Christopher mumbled.

"You might not but don't you know why they want you in those ballrooms? They are shopping for husbands. That is their main job."

"Well, they are not going to find a husband in either one of us. We are not ready for marriage." They laughed aloud. The sound sent a sense of lightness in the room.

"And what about you? I am sure that includes you, too." Anthony said.

"Yes, I suppose it does, but I am not available." He grinned.

"Really? How so?"

He chuckled softly. "Unfortunately, I cannot say as of yet."

"Katherine?"

Patrick's cheeks flamed as her name washed over him.

The Duke turned to face his sons. "Not another word. Let's get to work."

The morning flew by too swiftly, filled with a multitude of tasks. The ledgers were balanced, and it was an eye-opener for Patrick. He never realized the extent of detail that went into these books. It was quite complicated based on the individual family's monetary income, sustenance food, farm-produced consumption goods, and essential production factors. He was amazed by how much went into his father's responsibility for the welfare of the help hand families. Not to mention that he cared deeply about their children's education and health.

A complete log chronicled the buildings housing the farm animals and the help families' residences. Another log contained analysis and evaluation of all the systems required running the daily chores. He could see that it was a fascinating art between optimizing resources and achieving excellent results. Patrick sat back and rested his hands, palms down on the desk.

"Father, why are you doing all this by yourself? There are so many people around you, capable of handling all these tasks."

The Duke regarded him in silence before he replied.

"That is true, I do have many people, but I use them to do all the physical work and provide all the numbers that go into these ledgers keeping this estate going the right way. Your mother was adamant at being part of the growth when we first got married. She set up the ledgers and handled all the details. The estate became profitable beyond expectations, and that is when we decided to keep this part of the business in house rather than hand it out to solicitors. There is a certain satisfaction that derives from work well done."

Patrick's eyes lit with admiration for his father. He pulled together the payroll checks and set them aside in a small pile. "I guess we are done here, right?"

Somewhere in the house, a clock stroked out minutes and seconds as they rose to their feet and picked up their coats.

"Oh, look here are a few invitations for you," Anthony said and handed them to Patrick. His response was instant; he seized them and flung them into the hearth without looking at them. Flames enveloped them quickly.

Anthony gasped. "You didn't even check the names."

Christopher opened his mouth to voice his question, but Patrick beat him to it, forcing his lips straight. "There is no use. I wouldn't get myself anywhere near a ballroom."

Following a short meal and a very stimulating conversation about ballrooms, they pushed away from the table. Their exchanges had taken a rather amusing turn, for they regaled each other with funny stories. Patrick loved being home and spending time with his family. He could not help feeling a slight pang of sadness, knowing that his brothers had to go back to school. He wanted to spend more time with them and learn more about their activities during the six years he had missed. He noticed one thing. They had grown more thoughtful, intellectual, and charismatic. They were not the boys in short coats that he had left behind. "When are you going back to school?" he asked Christopher.

"Hmm, I think we have a fortnight left here." He met Anthony's gaze. "Am I right?"

"Yes, that's right," Anthony said after several seconds had passed. The Duke watched his sons for a short moment, and with a sigh, he waved them out the door. By the time they stepped outside, Maurice, the stable foreman, had the four massive greys saddled and waiting. Midday greeted them with the soft wind, and a few clouds still spotted the blue sky. Mounting, they settled in their saddles and cantered off.

Fields and meadows blooming with beautiful wildflowers and beautiful trees surrounded the estate. They rode through spacious pastures, hidden meadows, and into breathtaking ravines. Patrick pressed his heels to Pegasus's side and picked up speed. He felt the warm wind blow against his face and smiled wide. Riding Pegasus gave him an indescribable sense of freedom. They were all moving along winding paths and beautiful streams of running water. Their first stop was his parents' stud farm two-and-a-half miles to the east bordering the Weldon estate. Young lads were working, keeping the yard and the stalls in spotless condition. The freshly painted buildings housed the stables, and the fences were impeccable. They spent more than an hour there talking to the foreman and watching the fabulous Arabians and thoroughbreds trained by skillful hands.

Next, they visited the various locations and talked with the foremen and farm safety advisers. They provided information on the equipment status and details about places they assessed for potential danger to the animals and workers. Finally, the head foreman handed Anthony the paperwork for the sales, receipts, and expenses for the month. Patrick enjoyed being part of his father's activities and watched firsthand how effectively he communicated with everyone around him. He was very proud of his father and delighted that he had come out of his illness strong and healthy again. While they could comfortably ride for a couple more hours, they decided to head home. He glanced at the sun and noted that they had only about an hour before twilight.

His father, with an imperious gesture, led the way. Patrick, Christopher, and Anthony cantered side-by-side through the green fields keeping a close distance from their father. At the courtyard, they dismounted and handed the reins to the stable lads and strode into the house, dirty, sweaty, and tired. They headed back to their rooms to clean up and change for dinner. A hot bath had been prepared for him; he stepped into the tub, fully submerging himself in the warm water. Resting his arms against the edge of the tub, he closed his eyes. It had been a good day.

· · ·

Early the next morning, Patrick stood by the large window and pulled the curtains open to look at the sunrise. It was a perfect day. The sun peeked over the horizon, giving the sky a light yellow and orange tint. He smiled, unable to move his eyes away from the stunning sight. As the sun continued its journey upward, the sky turned a fantastic array of beautiful colors. The fields looked greener than he had ever seen them. He could even feel the sun's warmth encircling the earth. His thoughts turned to Kat. He could not stop mentally rearranging specifics, turning over every item, and figuring the best way to approach this issue.

Today he suspected that his friends would be arriving, and he was anxious to share the information he had gathered and establish a good plan. He turned and strode across the thick carpet. Slowly, he made his way to the bath. He washed, shaved, and dressed leisurely. Suddenly his attention was drawn by the sound of horse's hooves rapidly approaching. Running footsteps on the cobblestones of the courtyard brought him back to the window. He had suspected correctly, his friends had arrived. A wide smile crossed his face, when the riders came to a halt. They dismounted and threw the reins to the grooms who had come running up. George Theron MacDougall, Michael Gregory Norman, and Edward Anthony O'Connell stood for a few moments and looked around. Patrick chuckled out loud. They looked ready for action even though there was no enemy in sight. They were all tall, broad-shouldered, and dressed with elegance in beautifully cut coats over white shirts, with long legs encased in tight buckskin breeches that disappeared into polished black Hessians.

They did not look tired, but he knew that London's ride was a long and dusty one. The elegant cut of their morning clothes poorly hid the strength they possessed. Patrick knew that underneath the stylish clothes, they all bore the scars of the years they spent behind enemy lines.

Patrick went out the door, crossed the hallway in large strides, and descended the main staircase two steps at a time. The noise had brought Jacob and his mother to the foyer.

"Good morning Patrick. I think your friends are here."

The knock came before he had a chance to open his mouth. "Yes, Mother," he called out as he pulled the door wide open. They had not seen each other since they stepped away from the ship that brought them back to England. The hugs were firm and genuine. They rejoiced in their pride as part of the British spy groups that had handed victory to England.

Patrick moved on to introduce the group to his mother. She invited them to join the family for breakfast, and they were happy to accept her invitation. They walked into the breakfast room with a keen sense of hunger and anticipation for a great discussion. The room was filled with the beautiful scent of coffee, smoked ham, eggs, and toasted bread. Soon his brothers and father joined. Breakfast had never been so lively and so energetic. His father was a close friend with Gregory's father, the Marquess of Pendenton. That created some lengthy conversation between those two. They spooned mountains of eggs and worked through plates of ham and sausages. After a couple of coffee cups the glimmer in their eyes implied that they were enjoying themselves more than they typically did. After breakfast, they took their leave after thanking the Duke and the Duchess for their kindness.

Patrick professed that the library would be the perfect place for them to hold their meeting. He steered them down the long hallway and up the main staircase to the second floor. He stepped aside and let his friends enter before crossing the threshold and shutting the door behind him. The room was large but beautiful. The walls loaded with excellent leather-bound books in dark wood bookcases. Thick carpets covered the floor making their footsteps inaudible. A pair of leather sofas faced each other in front of a large fireplace, which was ablaze, making the room even cozier. Several large chairs were

set at critical spots of the room. They stripped their coats off and tossed them at a settee by the hearth. Patrick strolled to the sideboard and picked up the decanter full of the finest French brandy and offered to pour. With a full glass in hand, he gestured for them to sit. He then took his place behind his father's large desk. They took a sip of the brandy letting the dark liquid slide down their throats, sending warmth across their muscles.

"So, what's up, Patrick?" George asked evenly. "What is going on? We are eager to hear the urgency for this meeting."

Patrick seemed to twirl a pen between his fingers tensely as he glanced between his three friends and dragged in a long breath.

George raised an eyebrow, while Edward and Michael appeared cloaked in quiet anticipation.

"Well?" George asked again, eyes narrowed.

Patrick kept quiet for a short moment, and, when he spoke, his voice was measured. He lay out his concerns, and for the next hour, he provided all the details his father and Katherine had given him. He stopped and took a deep breath. "I am sure that there is more to the secret Bennett is holding. He is one of the most dishonest men I have ever met, and his son is even worse."

The men looked very intrigued and ready to help. "I think we need to move in steps," Edward suggested.

They all turned their attention to Edward, who continued. "I think that we need to set up surveillance in London on the few of the groups of criminals known to deliver extortion letters for money. We might find something."

"This took place so long ago. How would they ever know what happened then? I would be surprised at that," Patrick muttered.

"Patrick, these groups have been in business for years. The older recruit young boys and keep the cycle going."

"I have an idea," George added with a firm voice. "While you are checking the criminals for information, I will contact Andrew Fletcher." At the sound of the name, everything in their mind came to a screeching halt. From his office, Andrew Fletcher was their mentor and the person the secret military forces respected the most. Andrew reported to Paul Webster the commander who was obscured in Whitehall's depths, and directed the entire British spy networks, behind enemy lines, responsible for all covert operations. He was also the husband of Quinton's mistress.

"What could you possibly ask Andrew to do in this case?"

"I will ask him to find out if they arrested any extortionists around the same time your father and Weldon received the letter. If so, he will be able to check the details in their arrest files. He might even provide another avenue if all this fails."

A stony silence fell between them. These were two good routes to take, but they had to dig deeper.

"My take on this is a bit different," Michael offered.

" Michael, what's going on in there?" Patrick asked, pointing toward his head.

Pushing back his chair, he rose to his feet and walked around to face his friends. "I think that we need to search Bennett's home and find the document he used to get his son married to Katherine. We might also find other paperwork that would lead us to the men he worked with the night of the murder."

Patrick blinked, rose to his feet, hands behind his back, paced across the room. " Michael, you have a great point." He exclaimed. "We were the best in infiltrating people's residences and stealing documents during the war, so this should be easy."

"They decorated us as one of the best spy groups behind enemy lines," George added, laughing out loud, and his friends joined in. For the next couple of hours, they whispered and set up a plan. They decided that they would take all the steps above one at a time and work their way through each one until they resolved the issue, starting with the Bennett residence. They agreed that they would not get Andrew involved until they had no other avenue.

Edward clapped Patrick on the back. "Don't worry, my friend. We will have this problem resolved before you know it. We have experienced worse and come out on the winning side, so we should approach this like any other engagement." They all paused, considering Edward's words. Finally, they nodded in agreement, exchanging glances. There was more than a touch of uninhabited adventure in each of them, and they were extremely loyal to each other.

CHAPTER ELEVEN

*S*ilence fell in Duke Wingham's study as they all absorbed the steps considered. "Have you thought about facing Quinton? George asked, changing the subject. "You need to have a plan for that, too."

Patrick stifled a groan and drew a long breath. He hated Quinton with passion. In the past six years, he had carried this burden and could not wait to end it. Raking his hand through his hair, he walked around the desk to the walnut sideboard that held the brandy. One hand on the brandy decanter and the other cupping a glass, he suppressed an inner struggle. He poured a generous amount for all and gulped his down, wincing appreciatively. The stern liquid burned its way down his throat and irritation plucked at him again.

"Anything more?" George glanced around the room.

"One more thing we should discuss while we are together," Michael said.

George raised his brows. Curiosity propelled him. "What's on your mind?"

"When we landed in France and banded together behind enemy lines, we formed the Viper Group and swore loyalty forever. At the same time, I vividly remember that we came to a significant agreement. If we ever made it home alive, we would form a club with the same name. Well, here we are. You have to agree that we need a place to meet to exchange ideas, handle issues such as this one, or simply have a few drinks and enjoy time together." His gaze lifted and scanned their faces. He looked like his mind flashed on clips of memory. Michael paused, then added. "Well?"

George smiled wide. "I remember and love the idea. It would not hurt to have a few bedchambers in case..." he mused. "It would also serve as a barricade against the hungry mamas of the ton looking to unload their daughters to one of us." At his words, laughter filled the room.

Sipping his brandy, Patrick recalled his earlier conversation with his brothers and nodded. "It should be somewhere easily reachable but not known to anyone else but us." George tapped the desk in thought. He then looked at his friends, and all agreed to find the perfect place.

"Are we done?" George chuckled.

They drained their glasses and stood up. They agreed to go riding after they had something to eat. Patrick pulled the bell cord. A few minutes later, a soft knock drew their attention. Jacob opened the door and halted at the threshold. Patrick smiled kindly. "Jacob, please show my friends their rooms to have some private time."

Jacob glanced at Edward, George, and Michael and met

159

their gaze. "I had your luggage moved upstairs, and footmen are preparing hot baths for you."

They all looked pleasantly surprised. Slow, effortless smiles curved their lips. They inclined their heads. "Thank you, Jacob."

They picked up their coats, and together they strode out of the room. Patrick paused as they reached the top of the staircase. "I have to agree with Edward; we need to look for a London place that would fit our requirements. A place away from our homes to avoid servants' rumors spreading about our personal activities." He smiled, as they climbed the stairs and went into their appointed rooms.

A few hours later, they met downstairs, freshly washed, shaved, and dressed in elegant coats, tight buckskins, and gleaming Hessians. They strode down the corridor and reached the dining room in time to join the rest of the family for a delicious meal. Patrick and his friends' appearance snatched everyone's attention. The Duke acknowledged them with a soft smile. "Hello, come in." He rose to his feet and shook their proffered hands. They strolled to the sideboard exchanging warm greetings with Patrick's brothers and the Duchess. During the meal, the conversations drifted through various subjects, such as billiards, cards, fencing, and horse racing, overall general and lively.

The Duchess studied her son's face. "Are you going riding?"

He met her eyes and noticed a sudden intensity in her

expression that completely surprised him. He raised his brows, hesitated, and made a mental note to ask her about it later. "Yes, Mother, I thought this would be a great way to show my friends the estate." She nodded in agreement and looked down at her plate.

Christopher cleared his throat, drawing his attention. "Can we ride along?"

"Of course, you—" Sounds of horse hooves on the cobblestone courtyard echoed in his ears and stopped him midsentence. Muttered voices and a doorbell chime had drew everyone's attention away from the conversation.

They watched Jacob leave the room. A few minutes later, he returned. "Duchess Marianne Weldon and Lady Katherine Weldon are here to see you, my Lady." Duchess Wingham pushed away from the table, sending a soft smile toward Patrick, who had risen and stood staring at his mother in patent disbelief. What was Katherine doing here?

His reaction did not escape anyone in the room. His mother could almost feel the pressing weight of Patrick's gaze. "Please finish your meal," she muttered. "They are here on my invitation for afternoon tea."

Recovering his wits, he watched Katherine and her mother cross the threshold behind Jacob and stopped short as they immediately spotted the three young men they had never seen before. They stared at each other for the space of a moment. Patrick's mother rose to her feet in a rustle of silk and hurryingly approached her guests.

Katherine smiled at her and managed to find enough breath to speak evenly. "My Lady, your invitation to tea might have brought us here a bit early. We are sorry for interrupted your meal."

"No...No..." She exclaimed and waved her hand, dismissively. "I have been expecting you. Please come in and meet our guests."

The women turned and met the patently admiring gazes of the men. Katherine was breathtaking, clad in a light pink chiffon gown with beautiful spring designs and a lovely beaded bodice. Duchess Weldon was sure that the looks directed toward her beautiful daughter. Katherine was aware of the stir she was causing, and she struggled to keep the grin from her face. Patrick's blue eyes held hers, and she felt a warm sensation spread across her veins. His mouth curved, and his eyes seemed to light up. She inhaled sharply and released it on a lengthy inaudible sigh. She could almost see what he was thinking and averted her gaze quickly. Eyes are said to be the mirror of the soul.

Patrick moved with an unhurried grace and crossed the room. He took Duchess Weldon's gloved hand and pressed a kiss on the back of it. Then, he approached Katherine and lifted her fingers to his lips. Although she wore gloves as well, he could feel her skin's warmth as he pressed his mouth on the back of her hand. Along with his mother, he steered them further into the room, where everyone was now standing, their eyes focused on the two elegant women.

They greeted the Duke warmly along with his other sons. Patrick proceeded with the introductions of his friends. Both women were extremely enthralled in meeting George, Michael, and Edward. They were well aware that they belonged to an elite group that helped bring victory to England along with Patrick and William. That alone was awe-inspiring.

Duke Wingham pulled the fob from his coat pocket and checked the time. He moved with quiet grace. "Ladies, I must excuse myself. I have a meeting I need to prepare for."

Duchess Wingham hauled her gaze up to her husband. "A meeting?"

"Yes, my dear, Jonathan Ainsworth will be here in the next thirty minutes. I need to get all the paperwork ready for him." He leaned down and pressed a soft kiss to his wife's forehead.

He then inclined his head. "Please forgive me, my dear Marian. This meeting was preplanned. It was wonderful to see you."

She smiled and held out her hand. "It was good to see you, my Lord."

His hand closed around hers. "Please come back." He released her and bowed elegantly.

He drew his gaze from her and looked at Katherine. "You, my dear child, look as beautiful as always." He took his leave and strolled out of the room.

When he was out of sight, Patrick's mother turned toward the other ladies. "We do not need to be standing here talking when we can be more comfortable in the sitting room."

Duchess Marianne turned her attention toward the men. "It was very nice meeting you."

The men bowed elegantly and returned her kind words.

Katherine inclined her head and smiled politely. The gentlemen left the room to ready for their afternoon ride.

Patrick stayed behind. He glanced around the now empty room and hallway and watched as his mother led Katherine's mother toward the sitting room with Katherine on their heels, but just before she crossed the threshold, he reached for her hand and held her back. Katherine's blood raced through her veins until she was sure he could hear her heart pounding in her chest. He bent down and took her lips on a soft kiss. She moaned into his mouth. He then pulled away and gazed into her eyes.

"I am leaving tomorrow morning early for London," he said.

She hesitated, clearly considering if she should ask about his time away. She decided that this was the most urgent thing she wanted to know. "For how long?" Her words were breathless.

Patrick sensed her growing tension and took one step closer. He set one long finger under her chin, bringing her face much closer. His patient voice and quiet tone gave her solace. "Kat, I will be gone for a few days. We have to start working on the plan we discussed yesterday. I can't do that from here. We need to be close to the Bennett home to follow their activities."

Clutching his sleeve, she pulled herself closer. "Please be careful." Despite her effort to stay composed, she found herself ready to cry. But she knew that Patrick was working to whisk her away from Quinton and into his safe embrace.

"I will be back as soon as possible." He smiled intently.

"Where are you going now?" Her voice had lowered.

"We are going riding, and I will take my friends into town. I am sure we will not be back until much later."

She hmphed. Taking another look around, making sure there was no one in sight, Patrick stepped away from the doorway and pulled her closer, and bending down, covered her mouth with his. Her lips parted, and he surged eagerly into her mouth's softness, tasting her sweetness and seizing her soft lips' sensuousness. She moaned in his mouth, and the sound resonated deep into his very core. He angled his head and deepened the kiss, leaving Katherine utterly witless. She tunneled her fingers into his hair and clung to him in desperation. His brother's voice calling for him jolted him and jerked him back to sanity. "I have to go, my love." He pressed a soft kiss to her lips and let her go.

Katherine stumbled back, still lost in that kiss. Her gaze touched his face for one last time. Then she walked away toward the threshold of the sitting room and disappeared behind it. "There you are!" He heard Duchess Weldon call-out at the sight of her daughter.

He smiled and quickly moved toward the front door. A few minutes later, Katherine heard the thunder of receding hooves that soon faded away. She blinked against the sadness his absence created.

The men rode out across the rolling green hills of the estate. The sun lingered in the blue sky, sending rays that bathed the earth in pure gold. Patrick studied the horizon and smiled broadly. It was where he wanted to be for the rest of his life. There was a spectacular view in the short distance that drew their attention and took their breath away. They could see a river crossing the green fields from east to west. The sun's rays hit the water and created a breathtaking rainbow of blues and greens. They sped down the hills, through the trees until they reached the river. They crossed the small bridge and came to the top of the hill at the property's end.

The village of Wingham in the valley two miles away looked like it spread under their feet. William and Patrick often spoke about the tranquil town that promoted and moved many of their parents' products to adjacent towns. Descending the hill, they burst down the final stretch into the village square, kicking up dirt. They wanted to explore and check the market stalls with their bountiful offering of beautiful clothes and textiles and savor the tasty ale served in the local taverns. Their horses snorted as they pulled back on the reins and dismounted.

After they finished visiting the various textile locations, they decided to stop at the nearest tavern. From a slight distance, they heard intense discussions and laughter. It was now late in the afternoon, and locals began to assemble as they always did after work to gossip about their family and neighbors and enjoy a few drinks. With a nod of his head, Patrick led the way inside. Heads turned to watch the six elegantly dressed men take a corner table to avoid the bar's rush. George moved around the edge of the crowd slightly, trying to see what point they were at in the service. Soon the barmaid brought them drinks.

Edward spoke first. "I am aware that we all own a few elegant country homes but only one in London. So, as we discussed before, we need a commonplace. Where do you think we need to start looking?"

Patrick let his gaze stray over to the table next to them. He raised an eyebrow at the men who were leaning closer, trying to eavesdrop. "Can I help you?" his words fell slowly, distinctly, and marked by the most definite emphasis. There was not one of them that did not feel a low shudder run along their nerves. They immediately turned the other way and moved their chairs a little further away. Patrick chuckled inwardly. "Well, how about if we look at..." he started to say and turned to find five pairs of eyes peering down at him in anxious silence. "What?

"What was all that about?" his brother asked.

"They were trying to eavesdrop, and I let them know that I was not happy about it."

The men turned toward the table next to them, but the men had already moved. George shook his head and chuckled a rich, throaty laugh. He glanced between Anthony and Christopher, his lips turning up, "Your brother did this a lot in Paris."

Their eyes flew to Patrick. "Really? Why?"

"Why?" He was shocked by the question. He leaned forward, keeping his voice low. "Our conversations behind enemy lines were a matter of life and death. I was not a fan of people eavesdropping. I guess it is a habit that I need to work on now that the war is over." He chuckled. His gaze snapped up as if he remembered what he was about to say. He cleared his throat. "So, I thought we might look for a home on Baker Street, Gloucester Street, or Portman Square, the swarm of little streets nestling at the verge of Park Lane, and those lying between St. James's Street and the Great Park. What do you think?"

Gregory glanced sideways toward his friends and took a deep breath. "I like your ideas. There is also Grosvenor Square, and we might even look at Arlington Street. It overlooks Green Park, and that makes it nice as well."

They all agreed that those were some great ideas for the establishment of the Viper Club. The barmaid came back with a decanter full of ale and set it in the middle of the table. Patrick's gaze flitted between his brothers and his friends. "We can't wait this long to resolve the Bennett issue." His mind raced with thoughts as he picked up the decanter and filled the glasses to the brim. Silence filled the space between them.

George took a long sip and leaned forward, watching his friend over the brim of the glass. "What do you suggest?"

"First, let me say that I hope you understand the necessity of secrecy in our working together on this issue."

"But of course," they all replied in unison, nodding their heads.

"We can meet at my home at Oxford Street while we are looking for the new house. We will not be disturbed. Besides the few servants, there is no one else in the house, and they are very loyal to me. I know that you all have the same set up at your residences, but I also know that some of your family members visit regularly." They all nodded in agreement.

George swirled his glass before sipping his ale. "Surely, someone knows the truth about this whole arrangement," he added. "I smell a conspiracy; there is no way the whole scheme was put in place by Bennett."

They talked a bit more and sipped at their ale until they finally noticed that they were the only people left in the tavern, and their glasses were empty. A few locals were still there, but they were too drunk to move. "Anything I can get for you, sir?" the barmaid asked with a smile.

They looked around for a moment, down at their empty glasses, and back up at the barmaid. "No, thank you," Patrick said. The barmaid nodded her head in acknowledgment as they pushed away from the table and walked out. By the time they returned home, the sun was already setting on the horizon.

Morning sunshine flooded the dining room, where the family had an early, leisurely breakfast. The Duke sat forward, took a sip of his coffee, and pinned Edward, George, and Michael with his gaze. "I can't tell you how happy we are that we had the chance to meet you. Patrick spoke of you in his letters while in France and again when he came home. I am especially pleased and thankful that you have agreed to resolve this major issue plaguing the Weldon family and ours."

They smiled and nodded their heads. Theron was the one to speak. "The pleasure has been entirely ours."

The Duchess turned to Patrick. "What time are you leaving, dear?"

"As soon as we finish here."

At the front patio, he bid his parents and brothers goodbye. They quickly mounted their horses and slowly headed out of the cobblestone courtyard. When they cleared the gates, they galloped off toward London and hurriedly disappeared into the distance.

The road back to London seemed twice as long as Patrick felt the weight of the situation pressing down. He was thankful that his friends rode back with him, ready to assist in any way. His brothers didn't follow. They had to return to school the following week. Patrick's house at Oxford Street was exquisite. It sat on a large piece of land groomed and splendidly designed. It had a stable with twelve stalls, all refined oak and brass. Magnificent trees whose branches intertwined and formed a fabulous green tunnel adorned the driveway to the courtyard. They dismounted and handed the reins to the stable lads. They brushed off the dust from their coats and proceeded into the house. Patrick checked his watch. It was a quarter after one, which meant they had time to bathe and enjoy a late dinner before they gathered in the study.

"Let's take all the time needed to bathe and relax. I think we should have a light meal and then get to work." He looked at his friends straight in the eyes. "What do you think?"

"Sounds like a plan," Gregory said with a smile.

"Christian will show you to your chambers."

They climbed the main staircase together, chatting and joking. At the top of the landing, Patrick halted. "When you are ready to eat, just follow your nose. Jenifer is an amazing cook. The wonderful meal will be waiting for us in the dining room." He suppressed a laugh at his comment, but his friends found it quite amusing, and they broke out into hardy laughter.

CHAPTER TWELVE

Two hours later, Patrick walked into his study. No matter the weather outside, the evening always felt cold inside. He was the first one to arrive. He strolled over to the fireplace, removed the screen, picked up the poker, and stoked the fire, generating a huge flame. He then replaced the screen and walked to his desk. Soon the rest of the men arrived and took a seat in the cozy chairs around the office. They all knew why they were there, but they were missing the rules of engagement. Patrick pulled a map out of a bottom drawer and stretched it across the desktop.

"What is this?" Edward asked.

"This is a map my father drew showing every entrance and every detail of the Bennett residence,"

"But how? I thought they stopped being friends a long time ago."

"Yes, that is true, but Bennett and his wife bought this home when they were married. At that time, they had a very tight friendship with my parents and William's parents. The kids were all in short coats. There was no need for Bennett to use extortion like this until Quinton grew up to be a rake, a womanizer, and a gambler. He and his father gambled most of their fortune away, and that is where Katherine came in. Bennett wanted her fortune to pay off his debts."

Their faces grew hotter from outrage. "What a horrible human being," Edward scoffed.

"You are correct, Edward. I will not rest until Quinton and his father pay for what they have done. I only wish that Weldon and William were still alive to see them punished. Duke Weldon died from a broken heart. He could not forgive himself for giving his precious daughter to a man like Quinton." The men nodded their heads at the obvious contempt they heard in Patrick's voice.

He then swung around and sauntered to the center of the room to face his friends. His lips lifted briefly and his jaw set. He had to display a patience he didn't have. He wanted this over. He walked back and looked down at the map and then up again. "Before we study the map. "I want to thank you again for coming to support me as you all did behind enemy lines. I have been thinking about my family and William's family. I believe in honor and responsibility, and I know that without those, the rest is meaningless. I promised William that I would pursue this issue and whomever is involved even at great cost to everything I hold dear."

"Don't stress, Patrick. We are all here for you. I am sure that we don't understand your feeling's depth, but we are brothers, and we have sworn to support each other for the rest of our lives," Edward said.

Patrick closed his eyes briefly and nodded. "I must say that I have been consumed by this ever since I stepped foot on English soil."

They all leaned forward to examine the map. George twisted his lips and drummed his fingers along the edge of the desk. "So, what is the plan?"

"I have received little information. Alexander Bennett's wife has been staying in the country and will be there for another fortnight. I will bet that the disgraceful Bennett men are spending their time with their mistresses."

"So, you are saying that there would be no one there but for the servants?" Michael asked.

"That is what I am hoping. The servants' quarters are on the opposite side of the main house, so I am sure we will not be interrupted."

"Do you think that he is reckless enough to hide this type of information in his home?" George asked.

"I am sure of that. Quinton has disgraced himself in so many ways; He doesn't trust anyone and has no friends in the ton or London,"

"Do you think we can find a connection between Bennett and his conspirators?" Michael asked.

"Yes, he threatened Weldon with that information, so I hope that there is a journal or document buried in his study or library. It is worth searching for anything we can find in his home. Who knows? We might find names that will be helpful to us."

They went over the details on the map until they knew their way around the residence.

"What time is it now?" George asked.

Struggling to get his brain into gear, Patrick looked at his watch. "It is only eight o'clock" he replied. "I suggest that we do not leave until darkness can provide the protection that we need. I am bringing a couple of the matchboxes we purchased in France."

"We need a small bottle of sulfuric acid to light the matches if needed," Edward said.

"I have it right here," Patrick replied, pointing at the fireplace mantel.

The light outside began to fade away in the same gradual manner it had arisen, and soon the earth was again plunged in darkness. They moved as panthers seeking prey. The streets were shadowy and bare. They arrived on Grosvenor Avenue a little after midnight. The house looked black and empty, and it was apparent that the servants had retreated to their quarters. Gritting their teeth, they climbed over the gates and crept to the edge of the garden. Their adrenaline pumped hard as they walked at an agonizingly slow pace across the yard to the main door. They breached the lock, and tiptoeing, entered the empty foyer. Patrick and George ascended the dark staircase to the second floor. Michael and Edward moved on the other side of the house and took the back stairs that led from the kitchen to the second floor. Those stairs were cold and winding, and they slid their hands along the damp walls to feel their way up through the darkness.

. . .

They had uninterrupted access to the second floor. They stood in a dim hallway with several doors on either side, assessing the situation before moving. Using the map as a guide, they proceeded first to the study. Patrick reached for the handle and turned. The door was locked. He pulled with all his strength and yanked it wide open. The room was colder than the rest of the house. The curtain had not been shut all the way, letting a soft silver band of light slip through the corner of the window, which cast eerie shadows on the walls. They proceeded toward Bennett's desk. They roamed through every piece of paper in the desk drawers, looking for documentation on the extortion. The poorly lit room didn't affect their capable ability to work in the dark. It was something they had done many times while in France. The fourth drawer on the right was locked. George took out a small tool and opened it quietly. He thumbed through a pile of papers, and his eyes zeroed in what it looked like a false bottom drawer. His breath hitched as flashes of the war flooded his thoughts. While behind enemy lines, they infiltrated many secret compartments and recovered relevant enemy documents that helped save countless British lives. He removed it and pulled out a pile of papers. He asked Michael to light a match, and he thumped through them carefully. As his eyes moved down the pages, an explicit curse escaped his lips.

Everyone halted at his sound, and heads turned. "What?" Patrick asked, seeing the shocked expression on George's face.

"I see the names of a few well-known highwaymen on this page." His voice was hardly louder than a whisper.

"There are signatures of agreements. It appears to be an official document."

"Highwaymen?" Michael 's eyebrows lifted. "Really? I didn't think they were around any longer."

"Yes, they are," Edward said. "I heard that because of traveler robberies' decline during those days, they engaged in various other crimes. Extortion was on the top of their list."

They moved closer to the documents. Patrick struck another match and noticed Weldon and his father's names toward the third page's bottom. He took the papers from George, rage filling every fiber of his body. He glanced at the content again and let out a faint gasp. His brows shot straight up, shocked into stillness. The document contained a complete layout of every person involved, and every location visited to complete Bennett's horrible sham for a sum of a few hundred pounds. After they used several matches, they concluded that they had found the documents. " I think we have found what we need. Now we have to find these people and visit them," Patrick said.

"But they may not be in business today," Michael stated.

Patrick nodded thoughtfully. His lips stretched into a thin line. "I have a gut feeling that someone down in the docks knows more than we do."

Michael 's frown deepened. "I suggest that we go there, follow them, listen to their conversations, find their contacts, and then deal with them."

Patrick looked as if he were trying to grasp a thought that remained just within reach and scoffed. "The thugs in

176

charge are executioners without souls and scruples. Let's go."

They took the rest of the papers from the secret compartment, put it back in place, and locked the drawer. They removed the remains of several burned matches from the floor, put everything else back the way it was, and left the room, closing the door behind them. Halfway down the dark hallway, they froze at the echo of a loud footstep in the foyer. Soon the newcomer was climbing the main staircase. Their eyes scanned the darkness, but they could not see the man's features. It had to be either Quinton or his father returning home after their late escapades. Patrick motioned for them to move quickly toward the back steps that led outside through the kitchen. He watched the others reach the landing and spun around to check on the man already coming down the hallway. It had to be Quinton, as it seemed to be a young man.

He stopped to stare at the stranger standing by the hall table's side. An enormous bouquet in a vase obstructed Quinton's clear view of Patrick's face. For a long moment, he seemed to struggle with the situation in hand. Then suddenly, without a word, he hurtled into Patrick and slammed him against the table. Patrick's hip hit the corner of the table and sent it and him crashing to the ground. He was on his feet in a heartbeat; Quinton came at him again with his fists balled in the air, and Patrick raised his leg and kicked the man in the mid-section, sending him stumbling backward. But he recovered and kept coming at Patrick, who kicked him again with extreme force, and this time, he sent Quinton flying across the hallway. Quinton stood, and the blows between them were firm, quick, and swift like an arranged dance. Patrick did not want to delay this any longer. His hand came up with a striking cobra's speed, grabbed Quinton by the throat, and pushed his head against the wall. He tightened his hands around his esophagus. Quinton struggled to breathe; he stank of alcohol and tobacco. He gurgled, and Patrick tightened his grip until the man lost consciousness and fell to the floor. Patrick ran to the end of the hallway, where his friends waited to make sure he would not need assistance. Within a few minutes, they were outside. The full moon was silver, nestled like a bright jewel in the middle of the dark sky. They moved quickly down the road, and soon darkness swallowed them.

Back at the house, they settled in the study with a glass of brandy in hand and the fireplace in full force. The room soon became warm and cozy. Together, they went through the documents in great detail. It was a detailed log of names, places, and times. The calculating cruelty of the murder made it hard to believe that one man could be so dreadful. Patrick could see why a document like this in the authorities' hands could land someone in jail for the rest of his life or even be executed. And he could clearly understand now why Weldon gave in to Bennett's request. However, he wanted to know why Bennett went to such lengths to have this young man murdered and then kept the documents to use them for his protection. He was a very deceitful man.

"There has to be something here about Bennett and his desire to murder the young man," Patrick said.

"Here is something," Michael spoke, his voice measured. He kept staring at the document in his hand. Silence followed.

"For God's sake, Michael! What is it?" Edward said following Michael's long pause.

"I think this is what you are looking for," he finally said.

Patrick took a sip of his brandy, measuring the document now in his hand. "It is what I have been looking for!" He leaned back in his chair and started to read. The silence stretched between them. They watched Patrick and could see the anger beginning to show on his features. Another twenty minutes passed, and his angry voice broke the spell of silence as he spat out. "Oh My God! That son of a bitch."

"Will you let us in?" George asked eagerly. "What are you seeing?"

"It is unbelievable. There are several notes from various people involved with details of their activities. There was an attachment with a write up by the Morning Post." He took a deep breath and continued. "The first note is from a scum named Weston that worked for Randal Wyman, a crime group leader. Randal was hired by Alexander Bennett to find out everything he could about Jonathan Coulter, the Marquess of Salisbury."

Theron found himself scowling. "Jonathan Coulter? How does he fit in Alexander Bennett's sham?"

"You will not believe this. It gets more complicated as it

goes. It looks like Coulter bought several wagers directly from Alexander Bennett without Weldon or my father's knowledge. The bets made a lot of money, and Coulter was happy with Alexander Bennett's job for him. One day, he decided to bet his main residence and home in the country, more than he could afford. Bennett assured him that he was in for a huge gain. The wager was a sham, and Bennett knew there was not going to be any return. He took the man's money and destroyed his life and that of his family."

"How does that connect to the murder in hand?"

"The young man murdered that night was Coulter's seventeen-year-old son."

"He must have had something in hand to threaten Alexander Bennett and whoever else was involved."

"Yes, Coulter kept a record of all his wagers, and Bennett's name was all over them. Included here is the Post's write up, and it reads as follows: "The Authorities announced that an audit was to follow the recent demise of Jonathan Coulter, a very well-known wealthy nobleman. All documents in his residence needed to be gathered and surrendered to the police within a fortnight. The information collected might help the authorities to understand the reason he took his own life.'"

"Oh!" George exclaimed.

Patrick released a furious sigh and said, "We are now sure that his son hid the documentation to punish the people who destroyed his father. He wanted to take matters in his own hands, and that got the poor lad killed. Bennett knew that his name, and only his name, was all over those documents since Weldon and my father never had any dealings with Coulter. So, he needed to get those papers back before the authorities found them. He contacted Randal Wyman, who had created an outlaw group of thieves, extortionists, and murderers. The log shows that he met with Randal at his office, located at East End by the river docks. Bennett gave Randal two names, Henry Edward Wingham and Gregory Oswald Weldon. The night of the murder, Bennett notified Randal that his two friends were at White's gambling. Randal sent a messenger to find them and to deliver a note to meet someone at Hackney Street. The note said that they had important information for them."

"So, who killed the young lad?" Edward asked.

"This is the mystery we need to uncover. Three men waited inside the residence at Hackney Street to assist Bennett with his plan. We need to know the shooter. I am hoping to find that it was Bennett who pulled the trigger. This information will shatter his life."

The sound of a distant clock echoed. It was two o'clock. Patrick paused and looked at his friends. "We are all tired; we should go to bed. We will pay a visit to that location tomorrow after breakfast." His eyes were still searching the papers while the others headed for the door. Suddenly, they heard Patrick take a large intake of breath as he called out. "Wait! Wait!" They halted and turned to face their friend.

"What is it?"

"I found a smaller piece of paper that I missed. It looks like a bill of sales for a pistol." All at once, a new kind of tension flooded the room. They turned and took an automatic step forward. Patrick shared a fleeting glance with them before he looked back down at the paper in his hand. His eyes traced the bill of sale, searching for any small detail. "It looks like Bennett's signature."

"That is good news," George said. "If we can tie the pistol to the bullet in the young lad's body."

"Here is where we will need to contact Andrew Fletcher. He can access information from the Whitehall archives. I will send him a note tomorrow morning before we leave the house." They nodded in agreement.

They now had a plan, intent, and purpose. It had been a productive night.

Patrick had instructed Christian to make sure that the servants prepared the guest's beds and a roaring fire in each fireplace. He stared somewhere over the glowing orange flames in his own chamber for a moment, as though looking to the future. A sharp pain shot through his left shoulder, making him recoil. It was one of the various injuries he had received during the war. The pain affected him off and on, particularly on chilly nights. Right now, it was overwhelming him ruthlessly. His thoughts went back to the times behind enemy lines. He could vividly see the young British soldiers he met who went to war for England and never came home. They had probably never fallen in love or gotten drunk on a Saturday night with their friends. They had not been able to list their goals, let alone fulfill them. The thought broke his heart. He would carry the scars of war both inside and out for the rest of his life.

He sat up a long while, listening to the red coals hissing as the house's sounds quieted. His friends had already retired to their chambers, and the servants withdrew to their quarters. A mixture of wild thoughts played in his head. Some were of the war and others about the details of the documents. He drew in a long breath and let it out slowly again. A chill crept through his veins, and he turned toward the fireplace that appeared to have burned out. He stood up and strolled over to the hearth. He picked up the iron poker and stirred the ashes. He was surprised to find that there was still life in them. He threw a few twigs to get the flames ignited and added a couple of large logs on top. Soon the fire was roaring again. He pulled off his boots and flung himself on the bed. He stared at the orange shimmer created by the flames across the ceiling. Slowly, he drifted off to sleep.

The next morning, they met for breakfast. Warm dishes placed on the sideboard gave them a choice of various foods. They heaped the plates with ham and eggs and took a seat at the table. Patrick swallowed a mouthful of eggs before he asked "Are you ready to go out and see what we can find today?"

The men looked at one another. "We spent a very long time during war searching for secrets, conspirators, and schemers so we know how vile men can be. We have to be careful." Michael said. A footman appeared with a pot of coffee and left it on the table. Michael poured for all of them.

The sound of horse's hooves clopping along and kicking the cobblestones brought their heads around. "Are you expecting company?" George asked.

Patrick pulled a face and sighed. He didn't want company, and he had not invited anyone at all. The booted feet on the front steps and the robust rap of the brass handle on the oak door stunned them into silence. Soon Christian appeared at the threshold. "Andrew Fletcher, to see you, my Lord."

All four pairs of eyes went wide. Their mouths dropped open, but they didn't say anything. They were utterly stunned, but genuine pleasure ricocheted across their features.

Patrick stared at his friends perplexedly. "Did any of you tell Andrew that we were here?"

Before anyone could open his mouth, a distinguished man, with broad shoulders, bright green eyes, black hair, and a cheerful smile set off by his face's square handsomeness, stepped inside the room. During the war, the taskmaster of all spies in Europe had been Andrew, who became their support away from home. Andrew had saved their lives many times by giving them what they needed to do their job safely while behind enemy lines. Andrew flinched at their stunned expressions. He had never grown entirely accustomed to the attention he received from his military career and job title.

"Good morning, chaps," he called out before they had a chance to move. "It is nice to see you again. I didn't get an invite for this gathering." His crooked smile widened into a full grin. Four men shook off the shock of his visit and moved forward to shake his hand with extreme joy.

Patrick clapped Andrew on the back. "This is such a pleasant surprise. What brings you here?"

Andrew chuckled. "It certainly wasn't your invite."
They all chuckled at his words. "I didn't mean to intrude,
but I tried to reach you, Michael, for a question I had, and I
was told that you were visiting Patrick." He then turned to
George. "I ran into your solicitor, and he happened to
mention that you were coming here, too. I was sure that
Edward would be with you at the same place." He looked at
them, and the corners of his mouth lifted. "Something is
going on. Whatever that is, I want in." He laughed out loud,
and they all joined in.

"Would you like some breakfast?" Patrick offered.

"No, thank you, but I will take a cup of coffee." They
took their seats around the table once again. Patrick looked
at Andrew long and hard before he spoke. He explained the
issue on hand in a few words. He told him about the
information they retrieved from Bennett's residence.
Finally, Patrick brought him up to the present, and the plan
they had for the day.

"Who is the man you are looking for?" Andrew asked.

"We are not sure that he is still in business, but we are
determined to find out. His name is Randal Wyman,"
Patrick answered.

Andrew flinched. "Randal Wyman! The highwayman?"

"Yes, you know him?"

His lips curved as if the question gave him malicious
pleasure. "Is there a constable in England who does not
know him?"

Patrick sat very still. "Is he still in business?"

Andrew's mouth curled with contempt. "Yes," he said
matter-of–factly. "The man is now in his sixties, and he is

185

still running one of the biggest rings of thieves, robbers, extortionists, and I am sure, killings in the East End. He started as a street boy who embarked on a robbery career at one point in his early life. Someone advised him that it was a means by which he might live as a gentleman. No authority has been able to tie any of those criminal activities to him. They need proof of guilt, and he has been able to escape that for several years."

"There are other people involved in this. We don't necessarily have to devote our search to Randal. We can go after the others, too," Patrick said.

Andrew extended his hand. "May I take a look at the documents?" Patrick handed him a thick envelope from his coat pocket. Andrew thumbed through them slowly. He finally looked up. "Can I have a few minutes to look it over?" Patrick nodded, and the others continued finishing their breakfast.

After a little more than fifteen minutes, he stood up, keeping his gaze on the documents. "There are many cases never solved, buried in the depths of Whitehall. This murder might be one of them." He looked up and handed the documents back to Patrick. He pulled the fob out of his pocket and checked the time. "All right, I am all caught up with the details. I am ready to go with you if there are no objections. It will be like the old days." His mind was back in another time, which suited the current situation perfectly. There were no objections, only appreciation and brotherhood.

. . .

The morning sun lanced through the window, throwing a pool of light in the room as the five men walked toward the front door. They passed through the courtyard and through the gates, stepping onto the main street. Andrew and Michael fell into an in-depth discussion on a separate issue.

By this hour, people had begun to spill out into the streets as the warm sky shined brightly. They hailed two hackneys and gave the driver the address. The shocked look on the driver's face did not escape them. They didn't carry aristocrats to that part of town. Soon they headed for the most notorious slum area situated in East End. The address shown on the documents to be Randal's office in the old days was located in the crime-infested part of town close to the river docks. When they arrived, they paid and walked down a ragged and filthy street. The clatter of horses' hooves mixed with the loud talk of people and children filled the air. Dead animals littered the roads. Filth and rubbish often blocked the drains. The area was well known for extreme poverty, degradation, crime, and violence. A third of the households were without a male breadwinner, and women were forced to go out to work, leaving children as young as six to look after their younger siblings. The older children ran errands, swept the streets, and became thieves working for thugs like Randal to make very little money to buy a bit stale bread.

When they arrived at the dilapidated building, they approached the entrance. They had barely let the knocker fall when the sizeable dirty oak door swung open, revealing an aged man poorly dressed. He looked them up and down carefully. "Can I help you, sirs?" His breath stank of decay and ale.

"We are here to see Randal Wyman," Patrick said in a firm voice. The man opened the door to let them into a shabby waiting room. "Who may I say is asking?"

"Just tell him we need some information. We will pay handsomely." The man asked them to wait and disappeared down the hallway. Patrick turned and met Andrew's eyes as soon as the man was out of their direct sight. "How do you think we should play this?"

"Let's not get ahead of ourselves," Andrew said. "We still don't have any concrete evidence that he has any information. We have no witnesses, so we need to be patient. He could feel Patrick's frustration, but they needed to see what Randal knew. Andrew could analyze situations and provide valuable advice. The others trusted him implicitly, and they were excited he had decided to join them.

A few minutes passed, and soon, the man who answered the door returned and asked them to follow him. They went down the hallway toward the back and up the stairs to the second floor. The man approached the second door to the right and stepped aside to let them in.

CHAPTER THIRTEEN

*R*andal rose to his feet and walked around to stand in front of his desk. He was a tall, well-built man in his mid-sixties with curly, dark hair and brown eyes. The morning post was spread across the top of his desk. They saw the surprise in his eyes when they walked in. With his head raised and his back straight, he stepped forward. "Who are you?"

They introduced themselves, but their names did not register with him. He could tell they were aristocrats and would pay a high price for his services, but their names were not recognizable. "What can I do for you?" He asked, and he pointed at the dirty sofa and a couple of chairs for them to sit. They chose to stand.

"We want you to dig into your records and find the name of Duke Alexander Michael Bennett. He came to you a while back and asked for a couple of your people to help him carry out a horrible plan that ended in the murder of a young lad." Andrew said, with a firm tone in his voice.

The word murder did not seem to shake Randal. "You said a while ago. How long ago?" He ran his hand through his hair, trying to jog something free from his memory. They gave him time to process the question. He huffed out a breath, pacing the mud-colored carpet. His words came out in a rush. "It has been a very long time. I do not remember him or the particulars." His eyes wandered over the stern faces of five men. He sighed and shook his head. "I do not remember a Duke Bennett."

He walked back and took a seat behind his desk. He looked as if he was trying to get over a hangover or fatigue from being out half of the night. He picked up a half-eaten piece of something with his left hand and sipped his coffee with the other. The room was large but not very clean. The walls were dark to hide the dirt; dust lingered in the air. The room reeked of tobacco. There were folders, papers, and books everywhere. He wiped his forehead with a soiled handkerchief, and his eyes met Patrick's. "I told you I don't remember a Duke Alexander Bennett," he repeated. "I am sure I never had any dealings with a Duke."

"These documents say otherwise," Patrick said evenly.

"Let me see what you have there."

Patrick did not hand the documents to Randal. "It was a long time ago, and all we need to find are the men who assisted the Duke."

"Do you have their names?"

"No, we don't. We need you to search your records for the Bennett case. If you help us, we will make it worthwhile. But if you don't, we will charge you with accessory to murder since we have proof that these men worked for you. It is all here," Patrick said and shook his hand, holding the pile of documents.

Randal's face stiffened and he swallowed uncomfortably. "Are you the authorities?" he asked.

"No, we are not, but we can hand these documents to the authorities if we cannot get your assistance." Patrick's voice came out slow and harsh. Satisfied that his warning had the desired effect, Patrick stepped back and stood next to Theron.

After a short moment of silence, Randal spoke confidently. "All right, that is easy enough." He glanced at the five eager faces across from his desk. He stood up and walked to the back wall full of shelves that held bundles of paperwork, bound and alphabetized. He stood in front of the letter "B" and spent a while thumbing through the piles. "Here we go!" he called out and raised his hand, holding three papers clipped together. He came back slowly and stood behind his desk. He took a deep puff from his cigar, held it for a short moment, and blew out a smoke puff in the direction of the ceiling. He reached for his coffee cup. Patrick's eyes narrowed to slits. His hand moved and hovered over Randal's, preventing him from taking the cup. Randal looked up and met Patrick's gaze. He raised an eyebrow.

Patrick's face was shadowy; his voice came out cold. "Get on with it; we don't have all day."

Randal hmphed and cracked his knuckles. He thumbed through the pages. "Oh my! It was a long time ago. I was a young man then." He chuckled without looking up. He steepled one finger at his chin and grimaced. "Yes, it is coming to me now. Bennett asked three men to meet him at Hackney Street. I sent Albert Jones, Philip Thomas, and Wilson Harris. They were young lads but needed work. I had nothing to do with the murder, and I didn't even know there had been a murder."

"Are they still in business?" George asked.

"Yes, Albert and Wilson are partners. Their office is down the street. Philip went out on his own, and his office is further down on the same street but on the other side of the water."

"Can we have these papers?" Andrew asked, taking five pounds out of his pocket.

At the sight of money, Randal's eyes sparkled. "Yes, of course, be my guest." He handed the papers to Andrew.

Andrew threw the money on the desk. "For the documents and your trouble," he said, folding the papers and shoving them in his coat pocket. They exited the building with quick strides, and the door fell back into place with a loud thud. Crisp fresh air hit their nostrils, and they breathed in deeply. At the sidewalk, Patrick turned and slid his gaze upward toward the windows of the second floor. Randal was there watching them while sipping his coffee. The excitement was hard to contain, and it spread quickly among the five men. It had been a lot easier than they had thought. They had the names of the men involved, and best of all outcomes; they were about to visit them. They made their way along by the river toward their next stop through slums with buildings put up without foundations and yards and streets unpaved and walls just half a brick thick.

Thirty minutes later, they arrived at their destination. The nature of this building was no different from the previous one, except the dilapidated structure looked worse, and the class of the people loitering were the same. Waste littered the street in front of the door, and beggars stood on either side, hands stretched out. They crossed the street and moved closer to the door. Andrew peered in and noticed a narrow corridor leading to a room at the far end. He motioned for his friends to follow, and he led the way. The others were happy to let him take the lead. He had always been the guide and the man they trusted with their lives. The door was wide open.

This office was in worse condition than Randal's. Papers and folders were crammed on the wall shelves, and others lay scattered across the floor. There was no furniture other than the desk and one chair. Body odor stunk up the air. The man who occupied the only chair behind an old desk looked up, and his eyes widened in surprise. The five men standing in front of him were obviously of an exceptional caliber. They didn't belong in this neighborhood. He was also darn sure that they needed something. Panic churned through his body, and he found himself blinking at the men, wondering what it was all about. He knew he looked like hell. The years had not been kind to him, but he forced a casual brightness to his voice. "What can I do for you?"

"Are you Albert Jones?"

"No, I am not, and who may I ask wants to know?" His interest was piqued.

"Are you Philip Thomas?" Andrew ignored his question.

"Yeah, Yeah, Yeah. I'm Philip. Who are you?"

"Our names are of no importance to you. We are here to get some information." Andrew's voice was cold, a voice that made a person stop and pay attention.

"What is it that you need?"

"Oh, many things, I assure you." The smile he offered him hardly set Phillip at ease. "We have information that you, along with Albert Jones and Wilson Harris, were involved in a scheme that caused the murder of a young lad."

"Murder?" He choked, astonished at the accusation. "Murder? No, no," he mumbled. Suddenly, he shoved himself to his feet and grabbed his desk's edge, shaking his head vigorously. "I'm not a murderer. I'm many things but not a murderer."

"The young lad was shot. We need to know who pulled the trigger."

"I don't know anything about a murder," he said, squirming under Andrew's scrutiny.

"Do you think of me as a fool?" Andrew asked. Philip's lips trembled, and he shook his head. He opened his mouth, but Andrew spoke again before he could get anything out. "Good. Because I am not a fool, nor do I expect you are. So, let us drop the game of verbal cat-and-mouse."

Philip drew back, mouth agape. "Are you with the authorities?"

Andrew was silent for a long moment, considering his question. He glared at him and exhaled sharply through his teeth. "No, but we aim to get the answers one way or another." Five pairs of eyes observed Andrew as he pulled the bundle of papers from his coat pocket, keeping his gaze on Philip. "These documents put you and your friends at that location on the night the shooting took place."

Philip flinched at Andrew's sharp tone. "That does not mean that I murdered the lad."

"One of you did, and we are here to find out who pulled the trigger."

"Can I see those papers?"

The Viper group knew that this poor bastard was a suspect, but nothing had linked him so far directly to the murder. They were here to get the truth. He took the documents from Andrew and sat back down. They watched him tirelessly pore over the papers for several minutes. He finally glanced up, and his gaze ran over the five men standing in his office. "Are you serious?"

"What do you mean?"

"This was ages ago."

"That is true. However, the murder went unsolved, and the case is still open at Whitehall. Randal remembers vividly assigning the three of you to carry out the job for Duke Bennett. Are you saying you don't remember being part of this?"

"No, I'm not saying that. I remember that night as if it

was today." For a long moment, he merely stared somewhere in the distance.

"Go on." Andrew encouraged him to continue.

"The three of us had a simple job to do. We were to hide inside the house at Hackney Street and wait for Bennett and his friends to come inside. Bennett was to use a short sentence as a signal to let us know that it was time to knock his two friends unconscious." He stopped talking and blew out a weary sigh. He looked lost in thought, tired of being in this business. He had been running from the law since the time he was a youth. Nobody ever cared about him or how he survived from day to day. It seemed that his whole life was pressing down on him at that very moment. He did not know how long he held his breath.

"What was the sentence?" Andrew's voice jolted him out of his thoughts and pulled him back into the room. He rose to his feet and moved away from his desk and exhaled sharply.

"What?" he exclaimed with a start, his eyes meeting Andrew's.

"What was the sentence Bennett used?" Demanded Andrew.

He shrugged and looked confused. "Oh! The sentence." He was trying to remember more of it, but little pieces kept coming back. "'What do you want?' or maybe 'What is it that we can do for you.' It was something like that; I am not sure, it was so long ago. Once we knocked them out, Bennett shot the young lad and took some papers from him. He paid us our fee, and we left. We never knew what happened after that, and we never saw Bennett or his friends again. We didn't know his name was Bennett. Not until you just told me."

Andrew's voice was softer. "Please try and think. Is there anything else that you left out?"

"No, I swear that is all that I know. I am sure that Wilson and Albert will tell you the same story."

"How much did he pay you?"

"I don't know what he paid Randal, but we got paid six pounds each. That was a good night's work for us, and all we had to do was knock unconscious a couple guys and forget everything about that night."

"I'm going to write down a statement, and I want you to sign it. Will you do that for me?"

"Yeah, Yeah, I have no problem in doing that. It is the truth. I am sure that Albert and Wilson will be happy to do the same."

"Can you get them here?"

"Albert should be here soon, just gone down the street to meet with a client. I can send a messenger to get Wilson here. His office is just a stone throw away." He went to the door and called out. Soon a young lad showed up. Philip said something, and the boy left running down the hallway.

"We will pay you well for this information."

"I'm glad I could help." His voice sounded relieved. Loud footsteps approached the office. A man stopped short at the door and let out a startled gasp.

"What's going on in here?" he asked.

"Come in, Albert," Philip said in a flat voice. "These folks need some information based on these papers." He pointed to the papers on the desk.

"What are those papers?" Philip picked them up and gave them to Albert. He thumbed through them and looked dumbstruck. "Are you bloody kidding me? These are from centuries ago."

Philip slammed a palm on the desk. "Albert, please, we are implicated in a murder."

Albert's eyes widened in shock, "Murder? What the hell are you talking about?" He didn't look convinced. Philip flicked him an irritated glance then after a short discussion between them, and soon after that, Albert agreed to sign.

"Did you send for Wilson?"

Philip pressed his hands on his temples and drew a breath of stale air. "Yes, I sent Thomas to get him. He should be here in a few minutes."

A couple of hours later, the men made their way out of Philip's office. They had had an extraordinary day. Armed with the documentation that Bennett hired Randal's services on the night of the murder, a bill of sales for a pistol signed by Bennett, and a signed statement of admission by three men who performed Bennett's requests. They hailed a hackney and headed back to Oxford Street. Unfortunately, Patrick could not shake the notion that he should not underestimate the Bennetts. He was sure that he could force Bennett to accept the facts, but Quinton was a different story. He had nothing to do with the murder, and he was still married to Katherine.

"Patrick, what's on your mind ole chap?" Maybe it was the look on his face that drew Andrew's concern.

Patrick turned his gaze to his friend. "I am extremely pleased with the outcome. I am convinced that we can take care of Bennett with all that we have, but what about Quinton?"

"What is it about Quinton that is bothering you?"

"Well, he is still married to Katherine, and I am not sure how I will ever resolve this horrible union. I promised William."

"Stop being such a skeptic, Patrick," George said. "It's not like the world is coming to a sudden halt. We will figure something out, and what about his indiscretion with lady Webster?"

"Lady Webster?" Andrew's mouth dropped open in astonishment. He straightened up and narrowed his eyes at George. He tried to close his mouth as if the next words would leave an aftertaste on his lips. He finally came out with it. "Are you saying that Quinton and Lady Webster..." he waved his hand in the air, lost for words.

George took in the seriousness of Andrew's face. "Yes, Lady Webster and Quinton have been seeing each other for a while."

Andrew blinked, completely shocked, and shook his head. "Good God, this would bring him face to face with the most powerful man at Whitehall. It is a severe charge. The gossip mill's gears will start grinding when the police chief finds out about his wife's indiscretions. He will have to save face. It will not be the first time for him. He killed a man during a card game for calling him a cheat. But let me ask you. How can something like this be a secret for this long?" He glanced between his friends, looking for an answer.

Patrick spoke softly. "There are only a handful of people who know about this affair. Katherine is one of them. She has used this to keep him away from her bed."

This statement was even more stunning to Andrew. He tilted his head, confused. "He has not consummated the marriage?" His mind seemed to race with questions, but he remained silent. Patrick gave him a grave nod. "That is simply fascinating," Andrew added. "Well, as I see, it makes the issue with Quinton a challenge."

All four men chuckled, "Yes, it does," George stated. Patrick cleared his throat. Silence fell for a long moment; his next statement directed to Andrew changed the subject. "I thought you might want to know that the four of us are planning to find and purchase a home to use when we want to get away from the daily routine. We want to spend time together, have a few drinks, and handle business that comes up without assembling in one of our residences and worrying about being heard by the servants or watched by others. We will make it our private club."

"The Viper Club," Michael inserted in a happy tone.

"Wonderful idea," Andrew exclaimed cheerfully. His eyes filled with interest, his expression jubilant. "It sounds like a splendid idea. There have been many times that I have wanted to get away. Do you know where you want to search for this property?"

George spoke up. "We will be looking at one of the quieter areas but not too far from our main residences.

Even if we are not going to live there, we would like to have a couple or even a few bedchambers in case..."

"In case what?" Andrew asked with a grin in his face. He knew what George was trying to say, but he asked the question anyway.

"Well, in case we want to bring a lady," he said quietly. A wide smile of insinuation spread across his face. "Would you care to partake as well?"

Andrew laughed out loud and did not hesitate. "Oh, yes," he replied enthusiastically. "This is one of the best offers I have had so far." This statement brought laughter among the men.

"When do you plan to meet Quinton?" Andrew asked. "I want to be there."

"I was planning to do that tomorrow. Can you stay the night?" Patrick said.

Andrew extended his legs even further across the hackney he asked. "Are you all staying?" He lifted his eyebrows with a questioning look.

"Yes, we want to see this through." Andrew was surprised at the answer because he knew that they had inherited wealth, titles, and various properties, including beautiful homes in London, not too far from Patrick.

Andrew looked around the confined area. "Why is that?"

George raised a brow. "Why is what?"

"I mean, why are you all staying here if your homes are a stone throw away from Patrick's?"

George's lips curved. "We didn't have any more pressing engagements when Patrick called. We wanted to join him in gathering information, assessing it, and utilizing it. We are all experts in methods and tactics. So, we decided to stay up late, exchange intelligence on the events, share views, and enjoy the fact that we are still alive and on English soil. Well, you do know all that, what you don't know is that Patrick has a huge supply of French brandy." Laughter followed his last statement.

"Then, I am in." He leaned back against the seat and closed his eyes. "This will be a lot of fun." He said firmly. They remained silent and watched the beautiful full trees at the road's edge until the carriage rocked into a stop in front of Patrick's residence. The wind had picked up, and the air felt much crispier than normal around this time of the year.

They mounted the stairs and walked into the foyer. Patrick spoke softly to Christian. Soon a footman charged past them and up the main staircase to prepare another chamber for Andrew. "How about a late supper after you freshen up?" Patrick asked and they all nodded in agreement. Andrew found the footman waiting before a door in the upper hallway.

It was an hour later when they gathered in the dining room. The room boasted a blazing fire in the hearth and a healthy variety of foods laid out on the sideboard. Tumblers and wine glasses were placed for each person. Wine decanters and water bottles sat in the center of the table. The meal proved less than a quiet affair. There were several war stories exchanged, along with laughter and healthy discussions. The sound of clinking forks against plates as they were finished their meal was drowned out by their voices.

Andrew reached for the wine decanter and filled his glass one more time. He swirled the wine around the glass and watched as the fragrant liquid coating the glass. Putting the rim under his nose, drew in a deep breath and allowed the fumes to drift delightfully over his senses. He followed this ceremony with a delicate sip that provoked a sigh of pure delight.

Silence permeated the dining room. Patrick glanced up to see Andrew watching him thoughtfully. His eyebrows rose in question. "Do you have something to say?" Patrick asked.

Andrew put his empty glass down. "Yes, I do,"

"Well?"

"I want to know about Katherine. I am sure that I'm the only one in this room completely unaware of the details." He turned his gaze to the men sitting around the table. "Nonetheless, I would consider it a favor if you let me know what is going on. I'm sure that this is not only about William's request. Is it?"

Sighing, Patrick replied, "No, it is not. I've been in love with Katherine ever since we were kids. We all learned about the union with Quinton while behind enemy lines. I felt so helpless and so hurt. I was glad that I came home, but the truth is that without her in my life, it wouldn't make any difference if I didn't. I want to release her from this fake union with Quinton. I want to punish him for his indiscretions, for the embarrassment he has brought to this marriage and Katherine's honor. I want to hurt him with everything I have." Each word was a measured blow. A long silence ensued while Andrew seemed to ponder how to respond.

"You never mentioned it before, so I was unaware, but I do have a suggestion,"

Four pairs of eyes rested on his face. "Go on," Patrick said eagerly. "I'm listening."

"If I am right, Quinton's behavior provides a clear pattern. He must inhabit every hellhole, gambling establishment, soiree, and social gathering in London." Cocking their eyebrows, they were wondering what Andrew had in mind. He seemed to be taking over and coordinating the next move just as he did during the war. It was tremendously gratifying to the Viper group.

Patrick grinned. "I think you've described the rogue perfectly correct. So, what is your suggestion?"

He opened his mouth to respond, and suddenly closed it and thought for a moment before he spoke again. "I received several invites two days ago. The Ainsworth's and the Weston's are the top two socials going on tonight. My suggestion is that we attend if you don't have any other plans. I have a gut feeling that the corrupted version of Quinton might show up. If he is looking for another mistress or a short encounter, there will be a few young debutantes available for the take."

"Perfect!" The exclamation, louder than he intended, escaped Michael before he could stop it. They all turned to meet his eyes. "It sounds like a great plan. I don't think he would want to miss the top two socials of the day. By the way, I received the same invitations a couple of days back, but I didn't reply. Socials are not my thing either."

Andrew's gaze went over Edward and George. "How about you two?" They sent him a deliberate smile saying that they had received the same invitations. Holding up a hand to indicate he understood, he turned to Patrick.

"What about you?"

Patrick inhaled sharply, a bit surprised by the suggestion. Dances and soirees were not his types of pleasure. "I have no idea. There are several invitations upstairs on my desk. Many have been there since the first day I arrived home. I have not been interested in attending any social function."

Andrew came slowly to his feet, an inexplicable smile playing around his mouth. His gaze flicked over their faces. "This could turn out to be a very successful day all around if we run into Quinton. Are we in agreement that we go on the prowl tonight?" They inclined their heads in agreement. Andrew pulled the fob out of his pocket; it was only three in the afternoon. They had plenty of time before they had to get ready. "Does Quinton know anyone of you?" he proceeded.

"No," They replied in unison. "We do not know him, never met him."

"What about you, Patrick?"

"I have not seen him for years, so I am not sure. The night we stole the documents from his father's residence, I ran into him for a short moment, but he did not see my face. He was deep into his cups, and it was way too dark in that hallway."

Andrew stood. "In this case, Patrick, you are the only one that might know what he looks like today. We will hope that you can point him out. At the appropriate time, we will pull him away from the room and talk in private." They stood in silence for a moment, each weighing their thoughts. "We need to go and pick the appropriate attires for the night. I am sure it will not take more than a couple of hours for each one of us. Then we can come back and have a stiff drink before we leave the house. Our plan, even though it seems frantic and irresponsible, might just succeed."

Patrick bade them farewell. Grinning, he told them he would be right here waiting for them to get back. The house suddenly became very quiet. Going slowly up the stairs, he wondered what the evening was going to bring. He picked up a glass from the side table in his chambers and poured a healthy amount of brandy. With his other hand, he picked up the bundle of invitations from his desk and plunged into a well-stuffed leather armchair by the fireplace. He thumbed slowly through them, and after picking out the two that applied for the night, he threw the rest in the trash. He didn't know how long he had been sitting there when he heard the loud chime of a distant clock strike seven. He suddenly realized that he needed to get ready before his friends arrived.

It was nine o'clock when all five striking men gathered in the library. They were the personification of noblemen who possessed amazing qualities, powers, and abilities.

They were the type of men who accepted life's challenges and death with confidence like no other. They were well known in the ton and sought by every mama and papa with a young unmarried female from the moment they stepped foot on English soil after the war. The problem was that most of these girls had not outgrown their awkwardness of adolescence to make a brilliant match.

CHAPTER FOURTEEN

*T*he carriage took off, rocking gently at first as they rode through the narrow, winding streets. They arrived at the Ainsworth estate on the outskirts of Watlington. The place was brilliantly lit. Servants stood at the bottom of a massive staircase that led to the front entrance. There were also uniformed servants standing at either side of the door to check invitations, welcome guests, and announce their arrival. They reached the main entrance and handed over their invitations, and shortly, they found themselves standing on the top of the landing inside a huge foyer decorated with remarkable taste. The staircase led down to a massive ballroom filled with jubilant people dancing or standing around, chatting, and laughing. The conversations were loud, bouncing off the ballroom walls, creating a joyful mingle of reverberations.

The five men slowly descended the main stairs and stood at the edge of a dance floor crammed with satin, silk, muslin, and ivory lace. They gazed out into the moving wave of colors and heard the laughter and the loud chattering that nearly surpassed the soft music. The room revealed the accepted fashion, art, and social etiquette of the times. Their gaze lingered around the room over the well-born aristocrats clustering around the dance floor wearing their social smiles and carrying on casual conversations.

Lady Ainsworth approached them with a charming smile on her beautiful face. Extending her gloved hand, she welcomed each one of them into her home. Heads turned, and a silent moment passed as the mamas, papas, and giggly young girls gaped at the five tall, broad-shouldered, handsome, gentlemen whose strengths were imperfectly concealed by the elegant cut of their evening clothes.

They spent the next couple of hours meeting endless groups of people. The faces had all become a blur. They continued to nod and smile mindlessly while Patrick searched for that one face they all wanted to see. Several beautiful young women eager to dance with them tried to capture their attention, but they politely remained leaning against the wall watching the crowd. A waiter passed carrying a tray loaded with champagne; they reached out, taking one each. They continued waiting for Patrick's signal while sipping slowly. Suddenly, a stunned voice dragged Andrew's attention. "You! What are you doing here?"

Andrew pushed away from the wall, a small smile creasing his beautiful face. "Hello, Amanda."

"So wonderful to see you. Are you alone?" She knew a perfect opportunity when it came along, and she thought that she orchestrated this one beautifully.

"No," he replied.

She looked around to locate a female close to him, but all she could see four handsome men looking in her direction. Her emerald eyes went wide. "Who are you with?" She kept her gaze on him, refusing to turn away.

"Amanda, please go away." He could barely believe that he was rude, but this was not a good time to settle unpleasant issues from his past. She backed a few steps further from him, a bit stunned, and then she turned and walked away, her saffron silk skirts rustling. He turned and met his friends' inquisitive gazes and waved his hand dismissively.

They had been on the prowl for an hour. One and half hours to be exact, with hands tucked into their breeches' pockets leaning against the wall when they noticed that Patrick's eyes fastened on the ballroom entrance. He was not sure that he remembered Quinton, but the man who entered seemed familiar enough to create an uneasy feeling. Patrick's face wore a riled expression. They followed his gaze and saw a man in his late twenties, clad in grey breeches and blue velvet coat with an arrogant expression. They immediately knew it had to be Quinton. Patrick walked back to join his friends as the harps and violins gave the signal for a dance. Quinton did not waste a single moment. His eyes were on a young girl chatting with a group of friends in the middle of the room. He paused beside her, looked down, and smiled charmingly. He took her hand, leaned closer, and whispered in her ear. She flushed pink, and both laughed over some private joke. Resting one hand on her back, he claimed the next waltz.

Patrick fumed with rage. The sight of Quinton caused a fierce ache in his heart. His character was that of a rogue, a cheater, a scoundrel, but the ton was still the ton. The majority of the families resorted to marriages for money, titles, and many other inappropriate things. The London society viewed gambling, womanizing, and cheating an ordinary happening among the wealthy. However, Alexander Bennett went even further. He bled other noble families of their fortunes. Patrick drew in a deep breath just as the dance ended. He motioned to the others, and they opted for a silent approach until they went outside.

The dance ended, and Quinton walked the girl back to her friends. Patrick was the first on his side as Quinton squeezed the young girl's shoulder and said he would be back. He turned and came face to face with Patrick. He drew back, surprised at the closeness. He gaped at the man's audacity, and suddenly, Patrick spoke quietly, but his voice was cold as ice. "Quinton? We need to talk."

Quinton straightened up, narrowing his eyes at Patrick. He stared at his face for a long moment, and then he came out with several quick questions. "You seem vaguely familiar. Do I know you? What do you want?"

"Never mind that. We need to talk now."

"I'm not interested in whatever you have to say. Stay away from me." He stepped back and turned only to face a wall of bodies blocking his way. He looked at them with a startled expression, and taking in the seriousness of their faces, realized that he had no choice but to follow Patrick. Their booted feet clicked across the marble floor as they guided him through the front door. The loud chattering and the music kept their departure undetected. The night-blooming flowers' scent drifted, and the heat from the ballroom dissipated, leaving them chilled. They had reached the bottom of the front staircase, and Quinton seemed to understand that something unpleasant was about to go down. He never dreamed that all this was about Katherine or his father. He was sure that one of these men had to be the husband of one of the women he bedded. In a way, he wished he had never gotten out of bed that morning. His mind ran wild, trying to think of ways to get out of this.

"What is it that you want from me?" he said quietly, voice a bit shaky.

They headed down the dark sidewalk and did not stop until they reached the park at the end of the block. It was now completely deserted. The moon allowed a gentle mixture of light to bathe the trees and greenery sprawled in front of them. Patrick finally stopped and turned to face Quinton. His friends stood a few feet behind them. Quinton glanced around and made a face. "Now what?" he asked, startled by his own strangled voice.

"I want to know why you married Katherine?"

Quinton looked shocked and shook his head in disbelief. There were a lot of scenarios that had crossed his mind, but this was not one of them. He paused, gathering his thoughts. He was confused. Patrick's voice shook him out of his thoughts.

"What have you got to say?"

Suddenly, Quinton's gaze snapped to Patrick's, with eyes narrowed, lost track of his time and space. It was a type of suspension that crosses the boundaries of reality and blurs the thoughts. He didn't weigh his words before he spoke. "I don't think this is any of your business. Katherine is my wife and my property. I don't have to answer your questions or concerns."

An intense silence fell upon the group. Patrick moved a bit closer. "Ah, but this is where you are wrong. It is my business more than you will ever know," The words were like frozen liquid to Quinton's senses.

"Oh… Now I remember the face. You are Patrick Wingham," he said, rolling his eyes, pointing and waving his finger at Patrick. "Well, let me tell you something. Your concern about Katherine is not mine. I know that you have often longed to bed her," he said and chuckled. "But you left, so I am not sure what you want from me. Like I said before, my marriage to Katherine is none of your business."

Quinton's slow smile that spread across his features was a reaction Patrick did not expect. Quinton continued speaking, and the words came out like pure poison. "That bitch deserves what she got. Her family thought she was superior, but she was just a stuck-up bitch who thought she was too good for me."

Quinton's statement was toxic.

Patrick breathed deep as if he could not get enough air into his lungs. Bile rose in his throat, and fury welled up in his stomach before he could stop it. His tight fist connected with Quinton's chest catching him off guard; a loud shriek escaped him before losing his balance, and he flew several feet to the ground. Disbelief raced through Quinton. Why did Patrick care? He wasn't part of Katherine's family. Why this aggression? Panic slid through him. He got off the ground slowly and backed off a few feet. "What do you want from me? What is your interest in my marriage?"

Patrick leveled him with a determining gaze. "Marriage? You call this a marriage? It is a sham."

With a scowl, he realized they surrounded him. Unexpectedly his voice hardened. "Again, who gives you the right to get involved in my affairs?"

Patrick's jaw clenched. "We are not here to get your approval; we are here to let you know that you will dissolve this marriage at once. This issue is not open for discussion." His voice was even, but the undertone of anger was evident in his words.

Quinton's mouth dropped open, clearly shocked. He raked a hand through his hair and burst out in anger. "Why don't you tell me what's going on here. Who is going to make me do that?" He took another look at the group and waved his hand around, guffawing with distaste. "Who are you, people? Do I need to call a constable?" He pulled a whistle out of his coat pocket and moved it toward his lips.

"I wouldn't do that if I were you," Andrew added in a firm tone of voice.

"Who are you?"

"I am Andrew Fletcher."

Quinton's chest tightened, and Andrew's authority sent

his stomach-churning. There was not a soul in the British elite who was not familiar with his name. They may not know what he looked like, but they knew the name. His eyes closed for a brief second, wondering how far he was into trouble. He lowered his hand and put the whistle back in his coat. A vein pulsed near Quinton's temple. Wide-eyed, he turned to face Andrew. "Have I broken the law in some way?"

"Not directly."

"Then why are you interfering with my wife and my marriage?"

"Indirectly, you are involved in a sham."

"A sham? I may have done many things that are not acceptable by society, but I am not involved in any shams. Can you please enlighten me?"

Patrick now took the lead. "Your father has been involved in many schemes that destroyed individuals and their families. One of them was used against Weldon to get his approval for the horrid union between you and Katherine. It is the reason I am telling you that you have to let Katherine go."

"I don't know what my father does, and I don't care. I know that I asked for her hand, and she accepted."

"Quinton, she was forced to accept you. She does not love you, she does not want you, and the marriage was never consummated. Your marriage is a sham. In case you don't know, everyone in the ton is aware that you have never shared Katherine's bed."

A short span of silence fell between them. Quinton did not seem happy to have such information out there. It was like a tornado swept him up in a sea of confusion, and just as quickly, he came out of it. He was not going to be scared away by a few men who he had never met before. He released an exasperated breath. Arrested by an eerie sense of realization, he cursed inwardly and glared at Patrick stubbornly. "You can't force me to dissolve my marriage based on the senseless words you dished out."

Andrew strode toward him, purposely. "I know someone who can make you set Katherine free."

The words shot through him, an undertone of promise, and Quinton leaned closer to Andrew, slowly. "You lie."

Andrew's eyes went cold. He caught Quinton by the wrist in an iron grip. "Don't push me; I should call you out for calling me a liar. But I will let someone else do that."

Quinton shook his wrist free with extreme anger. "I am not scared of you. I don't care who you want to send my way. It won't be my first duel, and as you can see, I'm still here." He chose the wrong moment to be sarcastic.

Andrew stared at him with a coolly calculating eye.

"You selfish bastard. It will be your last duel when you face Paul Webster, the husband of your mistress." In a daze, Quinton stood still, not quite able to register what Andrew just said to him. Patrick thought that Quinton seemed to age a few years in a brief conversation with Andrew. Quinton hesitated, looking at the ground; a surge of fear shot through his veins, but it seemed to disappear quickly.

"What the bloody hell?" he demanded. "You seem to be throwing names out there, but I told you before, I'm not scared of you. Are we done here?" He leveled a hard stare at the five men and took a few steps back. "I am going home, and you can go to the devil for all I care." He spun on his heels and quickly disappeared into the night.

His pompous remarks cut deep, but they did not try to stop him. They already accomplished their purpose. He had been put on notice and warned about his indiscretions with Lady Webster. He will have no choice but to face her husband, the top marksmen in England. It was not going to end well for Quinton. It was quite late, so they had a decision to make. Returning to the ball was out of the question. None of the women they met had appealed to their particular tastes.

"I say that we visit Alexander Bennett tomorrow and put an end to the charade," Patrick said. They all agreed.

"Where to?" Michael asked, "White's, Boodle's, Brook's?" A unison decision made, they headed to their favorite place, White's, the most fashionable hellhole on St James's street. They climbed into the carriage, and when the door closed, it rattled away down the main drive. Inside, Patrick rested his head upon the leather cushions and closed his eyes. A wide smile spread across his face. His long-life dream was now within his grasp. When they arrived, the place was full of customers, most already well into their cups. It was the place for men of their standing to drink, carouse, and gamble as rowdily as the next common swindler. The loud sounds echoed across the great room and up to the domed roof. They could tell that wagers were set high, and it was a sure thing that by early the next morning, a few of the men would lose their fortunes. Gambling had long been ingrained in British society. It was late when the carriage pulled up in front of Patrick's home at Oxford Street. They headed to bed with no words.

As the sun rose the next morning, they lingered over breakfast as they passed the morning post. They look rested even though they hadn't arrived home until the morning hours. The activities of the previous night seemed to have suited them. "Two fortunes lost last night," Anthony said and handed the post to Andrew, who took a look at the article.

A long moment passed. "Any names?"

Andrew glanced pointedly at the paper he had just tossed down. "Yeah! Lord Abeworth and Duke Sterlington."

Michael's eyes went wide. "Duke Sterlington? He had a huge estate, considered filthy rich." He picked up the paper as if he wanted to verify the name. "How could he lose all that in one night? What about his family?"

Andrew shrugged and helped himself to the last piece of ham.

"I don't feel sorry for him or his family. They were known for being cruelly vicious to the servants. Sterlington was arrogant, proud, and disdainful; his temper was on another level. Maybe he got what he deserved." Patrick said quietly.

"You don't mean that," Edward said. "You appear somewhat out of sorts this morning. Are you feeling unwell?"

"No, I'm fine." He scowled his annoyance at Edward's acute remark. "To be truthful, at the moment, I am thinking about Quinton's father. I am still unsure about how to go about it and avoid physical conflict, despite the time I spent considering this meeting."

Andrew studied his somewhat agitated demeanor. "What is bothering you?"

"Alexander Bennett is a man of wealth and position thanks to Katherine's dowry. I am sure that I need to have someone higher than some amateur constable to accompany me or us to serve him with these papers. I'm not sure how he is going to react, so we need to be prepared."

Andrew stood up. "I had a great thought this morning when I got out of bed. I'd like to go and meet Paul Webster at his office. You can come with me, and together, we can discuss Quinton's indiscretions and show him the documentation we received from Randal." He glanced around the table. "I don't think there is a need for all of us to go just for appearances. But we do know how he operates. He will review the details carefully and make sure that we handle the matter within the law."

George inclined his head in acknowledgment. "I think you should go on, and the three of us go and hunt for the perfect place that we can use for the new club. I saw a few houses in the post that had accumulated more debt than the owner could ever pay, and we may get some great deals. They are located in lovely neighborhoods with parks very close. One, in particular, is located between Hyde Park and Kensington Gardens. The others on Regent Street, King Street, and Newgate Street."

Patrick cut a surprising glance toward them. "It sounds wonderful. I wish I could join you, but this is a bit more important." His smile broadened.

George straightened slowly, coming to his full height. His smile remained all reassurance. "We will try to find something suitable. After all, you have plenty on your plate right now."

"We better be going," Andrew said. "Let's meet here later on this evening."

Back in the courtyard, they climbed onto the carriage, then silence stretched between them. Patrick was trying to find his mental balance, determined to figure out where he was going with this issue. Not just in terms of the investigation into Alexander Bennett's sham but also about the personal quest of Katherine. Andrew and Patrick soon fell into an in-depth conversation about the documents in hand. Somehow that discussion and other topics lasted through the interval until they reach Bow Street. The Security office of the magistrates' court was tightly guarded. They showed their credentials to the guard at the entrance. He let them pass assuming, that these officers of his Royal Highness arrived for some secret or highly important issue. They proceeded to the second floor.

Paul's office had been located at the same place in the middle of a long hallway for the past twenty-five years. He sat in an armchair behind his desk, facing the door. On both sides of his desk, folders and loose papers were efficiently arranged. His face lit up at the sight of Andrew Fletcher. He rose to his feet with a wide smile. He came around with his hand extended and pulled Andrew into a bear hug. He was a tall middle-aged handsome man with light brown hair and green eyes. "What a great surprise." He said in a deep voice. When he stepped back, he turned to face Patrick.

Andrew pointed at Patrick with a smile. "This is Patrick Marcus Wingham, one of our top agents stationed in Paris. He's a member of the well-known Viper Group."

Paul's eyes went wide. He shook his hand with extreme pleasure. "I am so proud of your group. You all did an amazing job for his Highness and England. I am delighted that you made it home safely. I did hear that we lost William. I am sorry I never met him, but I did meet his father before he passed." Waving them to the chairs facing his desk, he went to resume his. "What do I own the honor of your visit?"

Patrick had never crossed paths with Paul, but he was well aware of this amazing man just as every man who worked behind enemy lines across Europe had been. They took a seat, and soon Andrew fell in a lengthy conversation with Paul about politics and old crimes buried in Whitehall's depths. Patrick stood up and took a moment to look around the office with interest. There were wall-to-wall bookcases filled with war books, maps, and what appeared to be essential documents. He walked along the bookcases reading book titles and with interest running his fingers across some of the beautiful leather spines. He was in awe of this important and powerful man.

He was unsure how much time had passed, but suddenly he became aware of the intense mood that blanketed the room. He turned to face Paul just as a harsh oath slipped his mouth. His face-hardened, and deep concern painted every line of his face. He turned to meet Andrew's gaze in astonishment. He had not heard what had made Paul so upset, but he started to understand that Andrew had already brought up the subject of Quinton and Lady Webster. Quickly, he returned and took his seat as Paul rose to his feet, shoved his hands in his pockets, and started to pace in the space behind his desk.

For a brief moment, it seemed as if he couldn't recall where he was, but quickly regained his sense of reality. Paul Webster was not sure which hurt the most: his wife cheating or his pride. His eyes shot icy flashes from their green depths, and he pounded the desk in front of him in frustration. He blew out a long breath and pinned Andrew with a firm glance. "Thank you, my dear friend. I'm going to handle this on my own as it is very personal." Andrew inclined his head and remained silent. "If I am reading both of you right, there is something else. "Both nodded at the same time.

"Indeed, there is," Patrick said. He paused as if selecting his words and then glanced at Paul. "We are here to provide you with documentation that will help you close out an old open murder case." Paul's eyes narrowed. He kept his gaze on Patrick while he concentrated taking in every word. Patrick took his time and went over every detail, describing the documents' recovery from the Bennett residence. He had to admit that they broke into the home while everyone was away, but Quinton had returned just before they were getting ready to leave.

"So, what happened?"

"Nothing. There was an altercation between Quinton and myself, but he was heavy in his cups, so he didn't recognize me. The next day we visited the man shown in the documents that Bennett hired. We now have signed proof that Bennett purchased the pistol, arranged for the meeting, and hired the thugs that helped him carry out his deadly plan, and he was the one who pulled the trigger."

Paul found himself holding his breath. He remembered the case exceptionally well. It had to do with a well-known privileged family in London. He was a newly hired young constable in those days. To his surprise, things for this murder were falling in place like a well put together puzzle. "Please continue," he said.

"Bennett hid the documents and blackmailed Duke Weldon and my father. They were left to believe that Weldon had pulled the trigger that killed the young lad. Bennett had dwindled his fortune with huge wagers, and he was on the brink of disaster. He thought that having Lady Katherine marry his thug of a son would give him the chance to get his hands on her dowry, which was quite substantial. He threatened Duke Weldon with imprisonment if he denied the union and threatened my father as an accessory to murder if he was to speak out about it. I promised William that I would resolve this issue with everything in my power and destroy Duke Bennett and his son."

By now, Paul Webster was inwardly fuming. His words bounced across the walls. "Please, let me see those papers."

Patrick pulled the documents out of his pocket. Paul

flipped the pages, scanned the list, and gave a disgusted groan while

thumping his fingers on the desk. He ran his hands through his hair and made a growl deep in his throat. He looked at Patrick with a determined glance. "The pistol sales slip will be the knife to the jugular for sure. We recovered the bullet from the young lad's body, and we will pair it to the pistol. Keep your fingers crossed that it will be a match. My gut tells me that his game will not end well for him."

Andrew gave Paul an avid look. "We will need a couple of your men to go and face Bennett with this information."

"Andrew, you will do no such thing. It is a personal matter and my murder case. I will be the one to arrest his sorry arse. You are welcome to come along, but you have to let me handle this."

CHAPTER FIFTEEN

he Bennetts' butler opened the door and was surprised to see a few men at the doorstep, including three constables. "Can I help you?" he asked in a somewhat shocked voice.

"We are here to see Duke and Lady Bennett."

"Lady Bennett is still out in the country, but Lord Bennett is here. May I say who is calling, sir?"

"Paul Webster, High Constable."

The butler's eyes went wide. "Yes, sir, please come in." He left the door open, turned on his heels, and disappeared with quick steps. Soon Duke Alexander Bennett came down the stairs wrapping the belt on his robe around his waist still in bed, possibly trying to repair the drinking mood from the night before. "Is there something wrong?" he asked with an irritable tone glancing at the constable in front of him.

A cold, firm voice drew his attention. "Yes, there is

something very wrong. You, sir, are under arrest for murder."

"Murder?" He swung around with the audible gasp. "What in the hell," he yelled out loud. He kept glancing at the men looking for an answer.

"Please step aside. I have a warrant to search your home. In the meantime, you need to go and get dressed. You are coming with us down at headquarters."

Bennett went pale. He knew that something was wrong, but his mind was unable to bring forward the murder of the young lad from so long ago. "I demand to know what on earth is going on. Why should I have to go with you? You shall regret this." He took a menacing step toward Paul. A steady hand behind him held him firmly in place. "Unhand me, sir, immediately." Paul made a motion to the constable, and he was released.

"As I said, you need to go and get dressed. We will discuss all the details down at headquarters." He could see sweat beaded on Bennett's forehead. With a wave of his finger, he called the butler to approach. The butler felt a cold shiver run up his spine, not for the first time since they showed up. He immediately approached. "I need you to show my men the library and the study. Give them access so they can search the rooms. Andrew, you and Patrick need to go home. I will let you know how it all worked out."

Patrick felt more than a little pleased with himself. The morning had been much more successful than he had hoped for when they set off. He and Andrew thanked Paul for his help, and they departed.

. . .

An hour later, after Paul's men had recovered a few small black books and several papers, they were on the way to Bow Street office that maintained a privileged position among the other offices of the metropolis. Three constables watched them walk past the main door. Inside Paul's office, Bennett tried to strike a conversation once again with a sinking feeling in his stomach. "Look, High Constable or whoever you are, who am I supposed to have murdered?"

Paul took the little black books and papers from the constable and set them on the desk. He glanced at Bennett with disdain. "Do you remember Duke Jonathan Coulter?" He did not wait for an answer. "We all know that he killed himself, but my concern is about his young son's murder, William Coulter, the third."

Bennett's eyes went round, and his mouth dropped open. He felt a terrible sense of fright creeping into his mind as he realized that he was about to encounter his fate. The memories of that horrible night flooded his thoughts, and terror gripped him by the throat. He tried to stop his voice from trembling. "You got the wrong man. You need to be talking to Duke Wingham now that Weldon has passed about this crime. I can prove that it was not me."

Paul gave a disgusted snort and stared at him like a bloodhound on the hunt. "I can prove that you, and only you, pulled the trigger that killed the young lad. You destroyed his father and took away his life, his family, and his dignity. And what about Randal Wyman, Albert Jones, Philip Thomas, and Wilson Harris? I suppose you will tell me that you do not know any of them. But I have proof," he pointed at a pile of papers in his hands. "You organized the whole sham, and you are the one who hired all those men. I have their signed confessions, and before you say anything else, I have the bill of sale for the pistol with your signature on it."

Bennett felt the shock that rippled through his body. He frowned as he pulled the memory free of the cobwebs in his mind. The rage built His temples started to pound, knowing that he was caught. He was also aware that he would be at a disadvantage at the trial if he did not get a note to his legal assistant as soon as possible. "I need to send a note to my wife and son."

Paul shot him a sharp glance. "You can send it after you meet the magistrate." He motioned at the two constables who

were standing on either side of his chair. They picked him up as he wrestled to get loose from their tight grip and took him away. Paul watched them go. His expression remained resolute as he released his death grip on the chair. He rose to his feet, strolled to a side table, picked up a teapot, and poured himself a cup. He took a long sip and let the warm liquid slide down his throat. The realization of what Quinton had done came in a blinding flash. It was a fool's game that went against society rules. His honor had been impugned now; he would have to challenge the man to a duel. He nearly jumped out of his skin at a constable's voice standing at the threshold.

"Is there anything that you need, my Lord?"

"Yes, I need you to send a detail to locate Quinton

Bennett. Ask around, he usually occupies the hellholes around London. I want to know where you find him."

"Do you want us to pick him up and bring him in?"

"No, this is a personal matter."

The constable nodded and left the room. Paul refilled his cup and continued to scan through the pages of the two little black books. He was not surprised that he found what he was hoping to find. There were details showing names, dates, types of bets, amounts of money, and the initials of the people who had placed the wagers. It also showed wins and losses. The exciting part was that the numbers were adjusted by Bennett to show more losses than wins. That was the main thing that made sense. By the time he reached the last page, he clearly understood that Bennett picked and chose whose fortune would be taken away, which life would be destroyed, and he did exactly that. One of the names was Duke Jonathan Coulter. He set the books back on his desk, and after flipping through the loose papers, he leaned back on his chair and closed his eyes. He was sure that the whole Bennett saga and their family drama would become the hottest news in London. It would fill every page of the morning post. A murder story was always popular, but it was even more significant when it involved a wealthy socialite. Soon his mind turned to his issue, and a wave of nausea threatened to engulf him. He was trying hard to still the irrational thumping on his pulse as he contemplated his next move with Quinton. He looked very thoughtful, and then he nodded as if he had solved some inner struggle.

. . .

Paul Webster's green eyes glittered as he guided his horse toward White's where Quinton was gambling. He did not take a coach because he intended to call him out for the next morning, not to bring him in. As he pulled up to the courtyard, a neatly dressed lad hurried forward to take the reins.

"Welcome, my Lord," the young lad grinned. Once inside, he spoke to the attendant at the door. The man nodded in Quinton's direction. Paul strode to the table and stood right behind him.

"Quinton George Bennett?" his voice bounced against the walls.

Quinton's head lifted a bit. "Who wants to know?"

"Stand up." Paul's voice was cold as ice. Everyone at the table stiffened at his tone. They stopped and looked up. A couple of those men recognized Paul Webster, and knowing the indiscretions of Quinton, they realized what was about to happen. They stood up and moved away from the table.

Quinton straightened his entire body and turned to face Paul. "Who are you?"

Paul grinned. "Your worst nightmare."

"Oh, I'm scared now," he guffawed. "Who the hell are you? Do they let anybody in this place? Get lost."

Many men in the room who knew exactly the power of this man met Quinton's last words with a gasp. Quinton looked around the table, surprised with the expressions he saw on their faces. His attention turned back to Paul. "Who the hell are you, and what do you want?"

Paul's mouth quirked a little. "My name is Paul

Webster." His voice was cold and firm. Complete silence blanketed the room. The elite was well aware of the most powerful man in London. Quinton's eyes went wide. He could not stop the surprise he displayed. Most men were already in their cups and had no idea what was going on, and others were too well-bred to look at Quinton's direction. Long seconds passed as Paul stood back and considered for a moment. His voice was loud when he spoke again, compared to the room's silence since he walked inside. "I believe you are well acquainted with my wife." Quinton could not seem to find his voice. All he could do was stare, struck by the man's presence. His next words drove a chill along his spine, and Quinton recoiled. He could swear that his blood stopped moving. "I challenge you to a duel. Be at Hyde Park at seven-thirty in the morning. Weapons will be pistols. Be on time." These were his last words as he turned and left the room.

It was a while before people started to move around, and whispered chatter filled the room. Quinton looked lost. Movement, breathing, everything was suspended. He left without looking back. He was only a few hours away from meeting his fate. He was well aware that Paul Webster was his Highness's top marksman, but he had never set eyes on him before tonight. He needed to get home as soon as possible and talk to his father. He had always been able to get him out of a lousy situation safely. He was utterly unaware that his father was under arrest.

. . .

Back at Oxford Street, the Viper Group celebrated the outcome of their undertaking. Patrick was ecstatic that he was about to have his promise to William come true. With the brandy poured and each with a glass at their fingertips, Patrick rose to his feet. "I am sure that I speak for all of us when I say I'm pleased that our plans were successful." He lifted his glass to his lips, and the others followed. His gaze fixed on the fireplace as if he could read in flames his next statement. "Tomorrow, we can visit the homes you found and finalize a purchase." There was a long silence; Patrick's face suddenly a portrait of edginess.

"What's wrong?" Michael's voice shook him out of his thoughts.

"I am wondering what happened between Paul and Quinton." Edward's eyebrows shot up at his words. Patrick noticed his surprise and tried to expand. "I mean that I am wondering if he called him out."

"I am sure that Paul would make this item his priority. He seemed to be utterly infuriated with the news." Edward said. Patrick smiled halfheartedly at the words.

"I guess I am eager to see this nightmare vanish forever. I want to move forward with a clean slate with Katherine." He sighed heavily and drank down the entire contents of his glass.

Andrew set his glass on the table beside him, a smile fixed to his mouth.

"Patrick, ole chap. It's almost over." They all nodded their heads in solemn confirmation. They emptied their glasses and agreed to meet the next morning for breakfast before they went house hunting.

For the first time since he left his friend, he allowed his thoughts to drift away from the Bennett issue. He shrugged out of his coat and threw it on the chair. He stripped off his clothes and threw back the bedcovers breathing in the fresh scent of clean linen. He slipped into bed, and only then he let himself think about Katherine. Passion rushed through his veins on a heated wave, and he felt the heat down to his toes. His desire for her got the best of him. It was now a matter of time before she would be free. Free to be his wife and bear his children. He fell asleep in the middle of this revelation.

The morning post was crammed page after page with the Bennett saga. Each one of the men held a copy of the paper captivated by the ghastly details. Paul had been present at Bennett's meeting with the magistrate, and proof had been a beautiful thing. The documentation the Vipers had provided backed up all the charges brought in court. Bennett's well paid lawyer was unable to argue any of the accusations. His sentence was quick and stiff. Punishment for murder was death. "He finally will pay for all the lives he destroyed," Andrew said. There would be no sympathy on his behalf shown by anyone in the ton.

Patrick finished the slice of toast and took a sip of coffee. He flipped to the second page, and his breath came out in a hiss. "Son of a bitch" Three pairs of eyes looked up and pinned him in shock. He jerked his gaze from the paper. He glanced at the clock on the wall; it was eight-fifteen. He shut his eyes with a sigh of relief. The Bennett saga was exhausting, and it had been enough to shred his nerves.

"What is it?" Andrew gave him a sideways glance.

Patrick's eyes fluttered open, and with a sharp flick of his wrist, he threw the paper on the table. Check the second page. "The duel was at seven-thirty this morning at Hyde Park.

Michael nearly choked on a mouthful of eggs. "What?"

A unison sound of shock from Edward and Andrew covered the room. Andrew glanced around. The story didn't sound remotely plausible to him. "I knew it would be soon but never realized it would be this soon. If that is true, I'm willing to put down a wager of 10,000 pounds that Quinton is either dead or severely wounded and near death."

Patrick grinned and slid him a mocking glance. "I was sure that Quinton could never measure up to Paul Webster. But we will know soon. After all, it's my entire future that's at stake based on the outcome." Heavy footsteps in the corridor drew their attention to the door. A footman stepped into the breakfast room and handed Patrick a note, addressed to him from Paul Webster. Patrick felt his heart skip but managed to maintain a placid expression. Patrick thanked the footman and dismissed him. As he made his way out, Patrick read the content and glanced up at his friends with a big smile spread across his face.

"What is it?" Andrew asked.

"A note from Paul Webster."

"Well?" Michael's voice was sharply filled with curiosity.

"He says that Quinton was wounded severely, and he is

in the hospital. However, the outcome is not known." His future stretched like a bright star before him. He folded the paper and said, "I did not expect anything different." He pursed his lips. "If anything, I am ashamed to say that I was hoping to hear that he was dead." The men exchanged glances, and laughter burst out, filling the room. The feeling was mutual.

When they finished breakfast, they surged to their feet, filled with excitement over their next search for the Viper Club location. At the courtyard, they climbed into Patrick's carriage and left Oxford Street as planned. They emerged onto South Street and headed down the road looking for the right house to establish their Viper Club. They made several stops and walked through some beautiful homes located next to lovely quiet parks such as Hyde, St. James, Richmond, and Regent's. The last house was perfect; it met all their requirements. They surveyed the magnificent two-story pink brick house that stood before them with its lovely marble curved window crowns. It was nothing less than a showplace. It had a vast library, a study, a boardroom, a large kitchen with a dining room, and five beautiful bedchambers overlooking the fantastic gardens surrounding it. They had decided on bedchambers if they wanted to bring ladies after hours and spend the night away from curious ton eyes. There were servant quarters on the north part of the house away from the main floor. Located at the northeast corner of Regent's Park, with the right price, they purchased it on the spot.

. . .

The four men walked away with huge smiles on their faces. They shook hands in the carriage, and the Viper Club was born at 330 Regent Street. They rested their heads against the squabs and closed their eyes in satisfaction with the outcome with a sigh. Eyes still closed, Patrick felt a wave of relief crashing through him, and a triumphant smile engulfed his face. He had more than enough to do the following day. Today had been a day of nothing but great results. At Oxford Street, the carriage stopped in front of the door. They swung down to the courtyard and climbed the steps. Patrick paused as they reached the door and fumbled through his pockets for the keys, patting them one by one. "I seem to have mislaid my keys again." He grabbed the brass knocker and gave it two sharp raps. Soon his friends were ready to depart for their estates. Before leaving, they agreed to let Andrew and George hire the servants and any other help they might need to make the new house agreeable. Michael and Edward wanted to be in charge of hiring a professional decorator and oversee the furniture purchases and decoration of each room. Patrick would hire the butler who would be entrusted with the household's care and be in charge of the staff. It was going to be the place each one of them would use to feel secure from the ton and, in their own time, find the ladies who would possibly become their wives. They left Oxford Street before the sunset hit the cobbles.

. . .

Over dinner that evening, Patrick remained cheerful and extremely excited about the next day and his visit with Katherine. He was nearly finished with his meal when his butler walked in. Patrick looked up and met his anxious look. "What is it, Christian?"

"I beg your pardon, my Lord, but I thought you might want to know." He stopped short of his last words.

"Know what?"

"Lord Quinton is dead." His words echoed throughout the dining room.

Patrick grinned and leaned against his chair, delighted with the update. He thanked Christian and dismissed him. He spent the rest of the evening in his study. Sipping his brandy, he recalled the past six-plus years of his life spent in the services of his Majesty, and the difficult times and enormous gains of the Viper group behind enemy lines all in the name of England. William was always at the forefront of his thoughts. He had given his life and left a big void in the group of brothers. He lost more than a friend; he lost a brother. He was extremely thankful to the Viper group and Paul Webster for how they rallied behind him to achieve the excellent results in the past couple of days and paved the road of his dreams. He felt tired and ready for bed. He left his study and walked down the hall, his booted feet striking the tiles of the foyer, and slowly he strode up the steps to his bedchamber. He shrugged out of his coat and let out a slow breath. The brandy had soothed his nerves enough that he fell into a deep sleep as soon as his head hit the pillow.

. . .

The next morning, he lay still for several moments just staring at the ceiling. Minutes ticked by, and soon he realized he had to get up and get going. He dressed carefully, knowing that he was about to meet his future wife. He headed downstairs to the breakfast room. He made his selections at the sideboard loaded with a vast variety of food and fruits and returned to the table. The morning post was in front of him, and again the news was all about the Bennett saga and Quinton's fatal injury following the duel with Lord Paul Webster. He was deep into the story when he heard Christian clearing his throat. Startled, he wondered how long he stood there, attempting to get his attention. "Yes," Patrick said.

"I was wondering, my Lord, if you would be leaving for Scunthbury this morning."

"Yes, can you please have Pegasus ready for me?" he asked as he poured himself a teacup. Christian nodded and left the room quickly. When finished with breakfast, he set aside the morning post, put his coat on, and walked out to the courtyard. The door closed behind him with a loud thud as he took a deep breath and looked around. Pegasus was waiting anxiously for a run. He saw Patrick approaching and let out a joyful nicker and shook his head back and forth, making Patrick laugh. Patrick set his palm on his neck, stroking him gently several times. He vaulted onto his back and gave him a gentle nudge. They set out on a low gallop toward Scunthbury and picked up speed gradually. He chuckled under his breath. Electrifying emotions filled his mind at the thought of his next encounter with Katherine.

. . .

It was a beautiful morning. The sun climbed the blue sky slowly, and the breeze gently stroked his face. A significant part of the sky was bright blue with no clouds in sight. As he moved further and further away from London, the terrain changed. Variegated foliage and plant species gave the eye a breathtaking view. He heard the leaves rustle as they moved on the trees and felt the dew's freshness from the damp grass. He passed a few small villages on the way. Cows and sheep lolled lazily together under huge trees and along the roadway. The sky beyond was a sapphire blue, and the air bathed in brilliant sunshine. He noticed every little thing around him because he was in love, and he could hardly wait to hold Katherine in his arms. He felt the vibration of its progress through the ground beneath Pegasus' hoofs.

It had been a while since he had left Oxford Street, and the sun's heat and glare had by now given place to the coolness of the evening. Long shadows of the trees, bushes, houses, and picket fences lay picturesquely on the dusty road's dim light. It was twilight when he reached the crossroad. The right path would take him to his parents' home; the left would lead to the Weldon estate. He did pull his watch from his breast pocket to check the time even though he knew that it was too late to show up at Katherine's doorstep. He shook his head, returned the watch to his pocket with a heavy heart, and continued to the right side. He would visit her first thing in the morning. His brothers had left for school, and his parents seemed eager to talk, and so they spent a good part of the evening going over all the details of Lord Bennett's death sentence and Quinton's attempt to take on the best marksman in England. Tears hovered in his father's eyes. Patrick raised his brows. "What is it?"

His gaze flicked to Patrick briefly then away somewhere in the distance. "I feel sad that Gregory is no longer here to see that dirty bastard who chose to make a hell of his friend's families get his due." His voice died to a whisper.

Patrick nodded. "I feel the same way about William. I miss him every day, and I would have loved him to see Quinton's miserable life end in humiliation."

His mother stood up. "We should be thankful for the results." Something sparked in her eyes, something behind the thankfulness, the anger, and the sorrow of the news. It was something that she kept to herself as she leaned over and pressed a kiss to her husband's temple. "Good night, dear," she said softly. She moved closer to Patrick, hugged him tightly, and took her leave. "I will see you both tomorrow at breakfast," she called out.

His father studied his son's face for a short moment. "I'm astonished that you didn't visit Katherine tonight."

Surprised, Patrick furrowed his eyebrows. "How did you know that I wanted to do that?"

The Duke resisted the urge to roll his eyes. With a shrug, he chuckled. "Your face has a special glow when you speak of Katherine."

"It does?"

"Yes."

"Well, that is what I wanted to do first, but it was way too late to show up announced by the time I reached the crossroad."

"You did well. Tomorrow will be a better day, and you can spend a lot of time together. She has been waiting for you."

Patrick's eyes widened. "Am I missing something?"

Taking that as his cue, he smiled at whatever thoughts crossed his mind. "I promised your mother I would not say anything, so do not out me to her. Katherine was here yesterday following all the news. She was happy and excited that her long miserable marriage to Quinton was over. She wished that you were here to share the news with her. Mother wanted you to hear that from Katherine, so she told me to keep quiet. Can you promise that you will not say a word?"

Patrick laughed. "Don't worry, Father; I will not say a word. But I must say, I can hardly wait to see her again." A shiver ran up his spine remembering the last kiss. His father heard the truth in his voice, read the sincerity in his eyes. Patrick rose to his feet. "I shall bid you a good night, Father. I will see you in the morning." He could not let emotion rule his night, but he was craving stability in his life with Katherine by his side. He left the study and sluggishly climbed the steps to the second floor. He slipped into a warm bath and rested his head on the tub's edge. She had caught his imagination from the first moment he had set eyes on her. He closed his eyes and took a deep breath. He lost track of time until he felt a cold shiver run through his body. He opened his eyes and realized the water had gone cold. Stepping out of the tub, wrapped in a large bath towel, he walked back into his room. He could feel the chill in the air. He grabbed the poker at the fireplace and stroked the fire, creating a massive flame. He stood in front of it until he felt his body warm-up. His face grew hotter, and he was sure it was not the newly stoked fire; it was the anticipation of asking Katherine to marry him. He got ready for bed and quickly slipped under the covers. Katherine's beautiful face was the last thought he had before deep sleep claimed him.

CHAPTER SIXTEEN

*H*e woke up feeling exceptionally well rested. Rays of sunlight slipped through the curtains and into the room, lighting up small portions of the carpet. He removed his arm from his eyes and looked at the clock on the end table. It was seven in the morning. He swung his legs over the edge of the bed, and slowly, he got to his feet. He walked to the window and pulled the curtains wide open, flooding the room with sunlight.

He took his time to get dressed. When finished, he looked at himself in the mirror. His features possessed a distinctly autocratic look, light brown hair with deep blue sapphire eyes. His broad shoulders and powerful thighs perfectly suited his clothes. His magnificently cut coat and beautiful buckskin breeches looked molded to him. His cravat tied perfectly, and his Hessians shone. Satisfied with his look, he left his room and headed down the stairs to meet his parents for breakfast. Glancing at the clock again on the wall, he smiled. He had enough time to enjoy breakfast and arrive at Katherine's at a decent time.

"Good morning!" He announced joyfully as he bent down and pressed a kiss to his mother's cheek. She flashed him a smile. He then proceeded to load his plate with all the goodies offered at the sideboard. His mother watched him as he took a seat across from her. "Good morning, dear, you look very nice. Are you headed to Katherine's this morning?"

Patrick raised his brows and then smiled. "Yes." His mother chuckled softly at his answer and looked down at her plate. He fixed his mother with a quizzical look. "Something on your mind, Mother?" She sighed and did not reply. "Have you been thinking about my meeting with Katherine?" he continued probing.

She broke out into a soft laugh. "Not just thinking about it, my dear. Are you going to ask her to marry you?"

Shocked at the question, he looked up from his plate and met his mother's gaze. He knew, absolutely and without question that in this case, given the news of the past few days, his reply should have been obvious. However, his mother looked as if she was expecting an answer. He finished a mouthful of eggs and took a sip of coffee. "Yes, Mother, I will ask her if I feel that it is the right time to do that." She looked at him in dawning hope and beamed delightfully at the prospect. "I'm not sure how she is going to handle Quinton's death. Everyone was aware that they did not live together as a married couple. They condemned Quinton's indiscretions, and they sympathized with Katherine. She will be welcomed by the ton no matter what

her decision might be, and I intend to be by her side."
Patrick said. His mother reached across and patted his hand
warmly. His father smiled and nodded in agreement.

He took a final assessment of his appearance and shut
the front door behind him. He gathered his thoughts away
from the delicious sensation pooling in his groin at the idea
of Katherine. Pegasus waited, ready for the ride. He vaulted
on his back, and they took off.

It had been over a year since Duke Weldon died. The house
was not draped in black crepe any longer, but there was a
stillness to it as if no one lived there. He chuckled at the
thought of his childhood. The boisterous presence of the
young boys and a blond-haired little girl was equally
absent. The stable foreman took Pegasus, and he mounted
the front steps. The sweet sounds of a pianoforte drifted
from the right-hand window as he gave the heavy iron
knocker two raps and waited. The door opened, and Henry
the butler showed him in. "Good morning, my Lord."
Patrick gave him his most charming smile and returned his
greeting. The butler lowered his head in reply and led him
into the entry hall and politely asked him to wait. Soon he
was back, and Patrick followed him down the hall and into
a cozy parlor.

Duchess Weldon came into the room with a smile on
her beautiful face. "Good morning, dear," she said,
smoothing the front of her morning gown and pulling a
white shawl tighter around her shoulders with her left hand.
She approached Patrick and held her hand for him to bow

over. "I'm so happy to see you. Katherine should be coming along shortly." She motioned for him to take a seat. He took a chair across from her settee, feeling a sudden twinge of anxiety.

A long sigh escaped her. "These past days have been anything but pleasant or easy. The news as horrible as it was, actually was very welcome to us." She chuckled softly. "The Bennett saga has been spread across the morning post each day, enthralling the ton's curious and gossipers."

There was a short silence while the maid brought the tea tray with crumpets. She poured a cup for each and took her leave. Patrick ran his hand through his hair. "I must say that people's emotions, actions, and feelings sink into their environment over time, especially those around them. The Bennett saga has infuriated and, at the same time, pleased people who already knew the cruelness of their existence. I woke up this morning, much happier. A great weight lifted off of me. I have kept my promise to William, and Katherine is now free to be happy." He took a sip of tea and cleared his throat. "How is she taking all this?"

The Duchess stared at him for a moment. "The truth is that she is happy and relieved that Quinton is gone, and so am I." Tears appeared in her eyes.

Patrick reached over and took her hand. His smile was tender. "I'm sorry about this situation. I guess I'm the one who put things in motion." Silence followed his words only interrupted by a clock striking the time somewhere in the house.

She looked down at the handkerchief, crumpled in her

hands. "Dear, Patrick, I am gratified to hear you say that. We are so thankful for everything you have done for this family. I'm sad that Gregory is not here to enjoy the outcome. I hurt deep inside because I know that he died from a broken heart. He held that secret to himself for many years. Forced to give Katherine away to that rogue of a man, he was torn to the edge of insanity. The horrid union sent him to his grave. The hurt was far more than he ever expected. He could not live with that anguish any longer." The Duchess took a deep breath and lifting her handkerchief, wiped the tears from her eyes.

Patrick straightened his shoulders and rose to his feet. "I'm so sorry. William and I felt the same pain when we received the letter. He knew that something was not right and that something made his father approve of that union. He vowed to find out the reason and dissolve the marriage when he came home." He looked at the Duchess, and abruptly, he began pacing back and forth. His voice had risen to a powerful, lecturing tone. "William was like a brother to me, and I had been in love with Katherine for as long as I can remember. So, I had to carry out William's wishes after his death." By now, the Duchess was crying. Patrick retook his seat, reached for her, and patted her hands softly. A paused ensued, then he said, "It is all over now. Please stop crying." The Duchess seemed to relax at his words, a soft smile spreading across her lips.

The double doors of the sitting room flung open, and Katherine sailed through. Patrick and the Duchess glanced at her direction. She was garbed in a magnificent and enticing morning silk gown of rose color. The skirt was full, and the corset was cut square under her lovely breast. Her white silken flesh rose from the gown creating a magnificent vision. Her eyes of a deep sapphire color shined bright, and her lips parted sensuously. Patrick stood transfixed. The look in his eyes was unashamedly predatory; by the time he could breathe enough to think, he was brought back to reality by the Duchess's soft voice. "There you are, my dear!" Katherine moved further into the sitting room, and, reaching down, she gave her mother a warm hug. Slowly, she straightened her shoulders and stared at his handsome, smooth-shaven face of powerful features and a fabulous square aristocratic jaw.

Blue on blue, their gaze locked and took their breaths away. "My lady," he prompted and reached for her. With her gaze still locked on his, she placed her hands in his outstretched hand. His fingers closed over hers, and he pulled her closer.

"Thank you." Her voice was soft. Patrick immediately knew why she was thankful. His eyes sparkled with joy.

The Duchess chuckled. "I suggest that you both go for a walk in the garden before lunch. I am sure you have a lot to discuss. Have an enjoyable time."

Patrick thanked the Duchess and offered his arm to Katherine. She slipped her hand inside the crook. Extreme love filled her lungs, free now to marry him and love him to the end of time. Fluffing out her skirts, she followed him outside, down the stairs and through the courtyard to the path that led into a breathtaking garden. They walked under the trees, feeling the warm breeze strike their skin. Patrick's hand tightened around her wrist, and she sensed desire that flooded every muscle of her body with liquid warmth. Heat and lust surged through him when he rested his other hand over hers and heard her quick intake of breath. The instinct to take her there under the trees in plain view surged within him, but he suppressed it. She looked down the long path, sloping toward the beautiful manmade lake. She steered her errant thoughts to the man next to her and smiled. He strolled beside her, his arm around her waist now, and his pace slowed to match hers with his gaze completely fixed on her. She glanced up at him, and heat surged within him. He stopped and pulled her body against him; his lips found her mouth and claimed it with pure hunger. The kiss threatened to shatter Katherine's control. He lifted his head and dragged in a shaky breath.

She reached up, placing her hand at the nape of his neck. She pulled him down to her hungrily. Desire burst out like a volcano, spilling scorching heat all over her body. Patrick sensed her heated passion when she circled his lip line with her tongue, landing inside his mouth and tasting his sweetness. His arms moved impatiently and held her to him. "Let's walk down to the lake," he murmured into her mouth. "I want you all to myself away from any prying eyes." She pulled back and quickly walked down into the thick vegetation that ended at the water's edge. He sat on the grass and pulled her down to sit next to him. "Let's talk about Quinton."

Katherine sucked in a breath and jerked her gaze to his. "Do we have to do that now?" her voice quivered. She could still remember the coldness, the icy feeling that had settled about her while standing at the altar across from

Quinton. The weight had become too much to endure. She tried for six years to rid of it, and all she wanted to do now was move on. She glanced at him for a short moment and frowned. Her eyes turned to the garden and remained silent.

Patrick gave her time reluctantly, but eventually, he went on. "Yes, I need to know what you plan to do about his burial and many details about your life with him while I was out of the country. I want to know about the days that followed your wedding day." She tried to stand up, but he held her down. "Please, Kat, I must know."

Katherine hesitated. She pulled her knees up and clasped her hands together tightly around them. She tried to ignore the compression in her chest and the tears that pooled in her eyes. Her voice came out in a low distant whisper. "I have hated Quinton and everything he stood for, from the very first moment I set eyes on him. I tried to tell my father how much I dreaded the marriage, but he said that I was too young to understand and that husbands were not necessarily faithful or perfect in any way. I asked him why he was faithful to my mother, and he looked at me lost for words. He unexpectedly left the room, and when he came back, he said there was nothing else to discuss. The decision was final. I remember crying myself to sleep for three nights in a row. I was sure that my father was hiding a deep secret that would destroy him if unearthed. I can see now that I was right." She stopped talking for a few moments and tried to focus on the increased throbbing of her heart. These memories were very upsetting. Patrick understood, but he needed to know. He watched her expression softened with sadness carefully.

She pursed her lips and continued. "We lived in London, the first year of our marriage, but I promised myself that I would guard it with my life." She swallowed hard as tears stung her eyes.

He reached for both her hands and kisses them one at a time. "What was that promise?"

"I was never going to give my body to Quinton because I had promised it to someone else. Our marriage was a sham."

At her words, he went utterly still. He moved his arm around her shoulders and pulled her closer to him. He was sure that she was talking about him. His lips curved slowly until a grin spread across his face. He drew a shuddering breath. "To whom did you promise your body?"

Hot blood rushed to Katherine's cheeks. He tilted his head when she did not answer him, and with that knee-weakening smile, he asked again. "Kat, to whom did you promise your body?"

She stared back at him, silence more telling than if she had spoken. She blinked, almost hypnotized by the sweet smile spread across his face. He could hardly wait for her answer. "You," she said softly. He made a muffled sound of pleasure deep in his throat at her reply. His hand slipped down from her shoulder to her collarbone. Her breath left her in a sigh. His hand caressed her bare neckline, and bursts of desire struck her, making her shiver with sensation. He leaned in and kissed her with a hungry mouth, gliding across her lips' smooth surface. A growl escaped from somewhere deep in his chest. His hand moved into her hair, grasping the silken gold mass with intensity. She wrapped her arms around him and clung to him as if her life depended on it.

He pushed her back softly. "What happened during that year?"

She arched a brow at him. "Whatever do you mean?"

Patrick opened his eyes wide. "I mean, what happened between you and Quinton while residing in London."

She held his gaze, and for a moment, silence reigned. There was another moment of hesitation, and she finally continued. "Quinton only came to the house for the first six months and then moved out, most likely with one of the women he was bedding. When the year was up and the ton season ended, I moved in with my parents, and I have lived here for the past four years. I have never attended any of the balls or soirees or gatherings. I always felt that I would be the center of criticism even though I knew through the help that the ton sympathized with me and not Quinton or his family." She blinked the tears that she could not control. She squeezed her eyes shut as if she was trying very hard to erase her mind's ugly memories.

Patrick held her tightly and forced her attention back to his question. "What about the funeral?"

Katherine stared. The thought made her chest constrict. She looked confused and appalled by the question. Her eyes went wide. "I'm not going to do anything about his burial. I'm not even going to attend. I don't know the man, and I am glad he is dead. His family can take care of his miserable body. I do not want anything to do with it, but I do feel sorry for his mother. She is a kind woman kept mostly in the dark about many things. She was never one to attend gatherings or soirees. She spent most of her time at their country estate, so she never knew details of her son's horrible indiscretions.

Patrick hmphed. He ran his fingers through his hair. "I'm sure she knows by now."

Her smile faded. "Yes, I'm sure she is devastated." Frowning slightly, she looked down, and the moment stretched.

He put his finger under her chin and lifted her face to his. Her eyes were full of tears again. "What is it, Kat?"

In response to his questioning look, she replied. "I am saddened by Bennett's handling of my dowry. Quinton and his father have nearly depleted everything my father gave them on wagers, women, and other dirty deeds." She blew her nose into a small handkerchief and turned to stare across the lake.

Patrick flinched. "Kat, please don't think about finances. Money is not an issue. I'll take care of you and your family."

Katherine pressed her lips together. "My mother is fine. My father was very successful and ensured that my mother and brothers would not want anything after being gone. I was only speaking about myself." She looked into his eyes and took a deep breath. "That is all that I want to say about my life. Do you have any more questions?"

Patrick smiled. "There is one more question."

She gave him a curious look. "And what might that be?"

Patrick took her hands and held her gaze for a long moment. Katherine shifted. "What?"

He looked into her eyes and leaned closer. Gently he framed her face with one hand, and, lowering his head, he brushed her lips with his. "Kat, please marry me. Make me the happiest man on earth," he whispered into her mouth.

Tears filled her eyes, tears of happiness. She pulled back, and her lips lifted slightly in a sensual smile. She had given him her heart and soul unconditionally long ago. Her voice was trembling when she replied. "Yes! Yes! I will marry you." He smiled slowly, the blue in his eyes sparkled with contentment, and he kissed her-a long warm kiss, one that stimulated their bodies and minds. She raised her hands, grabbed the lapels of his jacket, and drew him closer. She kissed him back with hunger and passion. "I love you, Patrick, I have always loved you." He tilted her head for better access to her mouth. His kiss, this time, was explosive. His heart was filled with joy and pride. Kat was going to be his wife.

"Kat, I hate to bring this up now, but you will have to sign papers to settle all that was between you and Quinton."

"I'm not sure what you mean."

"I will have Paul Webster help with this issue. I had a long talk with him about an unconsummated marriage."

Her eyes widened. "What about it?" Shaken by the new information, she waited breathlessly to hear more about it.

"When we were looking into your marriage to Quinton, we found out that you had a religious ceremony without civil registration. Based on our laws, that type of union is not legally binding. You might be able to have your union to Quinton annulled, even if he is dead. I'm sure there will be tons of papers to sign, but Paul will take care of all that."

Awareness sizzled between them as she regarded him with probability. She closed her eyes and exhaled deeply; she felt overwhelmed with relief and comfort for the first time in five years. "I don't want to raise my hopes, but that will be wonderful. I feel like I was a prisoner for all this time." She swallowed hard and let out a deep sigh.

The silence was deafening, and it could have stretched longer if Patrick hadn't started speaking again. "How about discussing something more pleasant?"

"Like what?"

"The season starts in another month, and I already have received many invitations for balls, soirees, and gatherings. I want you to attend with me. What do you think about that?"

"I feel like I am waking up from a horrible nightmare and walking into a fairyland. I would love to get back into the ton circle and spend time with my old friends. I kept everyone at a distance while Quinton was alive because I was ashamed of my circumstances. Now all I want is to be there with you by my side."

"Yes, my love, I will always be by your side." He kissed her again and held her tight. They both lay back on the grass and looked at the beautiful sky. They remained quiet for a long moment, savoring each other's company. "Do you know what I would love to do right now?" he murmured, his voice was husky full of desire.

"What?"

His hand came up, and he ran his finger down the side of her cheek. "I want to make love to you; I want to make you mine."

Katherine lifted herself on one elbow, looked down, and blinked at him. "Who is stopping you?"

His eyes went wide, and then he broke into a hearty laugh. He lightly swept his tongue between her lips, pressing his warm, soft lips to hers. "I am the one stopping me. I will make you mine in our chamber in our bed. I do not want to belittle our relationship by taking you on the grass as if you were a frivolous assignation."

"Do I have to wait until our wedding night?" The tone in her voice that of desperation brought another hard laugh on his part.

"Might as well forget any plans you have for the next couple of hours because I will keep you with me," he said. He chuckled and pressed her softly onto the grass. He lowered his head and took her mouth in a sizzling kiss. Katherine bowed upward, trying to get closer to his body. The kiss deepened. The passion in the kiss spun her into oblivion. He pulled back, and she gasped.

"Patrick, why are you doing this?"

He just could not stop laughing at her eagerness and loveliness. "I love you, Kat, I want you, and I will have you but not now. Not like this." She pouted, and he smiled. There was some talk, but mostly they lay back quietly, absorbing the sun indulgently.

The sun had reached the middle of the blue sky and sparkled like a piece of a priceless jewel. Millions of golden rays rained upon the earth and warmed every living thing on the ground. "Kat, we should be going back. I'm sure your mother will be expecting us. "Suddenly a soft rumbling noise left her stomach. She looked horrified, and he laughed out loud. "I guess it is time to feed you." He rose to his feet and pulled her up to him. He looked down at her without releasing her. His lips were soft and warm when they brushed hers, and she moved even closer. His hands wrapped about her waist and held her to him. His lips moved from hers and followed a hot path along her throat and across her shoulder. She clung to him, eager and in need. It occurred to him that they needed to go inside. He suppressed a groan and pressed a soft kiss on her lips before he pushed her softly away. "Let's go, my love. Your mother is waiting." She looked embarrassed for her weakness as she began to put the scattered pieces of herself back together. He was irresistible, and she was irrevocably in love with him. She straightened her skirts, and together they walked back up the path in complete silence.

His gaze lingered over her for a moment. "Are you hungry?" She realized that she was ravenously hungry. She had eaten a very light breakfast. She clenched the muscles of her stomach to stop it from rumbling again. She nodded in agreement.

CHAPTER SEVENTEEN

*P*atrick couldn't remember having a better day than he had that day. On the way home he recalled holding her close against him, lifting her face to his, and piercing through her sapphire eyes. He'd never felt so out of control but also so blissful. He broke into a smile that made him feel warm all over. She was his dream come true. This desire was beyond anything he had ever felt before or imagined that something like this existed. He wanted to love her, protect her, and spend every waking moment with her. By the time he arrived home, it was late, and he felt tired. He went to bed without dinner.

He spent the next week helping his father prepare the books for the solicitor. He also rode with him out to their estate's various locations to help him settle many unfinished businesses. His mother was exuberant having him home. He sent a note to Paul Webster about Quinton and the unconsummated marriage. He wanted him to look into the British law and see if Katherine could have the union annulled. He visited her several times, and they went for long walks discussing their future. Patrick assumed things would go smoothly, but nothing could be further from the truth.

After spending two blissful weeks in Scunthbury, he returned to London. He needed to attend to the new property he and his friends had purchased and help get it ready before the season started. He promised Kat that he would return and bring her back to sign the papers that Paul prepared. The invitations for the season balls and soirees had piled up on his desk. He would have trashed them all, but now having Katherine by his side, he would go through them, pick what he thought would be nice to attend, and throw the others away.

Patrick took his time after breakfast, strolling to his study. From the door, he cast a glance at the pile of invitations resting on his desk and lifted one side of his mouth in a disdainful smile. He despised the ton and the ballrooms, but this season, he had to put aside his feelings and make sure he reintroduced Kat as his own to the English society's elite group.

The window behind his desk was a large piece of exquisite stained glass. The sun's rays burst brilliantly through it and showed the beauty of the many colorful hues that weaved together and made the carpet sparkle creating a fantastic sight. He walked into the room, a slight frown in the depths of his sapphire blue eyes. He shrugged out of his coat, threw it on the sofa, and sank into the large leather chair behind the mahogany desk. Leaning forward, he took a handful of the invitations and started to go through them slowly. He put in a pile the ones he chose to accept. The rest he pushed off his desk and into the bin.

He was ready to stand up when he noticed that a small white envelope had drifted to the floor. It didn't seem to match any of the other invitations. His mouth twitched. He bent over, and his fingers tightened around it. He hmphed when he noticed the lousy spelling of his first name. He flipped it from one hand to the other over and over again. There was no return name or address. He kept staring at it as concern flashed in his deep blue eyes. He drummed his fingers on the desktop and finally opened it. His eyes widened as an uneasy feeling crept up his spine. The note was from Randal Wyman, the leader of the crime ring connected to the Bennett saga. "What in bloody hell does he want with me?" The words on the small, folded paper inside the envelope were full of spelling errors. "I mast see yu as soon as posible" His mouth dropped open, and an uncomfortable feeling surged through him. What could he possibly want?

He stared at the misspelled words for a few moments, and finally, he decided to find out what was going on. He rose to his feet, picked up his coat, and pulled the bell cord on the wall. Christian' son hurried into the room.

"Yes, my Lord!"

"Mathew, please have my curricle ready. I have to go out for a little while." Mathew left, and soon he was on his way. Thirty minutes later, he was walking through the dilapidated door of Randal's office. He found him sitting behind his desk, looking down at a pile of papers. He didn't hear Patrick come in until he was standing right in front of him. Patrick cleared his throat.

He looked up, and his eyes shot up in shock. "I'm sorry. I did not hear you come in." He started to stand, and Patrick motioned with his hand not to bother.

He produced Randal's note from his pocket and looked at him questionably. "What the devil does this mean?" Every word braced with inquisitiveness.

"I have some information that you need to know. I am trying to be upstanding here, all right?"

Patrick gave him an exasperated glare. "Our deal about Bennett's disgraceful behavior is over."

Randal scoffed. "But that is what I'm trying to tell you. It isn't over."

Patrick's gasp expressed his surprise at his words. "What else could there be? Bennett is in jail waiting for his execution day, and Quinton is dead. To me, that seems to be the end of the Bennett saga."

Randal cut him off. "I understand all that, but please hear me out."

He stared at Randal for several seconds, and he nodded in agreement. "All right, let's hear it."

"I was visited by the Marquess of Lavenham Jack Thorsten. He was looking for information on the whereabouts of Quinton's wife."

Patrick gasped out loud. "Whatever for?"

"Quinton placed a wager for Jack Thorsten worth 30,000 pounds. He now wants his money back. He knows the Bennett saga, but he said that he would get his money back from Lady Katherine. He will use everything in his power to do that."

Shock widened Patrick's eyes as he considered Randal's comments. "What did you tell him?"

"I couldn't tell him anything because I have no idea where Lady Katherine is living now. He pressed for information, but I had nothing to offer, so he left quite angry. He said that he would handle this by himself. I thought that you needed to know." Randal's voice was now but a whisper.

Patrick remained quiet for a very long moment. Randal cleared his throat, bringing Patrick back to reality. He rose to his feet, stunned by the news. "Thank you, Randal. I appreciate the information. Sorry for being so rude when I came in." Taking a few pounds out of his pocket, he set them on Randal's desk.

"You do not have to do this, my Lord, I'm just glad that you know. I wouldn't want anything to happen to Lady Katherine."

His mind was in turmoil as he thanked him again and left his office. He took a deep breath as the curricle rumbled down the road, his eyes fixed in front of him, pondering the uncertainty.

In his study, he decided to sit down and write a few notes. He sent them to Theron, Gregory, and Edward. He was calling on the Viper group for assistance. He also sent one to Andrew and Paul including all the information from Randal. He also sent a note to his mother asking her to visit

Katherine and her mother and alert them in case someone came looking for money. She was to direct them back to Patrick, and he would settle the debt.

He pulled the published database that listed all the elite members of the English society from his desk drawer and thumbed through the pages. He stopped on the fifth page, and his eyes locked on Jack Thorsten, the Marquess of Lavenham. He wrote down the address and put the book away. He imagined that his friends would arrive first thing in the morning and set his plan in motion. He would try and settle the debt while keeping Katherine out of it.

However, that was not Jack Thorsten's plan. He had already located Katherine's estate, and taking two of his thugs was on his way to collect his money. Katherine and her mother would not receive Patrick's warning note until later on that day or maybe the next morning. It was noon when Henry Weldon's butler answered the sharp raps at the door. Three men stood in the opening.

"Can I help you, sir?"

"We are here to see Lady Katherine."

"Is she expecting you?"

"No, please tell her it has to do with her late husband."

Henry flinched, but he asked them to come in and left them waiting at the sitting room. Soon he returned, followed by Duchess Weldon and Katherine. The Duchess kindly asked them to sit. Henry did not leave the room. He stood by the door with an unsettling feeling. Jack started to speak and explained about the wager and the money owed to him.

Katherine was the one who spoke this time. "Dear sir, I have been separated from my husband for more than four years, and I do not know about his gambling affairs. I do not have the money that you need. I am very sorry for your loss, but I can't be held responsible for your misfortune."

Jack's eyes narrowed, and he frowned. "I beg to differ with you. You are still his wife, and all the properties and sums of money are now yours. I demand my money." His voice rose in an intimidating manner. Henry moved into the room and stood in front of the ladies.

"Sir, I must ask you to leave the house."

Jack Thorsten pressed his lips tight and hung on to his temper. His eyes narrowed at Katherine, and she narrowed hers back at him, tipping up her chin. He growled with anger as he turned and walked out the door, followed by his two goons. "This is not over," he called out without turning. "I'm warning you that you will regret this. I'll get my money one way or another." When the door closed behind them, the two women looked at each other in shock.

"Henry, please send a footman to the Wingham residence." Katherine instructed. "Explain what took place here and ask the Duchess to notify Patrick. I am sure he will know what to do. In the meantime, let's go by our daily business and take this out of our minds. It is just another dirty job by Quinton. I am sure he has destroyed many men and many families."

· · ·

After a small snack, Katherine took a book from the library and made her way to the garden. She sat on the beautiful bench under a tree and let her gaze drink in the view's beauty. Her lips curved in pleasure as her mind absorbed the stillness in the air. She watched several singing birds make their way between the trees. Her eyes followed the butterflies that lingered over the myriad of colorful blooms.

Her eyes fell on the large pond that occupied the very center of this fantastic garden creating a piece of heaven. She narrowed her eyes against the brightness of the sunlight that illuminated the water with its beams, turning it into a million sparkling jewels and sending them to disappear, along with the sun's rays, into the pond basin. She closed her eyes, letting her ears enjoy the soothing sound of the flowing water. She smiled.

She never heard the footsteps approaching until they stopped right behind her. Before she had a chance to react, large male hands grabbed her; one of the men wrapped one arm around her neck and yanked her firmly off the bench, while the other clamped a cloth soaked in sulfuric ether over her mouth and nose.

Terror surged through her body, her lungs locked as she struggled to breathe, but there was no air supply. She kicked, pushed, and tried to scream, but it came out as a stifled shriek. She decided to escape from her attacker with all her might, and soon she surrendered to a smothering sensation and finally to unconsciousness. Her body went limp. They carried Katherine out of the garden and threw her inside a closed carriage. They took a glance around, making sure that they were not detected. At first, they were so overwhelmed that this was easier than they expected that for a long while remaining in stunned silence.

"Oh!" one of them finally exclaimed, unable to keep his excitement from spilling over. "That was too easy, and the easiest money we have ever made." They both glanced at Katherine's limp body.

Katherine opened her eyes gradually. Her brain was clouded and utterly disoriented. Her eyes moved sluggishly around the poorly lit room, but nothing seemed familiar. Her mind was blurry, filled with jumbled up images. She clenched her eyes shut, thinking she was dreaming, but the surroundings hadn't changed when she opened them again. Her brain cells seemed to be stripped of oxygen, she couldn't remember a thing, and she couldn't think straight. Where was she? She had no answers. She lifted her arms and clenched her fists, trying to amass her faculties.

Minutes seemed to tick by, and panic settled in, paralyzing every muscle in her body. Nothing made sense. The sensation deepened, and she tried to block the anxiety unsuccessfully. Something was wrong, but the wall between her physical body and consciousness seemed to be temporarily impenetrable. She lay on the strange bed motionless, but for how long, she wasn't sure. Muddling through her vague thoughts, she tried to make sense of her present situation. She searched around the room one more time and inhaled deeply. She couldn't gather her bearings.

The silence dragged for what she thought was a century.

Abruptly, the striking face of a man emerged from her soul's depths and found its way through to the forefront of her vision and jolted her mind to consciousness, startling her. "Patrick!" she cried out, brought back from oblivion to reality. She closed her eyes as a surge of warmth settled deep in the pit of her stomach. A wave of shattering pain ripped right through her body, leaving her scarred. Vivid memories started trickling into her brain. The last thing she remembered was fighting for breath. Someone had grabbed her while sitting on the bench in her garden. She recalled the frantic struggle to break free from her attacker's chokehold. She winced at the thought, and her body tensed as panic settled deep into her bones.

Supported by her elbows, she pushed against the bed and propped herself up gradually. She searched for something that appeared familiar, but nothing came to her. A wave of anguish ripped through her, ramming her heart into her throat. *"Where in the world am I?"*

She inhaled deeply, scrambling to distinguish between reality and a dream. Her eyes flicked to the window. *"Why am I in this strange room? Who would possibly want to keep me prisoner, and why?"* It didn't take long and, suddenly, she gasped for breath. The face of a man flashed in front of her like a bright neon sign, and icy fingers crawled down her spine slowly. Jack Thorsten. You will regret this; it's not over. I'll get my money one way or another were his last words as he left the house. Bile rose to her throat quickly, and nausea threatened.

She fell back on the bed; tears streamed down her face and into her ears as fear raced across her body. Reality crashed into her skull like a thunderbolt, and pressure generated a stinging pain behind her eyelids. She trembled with fright, knowing that she was alone and helpless against a crazy man. Forced gasps escaped her and scattered through the stillness of the room. The reality rushed back. Thorsten was using her for ransom to get back his 30,000 pounds owed to him by Quinton. She scrutinized her surroundings like a wild animal trapped in a steel cage. *Does anyone know that I have been abducted? Will they find me?* Desperation and terror seeped deep into her bone marrow, and her heart pounded the walls of her chest like a hammer. She couldn't just lie there; she had to do something to escape, but how? She sprang up and struggled to her feet only to almost collapse. The floor swayed beneath her, and she grabbed on to the bedpost to steady herself.

Trembling, she tried to bring in her mind a glimpse of what she was doing before all this took place. She was reading a book. She looked around, but she did not see the book anywhere. *If they did not take the book, someone would notice while searching for me.* She stood in the middle of the room unmoved, with many undefined, perplexing, and mixed feelings. The room was fully furnished. She felt isolated and desperate. Words couldn't define the rush of emotions that surged through her body and shook her thoughts. She was trying hard to embrace the uncertainty that was enveloping her, and all she could feel was her world crumbling at her feet and disappearing into another universe. She needed help; she needed the safe sanctuary of her family, the warmth of Patrick's embrace, and his soft voice telling her that everything would be fine.

Carefully, she searched around once again. She heard distant murmurs, but she couldn't distinguish a single word. The room was large and exquisitely furnished. A luxurious and very plush bedspread covered the four-poster bed. A small eloquent nightstand was right next to the bed. A five-drawer mahogany dresser was opposite from the bed, and a window dominated the other side of the room. Two leather armchairs were on either side of the window with a very delicate square table between them.

She walked toward a partly open door. Standing unmoved for a long moment, she finally reached up and pushed the door wide open. The light coming from the window gave her a clear view of a large washroom. She turned around and crept up to the door. Not sure if it would be locked, she had to try, and it was locked. Disappointment settled deep into her stomach, and she listened guardedly, putting her ear against the panel.

She caught a faint sound of a man speaking loudly, but the sound never sharpened into real words. Sweat seemed to seep through her skin, making her body feel damp. She rubbed her hands together and swallowed hard, overcoming the fear that crept through her mind. *Where in the world am I? How am I ever going to leave this place? How far from home am I?* Suddenly a clear voice came from behind the door somewhere. "I will inform Jack that she is here." She heard booted feet in the hallway, then a door opened and shut, and all was quiet again. She walked back and sat on the bed. There was nothing more to do but wait. She was jolted out of her thoughts when she heard booted feet approaching. A key inserted in the lock, then the bolt clicked, and the door opened. She remained utterly still as Jack walked into the room and stood in front of her.

"I am glad to see that you are alert and quiet because I hate distractions and yelling. Trust me, something like that would be entirely ineffective." His voice was harsh, and his gaze cold. She was sure that he was an aristocrat of English society. However, he was not a nice man. He watched her for a moment, and then he started to pace back and forth. Katherine remained utterly quiet staring at the floor. He stopped and looked at her.

"Look at me when I talk to you." His voice grew harder. "I have sent a note to your mother requesting my 30,000 pounds. I am sure that she wants to see you alive. I give you my word that you will suffer no injury from my friends or me while in my home." A long pause ensued. "However, if she does not comply, I will have to resort to other solutions to make my money back and maybe even more."

Katherine peered at his face with bewilderment in her eyes. She took a deep breath and finally said through clenched teeth. "What are you going to do? Are you going to kill me? How is that going to bring your money back?"

His voice was now icy cold. He stared for a long moment and then broke out into a hearty laugh. "Have you ever heard of the white slavers?" Katherine's eyes widened as she tried to swallow a gasp. "I will sell you to them for even more money. They do not have any preference for social status. All they care about are looks. You are a beautiful woman. However, I would rather go the other route. The money is mine, so I should have it back. I have given your mother twenty-four hours to come up with a firm answer." After a moment of silence, he swung on his heels and went out the door, throwing the bold shut.

Katherine held her breath until she heard the lock click in place, followed by booted feet fading down the hallway, and then again, it was complete silence. A trembling sigh escaped her lips as she walked over to the window and stood looking out. Giant trees and greenery blocked her view. She was not sure how long she stood there when she heard heavy footsteps. This time more than one person was coming. The male voices that came from the other side of the door seemed unfamiliar. She moved quickly and threw herself on the bed, shutting her eyes. She heard the key turn slowly, and the lock was released. The door opened, and male voices become clear and concise.

"Come and look at this, I think she is still unconscious! I thought Jack came to see her, but I guess I was wrong." A male voice said. The floor creaked under the weight of the heavy footsteps that approached the bed.

"She is beautiful! Do you think she would remember our faces?"

"How could she? She never saw us, and I am glad that she never did." Another voice replied. The silence stretched between the two voices again, and Katherine thought she would die if she had to stay still for much longer. Finally, their footsteps broke the silence as they moved farther away from the bed. Next, she heard the door slam shut, the key turn in the lock, and the footsteps faded away. Rising slowly once again, she swung her legs over the edge of the bed and taking a deep breath; she stood up. The thick greenery did very little to raise her mood as she gazed out the window. She approached gradually and, resting her hands on the windowsill, pressed her nose against the glass and remained still. Finally, she decided to approach the door once again. Her fingers traced over the door handle, gripped it tightly, and pulled as hard as possible. Nothing happened. The door wouldn't budge. She stood there, gazing at the door as hopelessness closed and a stinging stirred behind her eyelids. Tears pooled into her burning eyes and started to stream down her face once again. She was losing hope. What if her mother did not come up with the money in twenty-four hours? And Patrick did not get notified to help her out of this situation? What if he sold her to the white slavers? Fear sipped through her veins like a tornado through an open field.

She turned around and searched the room, looking for something to help her pry the lock. Suddenly, she froze in place. The sound of the door handle turning drove a cold chill down her spine. She hadn't heard footsteps approaching or the key turning. The door opened behind her, and someone stepped inside. Katherine spun around and came face to face with a strange man. He was alone. Surprise flickered in his eyes and shock crept over his face.

"What in bloody hell!" The man exclaimed. He didn't expect her to be standing right inside the door. Katherine's eyes widened, and her mouth dropped as she gasped in disbelief. She recognized the man as one of the two Jack Thorsten brought with him to her home a couple of days ago. She opened her mouth to say something but closed it back again. Words stuck in her throat, and the silence stretched for a few moments. He was still staring at her. He remembered the effect she had on him up close. She was quite beautiful. A lot more attractive than he remembered from the moment they saw her sitting in the garden. Her voice snapped him out of his crazy reverie.

"What do you want?" She breathed quietly.

"There is only one thing I want from you right now, which seems to be a perfect time," he said wickedly.

"I don't understand," she said irritably.

He moved one step closer and grabbed both of her bare arms. "Let's say that you will make this a lot easier for us if you just cooperate. No more talk," he said. Lifting his hand, he traced his finger down the side of her face. "Sit down," he ordered, pointing to the bed. She recoiled and gave him an icy stare. A furious flush crossed his eyes, noticing her repulsion. "You think you are too good for me, don't you?" he said, spitting out the words with clenched teeth.

"You're a thug," she said.

"Shut up and do as I say,"

"Or what?" Katherine snorted, not understanding where she got the nerve.

"He suddenly reached over and grabbed her throat tightly, giving her a meaningful glare. "I'll throw you on that bed and show you that you are nothing but a whore," he said through clenched teeth. She raised her hands and slapped his hand away from her throat. Fury flickered in his eyes, and he lifted his hand and backhanded her hard. The key he was holding tore her cheek, and pain shot right through her bones.

"Whore!" he growled again as he watched Katherine stagger back, losing her balance and dropping to the floor. Lifting her hands, she touched her cheek and felt something warm and wet. She knew she was bleeding. She pressed her lips together as wrath pooled deep in her stomach, and the blood rushed through her veins and pounded in her ears. She had to make her move now. She had to try and help herself out of this situation. Blocking the excruciating pain out of her mind, she leaped up and threw herself on him. Her balled hands caught him by surprise right between the eyes. Lifting her skirt, her knee connected perfectly with his groin. The reaction to her attack on him came both fast and furious. He doubled over in excruciating pain, holding his crotch and gasping for air. His lips moved, but no sound came out. Katherine released the breath she was holding and just stared at him with rebellion as he crumbled to the floor.

Amassing all the courage, she could find she took the key from his hand and darted out, shutting the door behind her. She turned the key, locked the door, and took a few steps back staring at the closed panels. Swiftly turning on her heels, she vaulted down the hallway toward the staircase. She scaled them two at a time. Reaching the landing, where she bolted right into a wall of muscles. She stumbled backward, lost her balance, and fell down the staircase. Her body bounced painfully off each step and finally landed on the marble floor with a loud thump. She groaned in sheer pain.

After leaving the room, the small spark of hope that slipped through her veins was now gone before she had time to decipher it. An expression of wretchedness flashed across her face. She was doomed. The pain was excruciating. She couldn't feel her limbs, her face burned, and her eye felt swollen. She closed her eyes, feeling trapped and discouraged. She wanted to run, but her legs wouldn't respond, and even if they did, where could she go? Her lungs seared, and she couldn't contemplate anything but how to escape. Her heart thudded so loud she could hear it pounding her chest. She listened to the man descending the steps unhurriedly. With a few short strides, he was standing right over her, and she swallowed nervously.

"What do we have here?" A man said in a stunned voice. Reaching down, he grabbed her by her arm and lifted her as if she weighed nothing at all. Mustering all the courage she had, she opened her eyes. Their faces were barely a few inches apart. He was the other thug Thorsten had with him. His lips were curved upward in an aggravating half-smile. Katherine stared at him in shock and gasped in surprise.

"Wh," he started to say but stopped mid-word when loud pounding came from somewhere above. He stiffened, and his eyes flicked toward the pounding sound and then swiftly returned to her. Astonishment filled his eyes, and he let out a low, throaty grunt. Fury seethed as awareness settled deep into his mind. Pinning her with an icy stare, he slammed her twice against the wall indignantly, discarding her like unwanted trash.

Katherine crashed to the floor once again, and an agonized groan escaped her lips. Something warm and coppery cascaded over her mouth, down her chin, and soaked the front of her beautiful dress. *Oh, God! Please help me.* Her face was on fire, her body ached severely, and her throat felt dry. The man stomped past her without looking back and headed up the stairs toward the room the desultory pounding originated from without looking back. Her heart sank, and hopelessness spread across every muscle in her body. Her plan of escape had skidded to a dreadful halt. Tears streamed down her face, burning the deep laceration on her cheek, creating a sharp bite. The pain was excruciating, but she couldn't stop crying. Her thoughts were revolving uncontrollably, unable to find the power to slow down long enough to figure out her next move. Did she have an upcoming move? Her victory had been short-lived and somewhat discouraging. Her mouth set into a straight line, and she tried to lift her hands to wipe her face, but the pain was unbearable. She drew in a deep breath, and her chest muscles screamed in discomfort. She concentrated on the pain, and her brain ordered her to try and crawl toward the exit but she could not move.

A loud voice from upstairs snapped her out of her stupor. "Jasper, what in bloody hell happened in here? Why are you on the floor? Did you let a woman make a joke out of you?"

"That bloody whore! Where is she?" he growled.

"She's still here, no thanks to you!" he scoffed. There was a short pause. "Get off the floor. What's wrong with you?" he spat out. The man on the floor was still holding his crotch. Agony and sweat covered his face as he tried to straighten up and failed. His eyes focused on his friend. His friend scrutinized every move he made carefully, eyes-wide-open, lips curling up into a smirking grin. "Oh! The old trick, perfect blow right into the groin," he furthered, unable to hide the amusement from his voice.

"Bloody hell! It's not funny, Walter. It hurts like hell," he growled and frowned, cursing out loud. "Where is she? I'll give her what she deserves," he said, looking around wildly and making a considerable effort to stand.

"I don't think you're in a position to give her anything right now," his friend said, and he leaned down and helped him to his feet. He watched him take a couple of steps, moaning painfully. His dark gaze flicked to Walter and scowled; he was unable to suppress his embarrassment.

"How in the hell did you let her come so close? What were you doing here, anyway?" Walter muttered quizzically.

"I just wanted to check on her," Jasper murmured awkwardly.

"You have to admire her for trying to escape," Walter said now, teasingly.

"What? You've got to be joking," he exclaimed.

" I was only kidding." He snorted and giving him a soft push; they headed out of the room.

"Well, where is she?" he asked again.

"Don't worry about her; she'll not be able to walk anywhere for a while.

"What do you mean?"

"She fell down the staircase, trying to escape, and she is in bad shape."

"How badly is she hurt?"

"She is a bloody mess," Walter continued.

"Well, Jack is not going to like this either; it might mess up his negotiations with her family." Jasper murmured thoughtfully.

"Um…what happened isn't our fault," Walter muttered. "She tried to escape and fell down the staircase. He'll understand that".

Standing over Katherine now, they stared down at her. She angled her head upward and gave them a flat stare; she wasn't going to provide them with the satisfaction of knowing how badly she was injured. She was afraid that her irregular gasping would reveal her state of mind. Gathering all the strength she could muster, she lifted her leg and kicked Jasper blindly right between his legs. It was a perfect blow to his groin once again.

Jasper let out a terrifying sound. Katherine stared at him, wide-eyed. There was a gasping sound as he finally took a mouthful of air. "Bloody ballocks," he shrieked, and his body doubled from pain. Walter tried to help him. "There was a shocking moment of silence, and then Walter let his right-hand fly as hard as he could and backhanded Katherine on her face. Her head jerked backward and hit the wall with a loud thud. Blood shot from the deep laceration on her face and sprayed the front of Walter's shirt. She groaned severely and closed her eyes. Walter grabbed the corner of his white shirt and stared at the bloodstains with utter disgust. Fury emanated from his eyes, and a deep growl escaped his mouth.

"I'll kill you," he hissed wrathfully and, pulling his hand back, he prepared to strike her once again. She shut her eyes to ready for the next blow. Stand silence fell, and darkness moved in. She had lost consciousness.

A strong arm grabbed Walter's hand in the air, just before it contacted with Katherine's face. "What in the devil are you doing? Are you out of your bloody mind?" Jack looked down at Katherine and gritted his teeth. "You need to take the girl back in the room and take care of her injuries, or I will kill you," he spat out in a voice filled with anger. Walter opened his mouth to explain, but he decided against it. He bent down, and, with ease, lifted Katherine into his arms and carried her back into the room. He laid her on the bed and stared down at her for a short moment. He shut his eyes at the unpleasant sight in front of him. The cut on her cheek was deep and bloody, her lips swollen, and her left eye was black and blue. Her body's exposed parts were severely bruised from the fall, and her beautiful gown was stained with blood. "Blazes," he said quietly

CHAPTER EIGHTEEN

*O*nce dinner concluded, Patrick headed to the library. He plunged into the depths of the leather armchair, hoping to hear something from his mother soon. The clock on the mantelpiece chimed seven times. "Bloody hell," he muttered grimly. He rose to his feet and strolled over to his polished mahogany table and picked up the brandy decanter. He poured himself a hefty portion and watched the expensive liquid slosh into the glass.

He walked over to the window, pushed back the heavy curtain, and stood there motionless. He took a sip watching the twilight descending slowly as the sun dipped below the horizon. A shooting star sailed across the sky and disappeared in the endless and infinite dusk that now covered the countryside. Time ticked away with no news. He turned away from the window and left the library, shutting the door behind him.

As he climbed the stairs to his bedchamber, he heard a

loud noise of hoofs hitting the courtyard's cobblestones. His head swiveled toward the sound, and he froze in place. He turned and hurried back downstairs and out the front door. A young man jumped off his horse quickly and ran in his direction, nearly knocking him down. "Good evening, my Lord," he said breathlessly.

Patrick knew something was wrong as soon as he saw the young man's face up close. He sensed a prevailing tension in his voice. He stared at him for a short moment. "Did my mother send you?"

"No, my Lord, I'm here to deliver a message to you from Duchess Weldon." He handed him a small sealed envelope. He stared at it briefly. When he looked up, the young man had not moved an inch.

His eyes widened. "Anything else?"

"Yes, my Lord, She is very distraught, and she asked for you to read it immediately and reply."

A cold wave washed through him, and for an almost undetectable second, he went shockingly still. He drew in a breath and opened the envelope. His breath caught sharply when his eyes fell on the content.

Patrick, we were visited by three men this morning. One of them introduced himself as Jack Thorsten. He asked for 30,000 pounds that were owed to him by Quinton. We tried to explain that we had not seen Quinton for more than four years, and we did not have that kind of money. He got furious and tried to intimidate us, but my foreman stepped in and asked him to leave. He took his goons and left screaming that he would get his money one way or another. I didn't receive your mother's note until after they were gone. This afternoon, Katherine went missing. She was in the garden reading her book as she does every day, and we have not seen her since. We found the book on the ground, but she is gone. I had every hand in the household search every inch of the estate; there is no sign of her. I am worried that something terrible has happened to her. Please help me find her.

Ice crept down his spine, and his heart stopped. His body felt like a stone, locking him in place despite the overwhelming impulse to race to the Weldon estate to look for clues and tear London apart. He asked the young lad to come inside while he wrote a quick note in reply. *Please don't worry, I will find her. I will make sure that I bring her home.* He sealed the envelope, and the footman left immediately. His footsteps faded as he dashed down the hall. He had been a man of control all his life. He had never allowed anything or anyone to take that away from him, and here he was, lost. He prepared three more notes for the Viper group. When finished, he walked to the wall and pulled the bell cord.

A few minutes later, Christian appeared at the door, a curious look in his eyes. "What's wrong?"

Sighing heavily, he pushed away from his desk and rose to his feet. "I have a major issue, Christian. They abducted Katherine." His voice broke.

Christian stared at Patrick in astonishment. "Abducted? By whom?"

"A man from Quinton's past. That bastard took her to collect some wager he had with that piece of rubbish. I will tear his heart out if he has harmed her in any way." He enunciated each word, his voice lined with pure venom. "I need for you to have these notes delivered immediately. They must come tonight. Every minute that goes by makes the situation harder to resolve."

Christian nodded, and without a word, he left, shutting the door behind him.

Patrick shifted restlessly and glanced at the published database on his desk with all the elite members of English society. Flipping through the pages once again, he located Thorsten's address and wrote it down. There was nothing more to do but wait for his friends to arrive. They would have to pay a visit to Jack tonight. There was no time to lose, but he would need his friends' assistance. He was unsure of how many thugs Thorsten kept at his residence. This would not be a job for one man even if Katherine's safety was at the very top of his concerns.

He was unsure how long it had been before he heard the first hoofs hit the cobblestones in the courtyard, and soon more of them followed. His friends had arrived, and he let out a sigh of relief. He ran to the door and pulled it wide open; three men climbed those stairs and pinned Patrick to the spot. He rubbed his arms to ward off a sudden chill, despite the warm summer air.

"Patrick, you look dreadful! What's wrong?" George asked. "Your note was urgent but did not give us any details."

"Katherine has been abducted," he said. A collective gasp went around. Three pairs of eyes stared back at him in apparent disbelief.

"Christ," Michael muttered under his breath.

Patrick looked at the clock on the foyer wall. It was eleven-thirty at night. The time had passed quickly, and now it was nearly midnight. "Do we know who is responsible?" George asked.

"Yes, the Marquess of Lavenham Jack Thorsten."

"What the devil for? And who is he? How is he connected with the Weldon family?"

"It is not the Weldon family. He had made a wager with Quinton for 30,000 pounds. Now that Quinton is dead, he aims to get his money back from Katherine. He visited them, and when they refused, he threatened Katherine and her mother. They had no idea that he was going to stoop to this level."

George regarded Patrick through narrowed eyes. "Even dead, that rogue is creating issues for people."

"What is your plan?" Edward asked curiously.

"I don't have one. But I thought we should pay a visit to Thorsten. His home is only about an hour away from here. I did not want to go alone thinking that there maybe several thugs in his home. I'm sure that he brought her there from her country estate since he doesn't believe that anyone in London will be looking for her."

"Do you know his address?"

"Yes, it is in the book of the elite," he said. "He lives on Southampton."

"The element of surprise," murmured Edward.

"All right then, let's go," Michael said. "I would suggest that you send for backup. Constables will be required to make an arrest or arrests based on this type of crime and how many might be involved."

Patrick called for Christian to handle the messenger to the authorities. He then calmly locked his pistol and slid it into the band of his trousers. An hour later and long before the first light of dawn, the Viper group arrived at Thorsten's residence. Quietly, they dismounted in the thick woods that surrounded the house, making it entirely private from curious neighborly eyes.

Their adrenaline pumped hard as they walked at an agonizingly slow pace and went in through the servants' entrance. They knew that at this late hour, the help would have withdrawn to the servant wing. When inside the house, they crept to the foyer and up the staircase. At the landing, they split up. Michael and George went to the right while Patrick and Edward followed the left. Patrick was sure the London location had been picked on purpose so that its inhabitants could go unnoticed for as long as he needed to achieve his poor results. They crept, like ghosts. They crept silently, stopping short at each door to listen for sounds. Quietly, they opened each door and checked inside. At the third door to the left, Patrick heard a loud snoring sound. He pushed the door open slowly and looked inside.

The person on the bed never made a move, so he backed up, closing it quietly. By the time they reached the last door to the left, Michael and George had joined them as they had found two men in deep sleep in two of the rooms on the right side, but Katherine was not in sight.

Patrick started to lose hope as they stood in front of the last door to the left. He placed his ear against the door and heard a low murmur. He could not make any sense of it, but he had a gut feeling that he needed to go inside. He turned the handle slowly and pushed, but the door did not give in. It was locked. His hope rose. He took a small tool out of his pocket, and soon they were inside the room. It was a large chamber. The room was bathed in the bright moonlight, making it easy for them to see the contents. They tried to locate the murmurs, and suddenly, Patrick's eyes zeroed on a small body coiled on the bed.

He took a matchbox out of his pocket, and, lifting his boot, he struck a match. He held it over the bed and opened his mouth to say something, but the words choked in his throat, and he closed it again as he allowed these ugly visions to bleed into his brain one after the other. The match in hand burned his flesh, and he jerked to reality. "It's Katherine," he whispered. He lit another match and stared down in stunned disbelief at her bloody face and bruised body exposed by her torn gown. Patrick's world crumbled, and his mind was frozen in place.

The pain in his chest expanded. He inhaled sharply, and for a short moment, he thought the floor swayed beneath his feet. His joy of finding her suddenly faded into horror. The most astonishingly beautiful image in his head had become the most gruesome. He bent down and set one hand flat on the bed to take a closer look. The bedsprings creaked under his weight. He shook his hand to rid of the match that was now burning his fingers once again. He then slipped his hands under Katherine's body, and, lifting her into his arms, he held her against his chest protectively. He felt his heart shattering into a million shards.

"Kat, I'm here... you're safe now," he murmured. "Can you hear me?" Katherine did not respond. He pressed a soft kiss to her forehead. "Oh God! Kat, please wake up, my love. I love you," he muttered despondently. The anguish that spread across every nerve in his body was tormenting. He was too worried about her condition to think straight.

George instinctively raised his hand and gripped Patrick's elbow, interrupting his tremulous thoughts. "Patrick, come on, man. We need to take her out of here before someone comes." His voice was firm but supportive.

Patrick turned to face George and nodded in agreement. His eyes narrowed, and his expression changed to that of a man in control of his faculties. He moved forward and froze. Voices filled the room as heavy footsteps came down the hallway. "I'm telling you that I heard a noise," a man's voice said. A door opened, and the same voice could be heard again. "Wake up the boss; someone is in the house."

The men looked at each other and decided to move into the washroom area to wait in silence. Soon three men burst into the room. "Where is she?" a man shouted.

"She was here an hour ago when I checked on her, and I locked the door behind me."

"The door was not locked when we came in. What the devil is going on?" another man said.

Silence stretched beyond terribly uncomfortable. Patrick remained entirely still, and a nervous smile painted his angry face. He turned to George. "Please take Katherine back to the house and make sure that constables are on their way," whispered even though he knew that Christian had followed his instructions to the letter. George nodded in agreement and reaching over, he took Katherine carefully from Patrick's arms. Michael, Edward, and Patrick stepped into the room, taking the other three by surprise. With Katherine in his arms, Theron moved quickly to the door, protected by his friends and disappeared into the hallway.

"You are going to pay for what you did." Patrick hissed.

The man who Patrick assumed to be Jack Thorsten stepped forward. "Who the devil are you? And what are you doing in my home?"

"I'm Patrick Marcus Wingham of Hartford, and you?"

"I'm Jack Thorsten, Marquess of Lavenham. Now that the introductions are over, what in bloody hell are you doing in my home? Answer before I alert the authorities."

"You don't have to do that. They are on the way. I notified them about you and the abduction of Lady Weldon."

"You have no idea who I am," Jack said with ice in his voice.

Patrick clenched his teeth, fire spitting out of his eyes. Every feature on his face was alarmingly full of resentment. His fists clenched against his body, and he looked ready to explode.

The silence stretched again for a long moment, and finally, Walter stepped in front of his boss and laughed uncontrollably. Jack, and Jasper, the other goon, turned and stared at him, not understanding the humor. Eventually, Walter stopped laughing and coughed, trying to clear his throat. He formed a stern look and let his gaze sweep over the three intruders. His lips lifted in a sarcastic smile. "So, you are going to kill us?" he scoffed. "Who is going to do that?" he asked and grinned wide. "You three?" His hand made a motion in the air between Patrick, Michael, and Edward. "Where are the rest of your mates?" he mocked. "And I sure do not see any constables busting down the doors." He then broke out into laughter once again, trying to keep the atmosphere as smug as possible. Jack and Jasper joined Walter in his bizarre hilarity.

Patrick, Michael, and Edward remained unmoved, stone-faced. They didn't share in the goons' enthusiasm and cheerfulness. Fire flashed through their angry eyes, scorching the laughter right out of the goons' throats. Walter moved first.

Sprinting forward, he pulled his right arm back, suspending his balled fist next to his ear, and with all the force he possessed, he sent it toward Patrick's face. Patrick dodged quickly, avoiding the blow. Missing his target, Walter tried to resist the forward force, but lost his balance and flew headfirst past Michael and Edward, bouncing off the opposite wall and collapsed.

Jack and Jasper watched in stunned silence. Totally humiliated, Walter bounced right back up, cursed out loud, as he breathed in frayed gasps, and his eyes glazed with rage. He threw his body weight as hard as he could against Patrick, sending him back a few feet.

Patrick stumbled but kept his balance. His clenched fist caught Walter right in the middle of the face and blood-spattered out of his mouth. His next blow caught Walter again in the middle of his face, blinding him. Walter shook his head and put his hands up, trying to brush the blood from his eyes. Walter's breath hissed, and Patrick lifted his other hand and hit him square in the face one last time. Walter dropped to the floor with a loud thud and appeared unconscious.

Shockwaves tore across Jack's and Jasper's faces as they watched Walter. "Wh…what," Jasper started to say but stopped mid-sentence when the realization of Walter's fight resonated through his mind. His thoughts shattered as if a grenade detonated inside his head. He blinked, and quickly, he pulled a pistol from the back of his belt, and, without thinking, fired. The bullet nicked Michael's upper arm, and he staggered backward but didn't fall. A small bloodstain appeared on his shirt, and slowly, it ran down his arm. His lips curled into a devilish smile, and he took a step forward. Jasper was a much taller man and quite husky. His face was dark, and his eyes narrowed to slits observing Michael. He gave him a cold smile, pointed the gun once again, and started to squeeze the trigger, but Edward leaped forward and snatched the gun away from his hand.

Silence fell in the room like a death screen, and Edward flung himself with fantastic speed and landed simultaneously one fist into the middle of Jasper's face and the other into his throat. Jasper sank to his knees, choking and moaning with rage, grasping his chest and trying to breathe. Edward didn't give him any time to recover. He reached down and, lifting this huge man, slammed his fist repeatedly into his face and chest with enormous force. Jasper groaned with every blow, and finally, crumpled to the ground, coughing mouthfuls of blood, unable to breathe. Edward finally had enough; he let him go, and he crumbled to the floor next to Walter.

Jack's eyes moved around wildly. He knew something was special about these men. Looking behind Patrick, he noticed that Michael was now on the floor on his knees and was holding his arm. He breathed in relief, thinking that they might decide to leave without any further incident. Jack glanced at Henry and Walter on the floor, and there was no way for him to get out of this room. He wet his lips. Pure, uncomfortable misery filled his pale face. He turned to Patrick and said firmly. "You have the girl, so there is no need for you to stay here any longer."

"Not so fast, Jack. The authorities are on the way, and you will pay for what you did."

Jack snorted. "The authorities can't touch me. Do you know who I am?" He had barely finished his statement when they heard booted feet running up the stairs and down the hallway. Three constables barreled through the door, pistols in hand, and stopped, surprised by the scene. A fourth man stepped inside the room.

Patrick looked up; Paul Webster had entered the room. Paul nodded toward Patrick, Michael, and Edward with a soft smile and stepped forward to stand in front of Jack Thorsten. "You want to tell me what happened?" His voice was cold as ice. He had been told by Christian about the situation, but he would do an additional interrogation.

Jack glared at Paul, debating his words and what he could say in reply. His eyes grew darker and angrier, and he barked out while pointing at Patrick, Michael, and Edward. "You want to tell me why you are here?" he countered.

Paul's eyebrows drew together in surprise. "We were notified that you kidnapped Lady Weldon."

He shrugged. "I have no idea what you are saying. These men broke into my house in the middle of the night. I don't know what they were looking for, but we had to defend ourselves." He let out a furious growl. "You need to question them, not me. I want to press charges."

Paul looked down at the two men on the floor and chuckled. "You didn't do a good job defending yourself. In any case, that is not the story I heard. I know all about the kidnapping."

"There is no girl here. You can search the premises. Anything you heard is a lie." Jack did not know that he was dealing with a stalwart man. He did not know the relationship between the men standing in the room, and he had no idea that Paul was in charge of the authorities in Whitehall. He had never seen him before. He moved forward and shoved Paul with his body to get him out of his way. Paul moved his leg and swept Jack's feet out from under him. Jack coughed, stumbled, and did a header onto the floor. His temple clipped one of the tables as he went down, and a resulting bit of blood-spattered onto Paul's breaches. Jack howled in pain, but the noise didn't bother anyone in the room.

Patrick's smile widened. Did the man really think that someone would believe his story? The two men were starting to come around. Jasper and Walter blinked up at the ceiling as though they didn't see it. Two constables moved and picked them up by the back of their shirt with one hand and slapped a set of handcuffs on them with the other. Paul bent down and picked up Jack by his nightshirt and yanked him up to his feet.

He motioned to the third constable behind him. They pushed all three men out the door, down the stairs, and out the front door into the back of a waiting wagon. Patrick shook Paul's hand and thanked him for coming out in the middle of the night. Paul slapped him on the back. "Go home and take care of Katherine. I will take care of them." He glanced over at the others and burst out in laughter. Patrick introduced the men to Paul, and he shook their hands with pleasure. "I guess there is action wherever you go. Sorry Andrew missed this; he would have enjoyed it," he added as he walked out the door.

Patrick's expression spoke volumes. His eyes lingered for a moment between his two friends, standing quietly, giving him time to grip all that had taken place a few minutes ago. He looked emotionally drained. "I appreciate all that you did tonight," he said and smiled thankfully.

They left the Thorsten residence and walked in the woods to retrieve their horses. Battling anger about Katherine's condition, Patrick focused on getting swiftly back to Oxford Street. "You can go home if you wish, Katherine will be with me for a couple of days. I will summon a doctor and have him take care of her before I take her home."

"No, we will go back with you to make sure she is all right, and then we will leave you alone," Michael said, voice firm. They rode quietly. At the house, he found George standing outside one of the bedchambers.

"How is she?" Patrick asked. "There is a carriage outside. Who is here?"

"I summon Dr. Edwards. He is inside with her."

"Thank you, George." They all waited eagerly to hear what the doctor had to say. A little later, an older man with silver hair and kind features walked out of the room, shutting the door behind him. Patrick extended his hand and moved forward. "I'm Patrick Wingham. How is she?" he asked anxiously.

"I'm Doctor Edwards," he said with a kind smile on his face. "Lady Weldon suffered numerous injuries on her body and face. She has several lacerations that needed sutures, and she took a dreadful blow to the head. I am sorry to say that she will have a small scar on her face, the cut is too deep." Patrick flinched at his words. The doctor patted him on the shoulder and continued. "With a little care along with the medication I am leaving with you, she should be up and around in a few days. I just administered a strong dose of pain reliever, and she should be sleeping peacefully very soon. I will be back to see her the day after tomorrow if that's all right with you."

"Thank you, doctor," Patrick murmured, glancing at him thankfully. "I guess I will see you soon." He shook his hand again, appreciatively, and he let Christian walk him to the door.

When he heard the front door close behind the doctor, he walked into the bedchamber followed by his friends.

.   .   .

The tapping of light footsteps and distant murmurs grabbed Katherine's attention. Her captivity's unwelcome memory made the blood run cold in her veins and sent shockwaves right through her brain. Two angry sets of eyes overcrowded her thoughts, and a chill crept down her spine. She suddenly recalled her escape attempt and the horrible beating she received by her captors, but she was still in a drab haze that obscured their faces' memory. Soon the shot that the doctor administered started to work. A robust calm surged through her brain and spread across her body like fire, and darkness consumed her.

Patrick moved close to the bed and gazed down at her. The upper part of her face was black and blue. Her swollen eyes were shut, and sutures covered a three-inch laceration on her left cheek. Immediately, blinding emotion of deep love and passion surged through his veins. He reached down and touched her face lightly by running his finger down her cheek, across her bottom-swollen lip, and back up again. He then bent down and pressed a soft kiss on her lips. He stepped back and pursed his lips at the agonizing thoughts; his chest pain was intense. He grimaced again, his fists clenched by his sides. He drew in a deep breath. "Oh my God," he whispered, and his face didn't hide his deep concern.

Patrick's gaze shifted to his friends. They had no idea how long they stood quietly, supporting their friend on the other side of the bed. "You don't have to stay any longer," he said softly. "I'm so thankful for your support tonight. I couldn't have done this without you."

"We are brothers Patrick. Your concerns are ours and

vice versa," George said. "Let us know if you need anything while Lady Weldon is staying here. We will be back to visit in a few days."

Patrick nodded and shook their hands again, enthusiastically. "Go home. I will send for her chambermaid, her mother and whatever she needs." He followed them out of the room and stood at the door unmoved, watching their backs until he couldn't see them any longer. He heard the front door shut, and shortly after that, hoofs hit the cobblestones and vanished in the early morning hours.

Patrick needed to send someone he trusted to the Weldon estate. He wrote a note to Duchess Weldon explaining in a few words what had taken place. He then called for Christian. "Please send Mathew to Wingham to deliver this note into the Duchess' hands and retrieve Katherine's maid. I am sure she will bring all the things she might need for the next few days while staying here."

He then moved a chair closer to the bed, and lifting Kat's hand, he brought it to his lips. He could feel the warmth from her soft skin, and a shiver coursed along his nerves from the sudden sensation. He kept his lips pressed on her hand and closed his eyes, and he groaned inwardly. He felt tired, angry, and worried. He was jolted awake by a low voice. His eyes sprang wide open, and, pushing back, he swung to face the person standing behind him. He was utterly disoriented.

"Patrick, my boy, you are exhausted!" Christian's soft

gaze met his. His gaze dropped to Kat. She was still sleeping. Patrick blinked and coughed to clear his throat. He coughed again. "Did I fall asleep?" he asked, his voice throaty.

"Yes," he replied, his expression composed.

"How long?" It was all he said. His body felt numb. He stood and stretched his limbs, trying to start the blood flowing through his veins again.

"A couple of hours. Why don't you go to bed for a while? I know you'll feel better after a warm bath and some fresh clothes."

He nodded in agreement. It was already morning, and the early light was slipping through the window. His eyes shifted to the bed once again, and he noticed Kat moving a little.

"Patrick," she murmured drowsily.

"Good morning, Kat, I'm here. I'm right here," he murmured, leaning over her bed and pressing his lips on her forehead. "How are you feeling this morning?"

"I hurt, and I still can't open my eyes," she whimpered.

"Soon, Kat, soon," he assured her and pressed a feather kiss on her lips.

"Patrick!" she whispered in apparent surprise. "How did I get here? How did you find me?"

He touched her lips softly with his finger, to keep her from talking. "Don't worry about all that. You are safe here with me, and I will not let anything happen to you."

"What in the world happened?" she pressed on.

"I will explain when you feel better."

"I'm fine." Pushing her emotions to the side, she managed a smile to reassure him.

He twined his fingers around hers as if to offer her some comfort should she need it. "You were abducted for ransom."

"Abducted?" Evident shock coated her voice. She remained quiet for a very long moment. Suddenly, all the ugly memories from that day flooded her brain. Tears rolled down the side of her face. "I can't open my eyes," she whimpered. "What is wrong with me?"

"Your face is a bit swollen, my love, but it is temporary. You took a hit on your face, and your eyes are swollen shut. You are still as beautiful as ever," he said joyfully. She smiled softly but didn't make another remark about her injuries.

"Patrick, please go get some rest. You have been up for hours," Christian said. "I will stay with Lady Katherine until you come back."

"Patrick, have you stayed by my side all this time?" she asked.

"Yes, he did," Christian interjected. " He appears exhausted. You need to make him go to his chambers to bathe, get a couple of hours of sleep, and put some fresh clothes on."

"Yes, Patrick, please do that for me."

"But I want to stay with you," he replied.

"Please go. Christian is here now."

"Yes, go, Patrick," Christian insisted. "Lady Katherine's chambermaid should be here soon."

"You sent for Cynthia?" Katherine's voice sounded relieved.

"Yes, I did, and I notified your mother that you are recovering and that you will be staying with me for a few days until you are well enough to travel."

"Thank you; I am happy that you did that. Now please go."

Patrick sighed. "All right, then. I'll go, and I'll come right back. Don't go anywhere until I return," he chuckled against her ear. His lips moved across her cheek over her jawline and up again, pressing a soft kiss on her forehead. "I love you, Kat," he murmured.

"Please wake me up in a couple of hours," he said to Christian as he left the room. In his bedchamber, he took a warm bath and lay in bed. He mulled over all that had taken place the day before and through the night. His eyes lingered on the ceiling for a long time; finally, with a weary sigh, he closed his heavy lids and slung his arm across his tired eyes. He was exhausted. There would be time to ponder the matter later, but he needed sleep, for it had been a long night. His body relaxed, and before he knew it, he was fast asleep.

His eyes snapped open, an uncanny feeling washed over him, bringing him to his senses. Slanting his unfocused eyes toward the clock, he blinked. He did a double-take and swallowed a curse. "Christ!" he screamed. "I'm bloody late!" He had slept through the morning. He jumped out of bed and grabbed clean clothes; he moved around the room like a tornado. Soon he was walking into Katherine's bedchamber. He approached her bed and, leaning down, he placed a loving kiss on her forehead. His hand clasped hers and squeezed it gently. "Hi, how are you feeling?"

"Better now that you're here," she murmured, and her lips curved slightly up. It was not long before Cynthia, her chambermaid, and the Duchess arrived. They were anxious to see her.

A soft hand landed on her forehead and a warm voice whispered in her ear. "Katherine darling, I'm right here, Cynthia is here, too."

"Mother!" She mumbled through her swollen lips. Tears flowed freely down her face while squeezing the hand that was clutching hers."

Christian had two additional chambers prepared for the two guests. It was a couple of days later when Katherine finally was able to open her eyes. She was much better, and everyone was thrilled to have her back to normal. The swelling was down, and the bruises had turned purple and yellow, slowly disappearing but for a small scar on her left cheek. She spent a lot of time walking through the beautiful gardens either with her mother or with Patrick. She had been at Oxford Street for more than a week. Patrick's friends had come and visited several times, and they were happy to see Katherine looking better each time. She was feeling quite well and heeling splendidly. She was ready to go back home and begin her new life.

. . .

On Monday morning, she planned to leave for Scunthbury with Cynthia and her mother. The issue with Jack Thorsten had been resolved, so there would be no more incidents. She opened her eyes and winced at the unexpected exposure to daylight. A ray of sunshine brushed across her face while still lost in a slumber haze. She threw her arm over her eyes to block the light. Why is it so bright in here? Her gaze drifted toward the window. The curtains had been pulled wide open. She blinked against the brightness of the day. What in the world?" Her glance drifted to the other side of the room. Cynthia was bending over Katherine's travel trunk, packing her gowns, and other personal effects of departing after breakfast. "Good morning, Cynthia."

"Good morning, my Lady, I didn't mean to wake you up, but your mother asked me to get you ready, and we can leave after breakfast."

"That's fine. I should get up and get ready."

"I have prepared your bath, my Lady."

"Oh, thank you, Cynthia. That's wonderful." She kicked the bed covers away and sat straight up. The sudden move sent a sharp pain ripping through her muscles like a cyclone, and the air whooshed out of her lungs, leaving her breathless. Her face paled, and she cringed at the pain. Quickly, she leaned back on the bed.

Cynthia watched the change on her face and ran to her side. "Are you all right, my Lady?"

"Yes, yes, I'm fine. I think I moved the wrong way. I'll be fine." She lay there for a moment until the pain subsided, and then she scrambled off the bed a bit slower. She took a bath, and with Cynthia's help, she dressed. "Is Lord Patrick up?"

"Yes, my Lady, he is in his study. He was waiting for you to wake up."

"Thank you," she said. "Tell my mother that we will meet her in the breakfast room."

She left the room, heading toward Patrick's study. She pushed the door open and peered into the room. He was sitting facing the large window away from her. He was leaning back, his feet crossed ankle-to-ankle, on the top of a chair. She could lose herself at this magnificent Adonis that was hers, she thought, and only hers. A shiver of lust coursed along her spine, and the intensity made her lips tremble. She leaned against the doorframe, crossed her arms in front of her, and waited silently. She drank him in, reining in her wits that seemed to be scattered all over that room. She cleared her throat. "Ready for breakfast?" she asked quietly. Patrick swiveled the chair around to face her, and he stilled. Their gaze locked, midnight blue to sapphire blue, a most intoxicating mixture of colors. His jaw dropped at the sight of her. Her gown was shiny silk of baby blue, cut very low, and the cap sleeves clung to her ivory perfect shoulders as though she had fallen from the clouds enveloped in a piece of the blue sky. Her neck was long. Her collarbone had that classic look of fresh snow. A lovely long golden chain held a spectacular blue stone that rested happily on her stunning cleavage. Her golden hair piled up high, brought out the extraordinary beauty of her face. His mouth went dry, and he gasped inwardly.

He pushed the chair away and rose to his feet, the corners of his lips quirked up in a sweet smile. His voice was breathy and shaky. "Good morning, how did you sleep?"

"Fine," she said, her voice soft. "Did you already have breakfast?"

"No, I have been waiting for you."

She advanced toward him, lips pursed, and Patrick's lungs locked. It was hard enough for him to stay away, but Katherine was relentless. She didn't understand what she was doing to him. She stopped in front of him, and he inhaled sharply. Seconds elapsed. She cleared her throat and smiled sweetly. "Mother is downstairs waiting for us. We are leaving for Scunthbury shortly after we finish breakfast."

He winced at her words. He didn't want her to go away, ever. "You know that you will be coming back in a couple of weeks. The season starts, and I want you to be with me. I want to show you off. You have been away for a very long time. Your friends will be happy to see you again."

She seemed to mull over his reply, and after a few moments, she said, "Yes, I remember. I am looking forward to getting back to a happy life. Did you hear back from your friend on the annulment? Were the papers approved and signed?"

"Yes, your marriage has been annulled. Jonathan will send me the papers. They will be here when you come back to London. Your wedding was never valid and technically never existed." Patrick stepped even closer. He towered over her, and she drew a deep breath. He lowered his gaze, and their eyes locked. She stood on her tippy toes and brushed her lips against his suggestively. He stroked the tip of one finger down the long column of her neck, leaving a fire trail in its wake. Slowly his lips curved, and, swooping down, he captured her lips in a soft, tender kiss. She immediately moved closer, breast to chest, to take advantage of the situation, and he chuckled into the kiss. His hands came up, and he slowly eased her away from his body.

Katherine drew a deep breath, stepped back, and blinked. She met his eyes once again and held his gaze with a puzzled expression on her face. "What was that for?" she asked, entirely frustrated.

"That was because I love you, and your mother is waiting."

" Not fair..." her voice trailed and, turning, she stomped toward the door. Patrick couldn't help it. He laughed out loud. He led her down the stairs, into the breakfast room where her mother waited. Patrick greeted the Duchess and helped Katherine to the sideboard containing a fabulously well-prepared breakfast with eggs, bacon, glazed ham, a variety of cheeses, and fruits. Peached, apples, and oranges were on display. During the meal, the conversation took a delightful tone. They discussed nothing of consequence as they exchanged tidbits of the past few days. Patrick reached for the peaches and presented a slice to Katherine. She leaned forward and sank her teeth into the fruit, her lips gently grazing his fingers' tip as she did so. Patrick held his breath, and finally, the air whooshed out of his chest in a shaky gasp. "Oh, God," he thought to himself. He should not have done that. Overwhelmed by desire, he looked away and tried to rein in his wild thoughts. The conversation was happy, and nobody discussed the abduction. He found sitting and conversing with the Duchess extremely pleasant. After breakfast, they were packed and ready for their journey back to the country. On the way to the courtyard, the Duchess spoke with enthusiasm about her daughter's recovery and showed extreme appreciation for Patrick's assistance in getting Katherine back alive.

CHAPTER NINETEEN

he Weldon family left for their country home as soon as they finished with breakfast. They could not have chosen a more beautiful day to make the trip back home. The air was warm and redolent with the fragrance of wildflowers. Patrick watched his guests leave with sadness in his heart. He did not want Katherine to be away from him, but he knew it would be only for a short time. Back in his study, he picked up the decanter from the side table and poured himself a generous portion of the potent liquid. He slumped down in his leather chair and stretched out his booted feet. He stared at his drink while drumming his fingers along the armrest. The silence was deafening; he sighed profoundly, feeling the house's emptiness without Katherine. His face took on an even more distant look if that was possible. She was his dream come true.

. . .

The next two weeks went by quickly. They were filled with meetings at the new location. The club was near completion, and the Viper group gathered to witness the final touches, which left them enthralled. They never really expected such a remarkable outcome; elegant furnishings adorned each room with impeccable taste. Once through the door, guests entered a beautiful foyer with a sweeping spiral staircase leading upstairs to the chambers. The walls were more impressive, painted with vibrant murals that appeared to come alive walking through the rooms. Magnificent and expensive portraits of exotic places adorned the chamber walls. The gardens were superb. Large trees provided a canopy that covered a vast portion of the garden's left side. More manicured bushes and flowerbeds graced the lawn that was tended carefully by the capable new hired hands. The smell of roses and jasmine captured one's senses. They met with the decorator and showed their appreciation for the incredible job. The bonus was substantial. Patrick was the last man the decorator shook hands with on his way out.

The group decided to have a drink and celebrate the occasion. They filled their glasses with the most wonderful French brandy and took a seat around the conference room's massive table. The conversation became livelier following the consumption of the third glass. The final question left them in shock. Silence fell as they tried to digest every word spoken. "Well?" Patrick asked again. "Who is going to get married after me?"

They all looked at each other with wonderment in their eyes. "You have all agreed to find your wives as well. We are not getting any younger. We have traveled and spend a substantial time in France serving his majesty behind enemy lines. By the time we returned to England, we had found out that we inherited properties and titles and considerable wealth. Now we all need to have the perfect woman who will complete our lives and complement our elite status. I have found mine in Katherine."

They shook their heads in agreement and did try to imagine the exceptional picture Patrick painted. "How do you suggest that we do that?" Edward asked.

"You will accompany Katherine and me to the ballrooms, and hopefully, the right woman will be attending at the same time. If not, then there will be the next season to make your choices." Patrick's words resonated through the group, and finally, laughter filled the room. They sat back and had a couple more drinks before leaving the club, agreeing to meet at the first and very prominent ball given by Duke and Duchess Kearsley.

Patrick returned home and found Katherine's annulment papers. He thumbed through the pages and stopped on the third page. His eyes went wide "That son of a bitch!" he called out. Victor Justin, the so called pastor who had blessed the union between Katherine and Quinton, was Bennett's solicitor. He was not a priest and never ordained by the church. Patrick immediately notified the press. It was something he wanted to see in the next morning's news. He made sure that her trusted old friends spread the rumors throughout the ton about the latest updates on the Bennett saga. He worked tirelessly to restore Katherine's entrance to London's elite society, completely absolved from her past. Marisa Thornwell, Kat's best friend, informed Patrick that invitations started arriving at Katherine's country home the day after the annulment and requested her attendance at every ball and every soiree arranged for the season. She was gorgeous, smart, and elegant. The fact remained that every gentleman knowing her availability would seek her out. She was a force to be reckoned with, not to be ignored. The thought made him cringe. He would have to make clear to all that he had offered for her hand. He had to wait a fortnight before Katherine and her family returned to their London home. The thought of Kat being so near to his house every day made him feel restless and strangely anxious. He shrugged off his conscience and decided to rein in his thoughts and move forward.

Patrick woke up suddenly; his instincts informed him that today was one of the most important days. A moment passed before he raised his head and opened his eyes. The room was still dark; he drew in a breath and dropped his head back into the soft pillows. Today Kat and her family were returning to their London home for the season. He hesitated for a few seconds, and finally, he raised himself on his elbow and shook his head to wake up. He threw the covers off to the side, swung his legs off the edge of the bed, and put his bare feet on the thick rug. He sat there for a few moments and finally decided that it was time to get up. He strolled to the window and pulled the curtains wide open. He squinted against the bright sunlight and felt the warmth of the golden rays against his bare chest. The season's balls were set to begin the very next weekend. He would be attending them with Kat by his side. He had the Duchess's approval for their marriage, and Katherine had accepted his proposal. Tomorrow he would visit her, and following the formal courting, he would take her on a ride at Hyde Park. A knock at the door interrupted his thoughts. "Come in."

Christian opened the door and walked in. "Good morning!" he said in a cheerful voice. "Good morning, Christian."

"Can I prepare your bath, my lord?"

"Yes, thank you, you came just in time. A bath is what I need right now to wake me up," his voice coated with enjoyment. "And please forget the titles in private; you have been like a father to me."

Christian smiled in appreciation and moved quickly with his son Mathew's help to fill the tub with hot water. Once they left, Patrick walked into the washroom. The polished marble tub with the sloping sides was full of hot steamy water. He sighed as he sank in the tub and closed his eyes for a long moment. He then reached for the sponge and soap and set to lathering it up. When finished, he emerged from the water feeling rested and toweled himself off. He shaved, pulled his tight breeches on, and shrugged into his greatcoat. Today should be an easy day. Hands in his greatcoat pockets, he strolled to the window again and stared down at the beautiful lawns surrounding his Oxford estate. He decided this morning to walk and explore the gardens; several men were pruning the bushes and cleaning the flowerbeds. He smiled with pleasure. He turned and took a last look around; he headed downstairs toward the breakfast room. He filled his plate at the sideboard and read the morning paper. He spent the rest of the day walking around the gardens, going over the books he received from his solicitor about his properties. After dinner, he picked up one of his favorite books and a glass of bourbon and sat quietly in his study, enjoying the peace he hadn't felt in a very long time.

The next morning, he picked up the reins and began moving the curricle through the streets toward Bond Street. A massive bouquet rested on the box seat next to him. It would be the first real engagement date with his future wife. He showed up at the Weldon home with his fashionable curricle drawn by a pair of magnificent bays. With the bouquet in his hand, he mounted the front steps and rapped the knocker three times. While waiting, he wandered around the patio, looking at the beautiful gardens. "Are those for me?" Her soft voice made him spin around and stop him dead in his tracks.

Katherine stood right in front of him, and even though it had only been a few days, he had forgotten how beautiful she was. Slowly, he approached her, his eyes drinking in every inch of her. She was stunning in her rose silk gown that adorned the most elegant curves God had ever made to tempt a man. In a few slow strides, he towered over her. She took the flowers and smiled wide as she became very aware of his masculinity. "They are beautiful; thank you," she murmured. He leaned forward; his body close to hers, he braced his hands on either side of her face; the warmth of his breath tickled her lips before he bent down and took her mouth in a hot, scorching kiss. She moaned, and her knees buckled. If not for his strong arms, she would have been on the ground. She stared at him, unable to utter a single word. She was simply mesmerized. His lips curved, his blue eyes held hers, and he pulled away. She called for the butler and asked him to place the flowers in a vase. He slid his fingers around her wrist, and everything within her stilled at his touch. He laid her hand on his sleeve and drew her to him. He stepped closer to stand beside her, and led her down the stairs toward his curricle. Dragging in a tight breath, she fell into step beside him. The arm beneath her fingers felt warm.

He helped her to the box seat and mounted the driving seat next to her. Soon they were off. When they reached the park gates, he turned into the carriage drive and led the curricle down the path at a steady pace under the beautiful trees. A light breeze stroked their faces, and she smiled with pleasure. Patrick watched Katherine out of the corner of his eyes. The park was busy as nursemaids tended their charges, young men exchanged the latest news, and young ladies promenaded along the walks with their suitors.

An inquisitive pause ensued as the curricle rolled along the path. The sight of Katherine's beauty caused an immediate impact. Heads turned and eyes followed them as they stepped down from the curricle to stroll about the well-tended lawns. Her lovely rose silk gown clung suggestively to her fabulous figure with the neckline scooped low over her breasts, creating a magnificent sight. Patrick's hands burned with the desire to caress those alluring curves. Their eyes met and held as the awareness that had started to sparkle between them threatened to burst into an inferno of desire. Moments ticked too slowly then too quickly before turning and looking away, her face blushing a rosy pink. A burning sensation settled in his loins. Her scent drifted through his veins and settled into his bone marrow. He decided to ignore his arousal driving his senses to a maddening crescendo, and instead, concentrated on a casual chat while strolling down the path. He lifted his arm and rubbed the muscles on the back of his neck with his hand. They fell into a conversation that drifted to various subjects. Patrick enjoyed their discussion thoroughly. She kept talking, and he kept smiling and nodding, wanting her to go on and on. "I'm so happy that you are back," she said suddenly.

He was quiet for a few minutes, and then he stopped. He turned, put his finger under her chin, and lifted her head to face him. His touch was warm and inviting. He stared into her bright blue eyes, blue on blue, and his lips curved up into a beautiful smile that filled her body with a strange desire. "I'm happy to be home, too. The years I spent away, I never stopped thinking, dreaming, and hoping that one day you would be mine, my wife, the woman that I want standing next to me until I take my last breath."

"I'm here now, Patrick. I have accepted to be your wife, and I will be with you until I take my last breath." His lips curved up, complete satisfaction painted his face. He had to fight the strong desire to pull her into his arms and kiss her. The parks were far too public for such a display of affection.

He stepped back, and they started down the path once again. When they returned, he pressed a soft kiss on her lips and left her with a heavy heart back at the house. The more time he spent with her, the more he hated going home alone. She was the most amazing woman he had ever met. He could still taste her sensual lips. Just the thought of holding her in his arms filled him with a feeling of complete exhilaration.

After Katherine had taken a bath and gotten ready for bed, she realized that she could not wipe the blissful smile from her face. Heat coursed through her veins as she remembered his lips moving against hers with hunger and passion.

In the next weeks, they took more drives to the park and spent time together, getting to know each other better with each day that passed. When they day of the first ball arrived, Katherine was filled with excitement mixed with anxiousness for being seen in a ballroom for the first time in five years. Her marriage had been a sham. She was not sure about the people's reaction when she showed up with another man. But this was a step she had to take to enter this new phase in her life. On the day of the ball, she took a long time to get ready. She wanted to make sure that she looked beautiful for Patrick and her friends. She knew that this would be a validation of the rest of her life.

He arrived at Katherine's home in the family coach a half an hour early, unable to wait any longer. The Duchess invited him to the drawing room while Katherine finished getting ready. They carried on a lovely conversation. She adored him, and she could not hold back her pleasure at Patrick becoming her son-in-law. Suddenly, Katherine entered the room, and Patrick's breath left him in a single painful gust, and he stared, struggling for equilibrium. She was stunning. He rose to his feet and closed his eyes, fighting to summon his wits. She was gowned in a creation of substantial grace. Fabulous light blue silk had been splendidly cut to compliment all the beautiful curves of her sizzling body. The French silk's movement, the drape of the low neckline, and the beautiful woman in front of him made his wits scatter. The pearls at her throat were simply stunning. It seemed that each time he saw her, she was more beautiful than the last time. For a full minute, not a muscle moved in his gorgeous face. Katherine walked up to her mother and pressed a soft kiss to her forehead.

"Hello, Mother."

"Hello dear, you look beautiful. Are you ready to go?" Katherine nodded with a smile. "Make sure to say hello to Laura from me. We will meet for tea very soon." Laura Kearsley was one of the Duchess's best friends.

"Yes, Mother, I will let her know." She then turned to face Patrick, who was standing now very close to her. His lips curved upward in evident appreciation. His hand closed about hers and set it on his sleeve. "Are you ready, my dear?"

She kept her eyes on his. "Yes," she simply replied.

Once settled in the carriage, he pulled her closer to press a soft kiss on her lips. She gazed up at him with a skeptical look. "What is it, Kat?"

"Am I a widow?"

His brows rose. "What?"

"Am I considered a widow?" There seemed to be a wealth of meaning in this short sentence.

"No, dear. Your marriage was not real. It was a forced marriage, never consummated. Furthermore, the church did not ordain the priest who blessed the so-called union; he worked for Bennett. So, the union was a hoax all the way around."

"I wonder if the ton knows that." She looked flustered.

His lips curved. "Yes, they do. I made sure that the Post printed all the details as soon as Paul informed me. Please do not worry about this. It was in the Post several days in a row." He lifted her hand and raised it to his lips. The coach stopped in front of the Kearsley estate. She smiled, not just with her lips, but also with those beautiful blue eyes. She was now at ease.

Drawing a deep breath, holding her head high, Katherine entered the ballroom on Patrick's arm, and they stood on the top of the large staircase that led down to the dance floor. The bright light from the glittering chandeliers beamed over the extravagant silk gowns creating a moving sea of vivacious shades as the ladies moved gracefully around the dance floor. Draped in gold and diamond glitter, they created a stunning illumination. Laughter and conversation covered the ballroom. A mixture of fragrances filled the air. The music ended, and the crowd moved away from the dance floor. The orchestra was on a short break, waiting to deliver once again the beautiful sounds of famous waltzes.

The announcement of their arrival made heads turn. Patrick felt Katherine's slight wobble and placed a steady arm on the low of her back. She was suddenly aware of his strength, sheer masculine power close by her side, and felt reassured. The arm beneath her fingers felt like steel, but warm and alive. Katherine was breathtaking in her gorgeous blue silk gown. He was one of the most sought-after men of the ton. He towered over Katherine and held his head up. His square chin stamped him as an aristocrat who possessed a beautifully chiseled face of an Adonis stylishly attired in a black evening coat molded to his body. A pristine white shirt with a perfectly tied cravat, black buckskin trousers that showed not a crease, and shining top boots completed the picture of an exquisite man. Everything seemed to be in perfect proportion to his height, from his shoulders' extensiveness to his long legs' length. Even if the first ball was not in their honor, their presence announced Katherine's return to the ton and their wedding to take place soon. Patrick's eyes rested on Katherine, and everyone could tell that she was the one he had chosen.

Duchess Kearsley rose to her feet and practically ran over to welcome them both with open arms. She had a special place in her heart for Katherine. She had watched her grow from a sweet little girl to this fantastic, kind, and talented woman. She spoke four languages and played the piano beautifully. She had cried along with Katherine's mother over her union with Quinton. She had been utterly puzzled at the events that led to this horrid marriage. But at the time, no person had an explanation other than the rumors. So now with all the secrecy with the Bennett saga exposed, she was thrilled to death to have Katherine back. "We missed you, my dear," she said and held her in a tight hug for a long moment. "Thank you for coming. Henry can't wait to see you." She spoke of her husband, Duke Kearsley. "How is your mother? I have not seen her for a fortnight."

"She is fine; thank you. She told me to say hello, and that you should have tea together very soon."

The Duchess smiled warmly. "Yes, we should do that." She then turned to Patrick. "You, my boy, you have made us all proud to be British. We are all aware of his majesty's great achievements and triumphs and the losses we suffered at the hands of the French. We are extremely thankful for your sacrifices and saddened over William's death. I am so happy to see you back in England, safe and sound." Patrick smiled thankfully and returned her hug.

"I do want to ask of you a favor," she said in a low voice, glancing between them.

"Anything," Patrick replied.

"This is the first dance for this season, and it will be my honor if you let me announce your engagement during dinner." They both looked surprised.

Patrick glanced down at Katherine, requesting her

approval. She remained silent for a short moment and then nodded in agreement. "Fabulous!" exclaimed the Duchess who clapped her hands with pleasure. She then took Katherine's hand, and with Patrick in tow, she presented them to every person that they had not met before.

In the past, his resistance to attending balls came from the egotistical rogues only enthralled in their own welfares, omitting everyone else around them. He was pleasantly surprised to discover that not all the men in attendance tonight were what he assumed them to be. A large group of men came from various major regiments and different branches of services, and they were well-bred and quite impressive. They, too, had just returned home from active duty. He carried on small conversations about England's loss on foreign soils with a glass in hand, which brought empathizing smiles on their faces. It all sounded too familiar, and he needed to move away and look for his friends who had not shown up as of yet. Not that he blamed them for avoiding this type of gathering, but they did say they were going to make an effort. Draining his glass, he set it on the nearest sideboard and moved toward the center of the room looking for Katherine, who had found her old friends and seemed absorbed in the chitchat flowing between them. Patrick smiled. As he moved from group to group, he surveyed the room for familiar faces. Andrew Fletcher was the last man he expected to see tonight. But there he was with his beautiful girlfriend, Alice, by his side. He reached for her elbow, and he steered her toward Patrick. They were happy to see each other. They exchanged a warm handshake, and Andrew introduced him to her. Patrick bowed and pressed a soft kiss on the back of her proffered hand.

"Where is Katherine?" she asked, looking around.

Curiosity propelled Patrick. "You know Katherine?"

"Yes, of course," she replied. "We became close friends in the last two years of secondary school. We spent a lot of time together until Quinton took her away from everyone she knew." Disdain coated her voice.

"I apologize for not knowing about your friendship, but things have been quite hectic since I returned home. I am sure that you have seen most of the details in the daily post." He chuckled softly.

With a polite nod, Alice smiled. She was charming.

Patrick raised his hand and pointed in Katherine's direction. The women were in a noisy tight circle, totally unaware of anyone or anything around them. Patrick started to say something, but suddenly he noticed that Alice had left Andrew's side, and she was now right in the middle of that circle, welcomed by the other women.

Shaking their heads, the two men moved away from the dance floor. A servant passed with a Champaign tray. Taking a glass each, they leaned against the wall. "Do you think that your mates will show up?" Andrew asked.

"Not sure, they said they would, but who knows. The fact is they face the need to marry and even the greater need to find the perfect wife. Unfortunately, these places might give them that chance and then might not." Andrew shifted his gaze from the center of the room to Patrick's face.

"Are they looking for wives?"

Patrick chuckled. "They do not even want to think about marriage. Let me ask you, would you have attended this dance if not for Alice?"

Andrew shook his head and laughed. "No, I would not. I hate this type of gathering. I always have." Both men fell into a very comfortable conversation. Soon they were head down, back in the memory lane of war. They never saw Michael, George, and Edward until they were standing right next to them. They seemed extremely pleased to see Andrew.

"Have you been here long?" Michael asked.

"About an hour or so," Andrew replied. Big smiles, warm handshakes, and lively conversation followed. The men drew a lot of the female attention in the room, but they did not seem interested in engaging.

Their friends still surrounded Katherine and Alice. They were all happy to have Katherine back in their circles. Patrick leaned against the wall with his friends and kept her in his sight. She moved with effortless grace through the ballroom, her fabulous gold hair catching the light from the chandeliers. Her gorgeous elegant gown hugged her lush curves, and her skirt swayed over her hips as she walked. He had a hard time taking his eyes off her as she moved from one group to the next with her best friends in tow. He noticed men approach her, trying to get her attention, but she was too busy with all the chitchatt around her. The musicians returned and the sound of a waltz filled the ballroom. She turned and stared into his eyes as her beautiful lips parted in a stunning smile. He reached her with a few fast strides and swung her into his arms; then they were twirling around the dance floor. He noticed Andrew with Alice in his arms across the room. To his explicit pleasure, all the others had already chosen dance partners.

Patrick met her gaze and smiled. "I did not want to be away from you any longer. I hope that you do not mind." His gaze fell on her lips as she brushed her tongue over them and desire shot through him, sheering every muscle in his body. His thoughts scattered once again, and he tried unsuccessfully to control his faculties. They were moving on the floor gracefully, effortlessly while his arms pulled her closer to him.

"Why would I mind?" her voice broke in. She stared up as they moved around the dance floor. He remained silent. She finally chuckled at his obvious befuddlement. "Why would I mind?" she repeated.

His striking blue eyes bored into hers, and her gaze fell on his mouth's masculine curve. He suddenly found his voice and answered her question. "Taking you away from your friends and all those men trying to get your attention."

Her eyes went wide. "What men?"

He laughed out loud as he pulled her closer. "Oh, my sweet Kat," he murmured in her ear. You have been away from the ton for a very long time. I can tell."

Katherine felt his hot palm on the small of her back and found breathing difficult but was determined not to let it show. He met her gaze and smiled.

"Well, I do not know about all those men. I'm only interested in one man." Her voice dropped to a strained whisper.

Patrick shifted closer, and his lips grazed her ear. "And who is this man?"

She looked up at him, and he caught that scorching glance and held it. Her lips parted when he swung her around, and his muscular thighs crushed against her. The hard ridge between them pressed up against her. Instinctively, she arched against him, drawing a soft groan as he pushed her closer. "I love you, Kat," he murmured for her ears only. "You are mine. I can't wait to make you my wife."

She looked into his eyes, and her gown tightened over her breasts as she dragged in a deep breath. "I love you, too," she replied in a soft tone. They were silent for a long moment, lost in thought.

"Are you comfortable with the Duchess announcing our engagement even though your mother is not here?"

"Yes, it is fine. Mother would not mind at all. She's extremely stressed with the Bennett issue. I am sure she will be happy knowing that they welcomed me with opened arms."

"Fine, I just want to make sure that you have no issue with this."

CHAPTER TWENTY

*K*atherine's dance card showed only one name; however, his friends stole a couple of dances, each with Patrick's approval. At dinnertime, they enjoyed a splendid variety of foods and desserts. After dinner, the Duchess rose to her feet and held her champagne glass high. Silence fell in the room, waiting for her to speak. Her voice was filled with apparent pleasure as she made the engagement announcement. The news was greeted with many cheers and congratulations as everyone's head swiveled in unison to regard Katherine and Patrick. It seemed like a dream. Katherine never thought in a million years that her life would take a remarkable turn of that magnitude. Patrick lifted her hand to his lips and placed a soft kiss on her fingers. The Duchess next request came as a considerable surprise to Katherine. "I would love for Katherine to entertain us at the pianoforte in honor of her engagement. Will you do that for me, dear?"

Katherine's jaw dropped as she stared into Patrick's bright eyes.

"Oh, I couldn't possibly!" She was incredibly good with the pianoforte but timid, and at this moment, all she wanted to do was be alone with Patrick somewhere away from everyone and everything.

"You play very well, Katherine," the Duchess indulgently said.

She knew that she had to play in return for the Duchess' kindness. "I shall be pleased to play for you," she accepted at last. She rose to her feet and followed the crowd to the drawing-room, approached the pianoforte slowly, and sat on the cushioned stool before it. Patrick moved closer and hovered affectionately over her shoulder and offered to turn the pages. People gathered around to listen. Soon her fingers started to move across the smooth mother-of-pearl keys filling the room with Chopin's extraordinary sounds. The keys dropped beneath her fingers and bounced right back up again. She played a couple compositions, and she noticed the pleasure on the crowd's faces. When she finished, applause filled the room, and she nodded in appreciation as she stood and moved away from the piano with Patrick on her heels. "My dear!" called out the Duchess. "You were magnificent! Thank you." She approached Katherine, and they embraced.

"Thank you for the warm welcome," Katherine whispered. "You have always been like a second mother to me, and I love you."

"My dear, you have no idea how worried Henry and I have been over your unfortunate mix up with horrid

Quinton. We are happy to see you back and free of every unhappy moment you had in the past five years. It is as if not a single moment has passed since the last time we were together." She stood back, holding Katherine at arm's length. "Here you are, my dear, better and stronger than before with an amazing man by your side. I am sure your wedding will be magnificent." The Duchess glanced up at Patrick and smiled thankfully for making Katherine happy again. A friend approached and hugged Katherine warmly. Patrick noticed his friends waiting at the front door.

"We must go," Patrick said in a soft voice. "It has been a fabulous night. Thank you for making it so special for both of us." After a few more hugs and many good wishes from the crowd, they took their leave. Just before they crossed the threshold, a couple approached. They were old friends of her parents.

"When is the big day?" the woman asked.

Patrick hugged Katherine to his side and took charge of the answer. "We will let you know as soon as we have a date. We have to go as it is getting very late," he replied with his disarming charm. From his perspective, it had been a successful first outing for Katherine, and she had been a real treasure. She did look tired, and it was getting late. Outside they bid goodbye to his friends making plans to meet at the Viper club in a couple of days.

In the coach, she leaned her head against his shoulder and left her hand in his. She was happy beyond measure.

"You look tired," he said, and bending down, he pressed a soft kiss on her lips.

"I am, but I don't want to go home," she murmured. "Not just yet."

His eyes went round surprise, painted his face. "Where would you like to go?"

"I want to go with you." She moved closer to him and lifted her head; she pressed her wet lips to set him on fire. A moment passed, pregnant with expectation.

Patrick heard the answer but didn't quite know how to reply. His senses conveyed the want in her husky voice. What his mind told him, the rational part of his brain knew to be improbable. Silence fell and held. Finally, his voice came out strained. "No. I must take you home," he said gently.

Katherine nodded but barely heard a word of what he said. He took her hands and held her gaze to his. "Kat, please listen to me, I know that you may disagree with my decision, but I waited for you for more than six years. I want this marriage done the proper way. There is nothing that I want more right now than to take you to bed, but I know the motivation is guided by the alcohol we consumed tonight and not a clear mind." Frustration coated his voice. He felt like a bloody arse, but deep inside, he knew it was the right thing. They were silent for a long moment; bodies close, and his thumbs tenderly stroked her knuckles. She found a smile for him, but it faded before the moment was gone. He tilted his head to the side, and his eyebrows furrowed. "Why are you so upset?" His arms came about her and pulled her softly back into his embrace.

"Because I want you," she whimpered.

Patrick shook his head and closed his eyes tightly. "Oh

God, Kat, you have no idea what these years have been for me."

"For you?" she exclaimed. "What about me?"

"There is nothing in this world that I want more than you," he murmured. Katherine seemed to mull over his reply. "Do you know that you were the most beautiful woman at the ball?" He stroked her cheek, and she chuckled. It was a quiet ride with both of them lost in their thoughts until the coach rocked to a stop this time in front of the Weldon residence. He led her up the stairs to her front door and held her against him. It was a very difficult goodnight for both. They did not want to let go of each other, lips still locked in a hot kiss. He finally pushed her back softly. "Kat, you have to go inside. I will see you tomorrow." She let go unwillingly and started to walk to the door. "I love you, Kat." His voice was warm and sensual.

She looked back and smiled. "I love you, too."

For the next three months, the Viper group remained busy with endless parades of social entertainments, balls, theatre, parties, and many other social pleasures. Patrick courted Kat unchaperoned at a variety of shows because of their upcoming marriage. All noted his devotion was only for her and her alone. Patrick's friends joined them in many of those balls, hoping to find the girl of their dreams. London's most exclusive families presented their unmarried daughters to the ton to meet eligible partners and arrange successful marriages. The young ladies seemed to appreciate their elegance, title, and exquisite looks, but the men gave them barely adequate time. They did not seem to find what they were looking for, so they spent a lot of their time socializing, playing cards and dice and attending horse racing. Paul also called on the Viper group to assist with a few severe murder cases. Their ability to resolve those types of issues was very well known and very vital in Whitehall.

Toward the end of the season, they tired of the socials. They knew that there was always next year.

With two weeks left until the wedding day, Katherine's excitement rose. Every time she looked at Patrick, she thought she was living a dream. She couldn't believe that life had changed for her in such a drastic way. There was a gleam of excitement in Patrick's blue eyes that filled her heart with warmth and anticipation. She was now even closer to taking this exciting step toward the dream she held ever since she was a little girl.

The Viper group prepared to celebrate Patrick's bachelor party memorably. They had not partied hard for anyone before Patrick. It was going to be a party of brotherhood.

The invitations for the wedding went out, and everyone on the list, from family members to business associates and friends, had accepted. They were looking at a huge crowd, and Katherine was thrilled. If possible, she would choose to share this extraordinary moment with every person on earth. Patrick didn't want Katherine to worry about the wedding expenses, and he made sure that it would be remarkable.

. . .

ON THE DAY OF her wedding, Katherine woke up late. The morning sunlight slipping through the sliver between the curtain and the window edge shot bright light on her face. Her eyes fluttered and opened slightly. It was not odd that she overslept on a day like this, because she had celebrated with her friends until the morning hours. Her head pounded, and the effects of that tugged at her eyelids. She pulled the covers over her head. *One more minute*, she thought.

She finally flung the covers away and slowly sat up cross-legged in the middle of her huge bed. With a soft sigh, she dropped her chin onto her hands and closed her eyes. Her foggy mind instantly came alive. She giggled blissfully. *I'm getting married today.* Just the thought of Patrick, and the very concept of marriage, made her body tense. She felt giddy, reeling from the warm sensation that erupted inside her. The sheer notion that tonight she would be sharing a bed with her husband sent delicious shivers down her spine. The word husband was a seductive murmur that rippled across her body and settled in her marrow's depths.

Less than twenty minutes later, she'd bathed, dressed, and made her way downstairs to look for her mother. She entered the kitchen and found her and her brothers at the breakfast table.

"Something smells good," she called joyfully.

"There you are," her mother said, turning to face her. "Did you sleep well, darling?"

"Yes, thank you, Mother," she replied with a soft yawn. Closing the distance between them, she fell into her mother's open arms. Her brothers hugged her tightly and pressed a kiss to her cheeks.

"Today's the big day!" her brother Nicholas chuckled. "You'll be the prettiest bride ever," The Duchess choked tears as she held her tightly.

"I love you, Mother," Katherine whispered.

Her mother cleared her throat, drew a tight breath, unable to disguise her emotions. "Would you like something to eat?"

"Yes, please, I'm famished."

"How about some eggs and bacon?"

"Mmmm, that sounds wonderful," Katherine said. She took a seat between her brothers. "How I wish that Father and William were here," she said, gazing across the room. "I know William would have been Patrick's best man, and Father would have walked me down the aisle." A shadow covered her beautiful face, and her eyes took a distant look. She knew that her father and brother would have loved to see her marry Patrick. She could hear herself saying, "I am a bit nervous, Father" and he would have replied in his soothing voice. "There is nothing to be nervous about, pumpkin." It was the nickname her father had given her as a little girl. She looked down at her plate, ready to enjoy a mound of fluffy eggs and bacon. She sighed inwardly and picked up her fork. Five more hours before she set her eyes on the man who'd turned her life into a beautiful, magical dream.

It was now 4:00, and the house was a bustle of excitement, and her mother was blissful. The wedding was scheduled for 6:00, and Katherine had arranged to meet her best friend Marisa and her bridesmaids Victoria, Alice, Isabella, and Evelyn at the church at 4:30 with a room reserved for them to get ready. The men would be there a little earlier in a different part of the church so they wouldn't run into each other before the ceremony.

Patrick entered first. He heard swishing and soft whispering, but he didn't look at the guests. He took his place on the right-hand side to the altar's left. Patrick's gaze swept the front pew, and he found his mother and two brothers who chose to let the Viper brothers take a more significant part in Patrick's big day. He wondered why his father was not with them. On the other side of the aisle, he saw Katherine's mother and her two brothers. Two seats held next to her, one for her late husband and the other for William. His heart was breaking that his best friend was not there.

The bridal music sounded, and every eye in the church turned to look down the aisle. Happy whispers broke the silence, and Patrick's mouth dropped. He did not know that his father had requested to walk Katherine down the aisle in the absence of her father and very best friend Henry Edward Wingham Duke of Scunthbury. Tears of joy filled his eyes.

Katherine garbed in a beautiful silk yellow dress, trimmed with small diamonds around the edges. The satin had been imported from the Far East and manufactured in

Paris with a magnificent spray of brilliant stones all over the skirt. The design had been drawn expressly for her wedding and surpassed her expectations. The headdress was a gorgeous tiara trimmed with diamonds.

Marisa, Katherine's best friend and maid of honor, soon walked with Edward, Patrick's best man and took their place Marisa on the altar's right side next to Katherine. Edward on the altar's left side next to Patrick. George followed with Victoria by his side; Andrew came next with Alice, and Michael with Isabella. The men took their place on the left and the girls on the right. The bridesmaids wore blue muslin dresses and brilliant diamonds throughout the material, giving it a Regency era look. The color of their dresses had been Katherine's choice to reflect the brilliance of Patrick's eyes. Bouquets of freshly cut flowers adorned the aisles, filling the air with a breathtaking aroma. Katherine's eyes fell on the man who'd made her dreams come true. A knot tightened in the pit of her stomach. He was stunningly beautiful. He looked so dignified, tall, with broad shoulders, long muscular legs, and an aura of elegance and masculine beauty. She drank him in with her eyes. At the sight of Katherine, Patrick couldn't breathe or pull his gaze away from her. She was a vision to make any man lose control of his wits. He never saw a woman so utterly beautiful. He was aware that all eyes were on her. He drew a breath when she approached; she was stunningly beautiful. Patrick struggled to breathe as he vaguely heard the priest's voice.

"Who gives this woman away?"

"I do," Patrick's father replied and placed her hand into

Patrick's. Soft, warm fingers gripped his hand, and he looked down into her eyes. A dazzling smile painted her luscious lips, and in a daze, he smiled back.

They turned to face the pastor, and Patrick kept her hand protectively in his. Shifting his grip, he weaved their fingers.

Still, in a haze, he repeated after the pastor the essential phrases. Then Katherine took Patrick's ring from Marisa and slid it on his finger as she spoke her vows.

"I, Katherine, take you, Patrick, to share my life, to be my husband, my lover, and my friend in the presence of God, our families, and friends. I offer you my heart, soul, and solemn vow to be faithful and be yours in joy and sorrow. I promise to love you until my last breath. You are the most wonderful, generous, and unselfish man, and I'll love you for as long as I live."

Edward handed Patrick Katherine's ring, and he turned to her. She extended her hand, and he closed his fingers about hers. He slid the ring on her finger. It was a perfect fit. He looked down into her eyes, and their gazes locked. Passion scorched. He was now ready to vow his love and promise to her.

"I, Patrick, take you, Katherine, to be my wife, my best friend, and my lover. My life didn't begin until you agreed to marry me, the sun didn't shine until I looked in your eyes, and the stars didn't come out at night until your smile appeared in front of me. I can't breathe if you are not with me, and I can't comprehend a world without you. You're enchanting, funny, sensual, and affectionate, and you make the earth rotate, bring the sunshine, and feel right when you're next to me. I promise to love you, protect you, support your goals, and make you utterly happy with all the power I hold. I couldn't wait for this day, and now here we are."

The pastor smiled kindly and pronounced them husband and wife. "You may now kiss your bride."

Patrick stepped closer, slid his hand about her waist, and drew her to him. Lifting her eyes, she met his gaze. He pulled her lips to his. It should've been a gentle kiss; after all, they were standing in front of a crowded congregation, but it wasn't. It turned passionate, and the weeklong separation made it powerful.

The pastor cleared his throat, reminding them that they were still standing at the altar. Embarrassed, they pulled apart though everything inside them screamed against ending the kiss. Soft laughter and enthusiastic clapping filled the church as they turned to face the crowd. Hand-in-hand, they walked back up the aisle, smiling at their friends' and families' warm wishes.

Patrick leaned close and murmured, "You look stunning. I missed you desperately, and you're in deep trouble."

Katherine blushed at his words. "I missed you, too," she murmured. He pulled her closer to his side. They were still breathless from the kiss.

At the reception hall, they greeted their guests as they came into the room. They had some of the most delightful moments with everyone before departing for their private quarters. Once in the carriage, Patrick gave instructions to the driver. He leaned back on the leather seat, pulled

Katherine hard against him, and, parting her lips with his tongue, plundered deep and hard. Their breathing increased, and her perfume dragged at his senses. He heard her soft sigh and drew a deep breath. Her breath brushed his skin, and his desire was barely restrained.

"I can't wait to take my wife to bed and show her how much I love her," he murmured.

Her gaze fell on the beautiful firm curve of his mouth, and her breath hitched. "Oh! Is she waiting for you at your house?"

With a low growl, he leaned in and crushed his mouth on hers. "You're beautiful. I promise that I will take you to the moon and back, slowly and passionately," he breathed against her lips.

"We're going to the moon?" She feigned shock. "Don't tell me I am to get ready for the long journey." She was unable to wipe the grin off of her face.

Patrick laughed out loud and dropped a kiss on her lips. "One thing I can promise you, it'll be a very long and pleasurable journey for both of us," he murmured seductively.

"Oh, my!" she breathed as she read the raw hunger in his deep blue eyes. Lifting his finger, he traced an upward curve to her cheekbone. The soft satin skin sent a thrill from his finger's tip to his growing, and he moaned softly. His lips curved appreciatively, and a muscle flickered along his jaw.

CHAPTER TWENTY-ONE

 *T*he coach wheels rolled over the courtyard cobblestones, and soon they were heading down the street toward Oxford Street. She pulled herself as close to him as possible and let him encircle her in his warm embrace. He rested his head back against the seat and closed his eyes. Suddenly, he felt his lungs compress, and the air left his mouth through his teeth in a hissing sound. Her fingers moved slowly over his chest, down his abdomen, and stopped when she reached his waistband. *Oh My God*, he had not finished with the thought when she reached for his mouth. Patrick grew harder. He grabbed her wrist and brought it up to his lips. The kiss was long and sweet. Excitement pulled between his legs and he moaned deeply into her mouth. Suddenly he pulled back. "Stop!" he scolded her softly. "I'm not going to take you in here right now, but if you continue with this assault, I may not be able to prevent the outcome."

. . .

Once at Oxford Street, he lifted her into his arms and laughed joyously. Her heart skipped several beats, and her breath caught at the sizzling look in his eyes.

"Is this where you're going to take me on that long journey?" she giggled. Her laughter echoed around them. He scaled the steps two at a time. "I am perfectly capable of walking," she said.

"And, I prefer to carry you to our bedchamber." When he crossed the threshold, he carefully set her down and kissed her gently on the cheeks and ever so softly on the lips. He shut the door behind them and threw the lockdown, never leaving Kat's frame out of sight.

Patrick rubbed his chin thoughtfully. He stood behind her and slowly painfully unbuttoned her wedding gown. It wasn't long before he had her out of the gown. Taking his time, he took out the pins that held her blond hair up and ran his fingers through the silky locks as they fell about her shoulders. His heart beat fiercely in his chest at the sight of her naked body, and he thought he might not be breathing. He proceeded to undress, and she stood spellbound as his shirt came off, and soon he was standing in front of her naked with an eager look in his eyes, looking like Michelangelo's statue of David. He was magnificent, and she was speechless. She reached up with hungry anticipation and pulled him toward her. Waves of barren desire rippled across every muscle and every vein when their bare bodies touched. She was soft, sensual, and indulgent. He was all hard muscle, body full of alluring appeal. He panted hard, and his pulse pounded. The feel of his skin against hers shattered her senses. His hands ran over every curve of her body. She moved into him, sending ripples of heat where they touched. His arms slipped around her and enclosed her body tightly against his. She stopped breathing. Dragging in a deep breath, he pulled back and looked deep into those blue eyes filled with passionate desire. He wanted her with an intensity that startled him. He bent his head and took her mouth in a scorching kiss, slanting his head as she gave him complete access to her mouth. She tasted of vanilla and cloves. His desire grew, and her eyes closed in sheer bliss. He scooped her up and carried her to his bed. He gently laid her down and slowly slid on the soft sheets until her head touched the pillows. She heard his breath catch. A fire raged through Katherine, leaving her burned, gasping, and hungry for his body. His name was on her lips; he slid down her length, the hard muscles of his body pressing against her soft skin beneath him. His lips captured her mouth again, and his tongue set up a slow dance of thrusts. Slowly he moved, and his tongue circled the soft earlobe, and Katherine moved suggestively against him. A low growl left his lips. His arms came around, cupping her breasts in his hands, kneading, rubbing, and squeezing. His thumbs brushed across the hard nipples torturing them for a while before his palms moved sluggishly over her abdomen. Slowly they moved around her hips very close to her world's very center. She cried out his name, pleasure burning deep in her core.

"What do you want, my love?" he whispered against her ear.

"I want you," she whimpered.

"Patience, my love." His lips twisted in a mocking smile. She reached around his neck, placed her hand on the nape of his neck, and pulled herself up to meet his lips in a hungry kiss. She didn't bother to answer his question. She had waited long enough for this man, and she was not going to wait another moment. Her skin burned, and her body trembled with longing. All she could think of was how much she wanted to make love with him. She held herself tightly against his body, and her hands stroked the planes of his back. His lips moved methodically from her lips to the side of her face, across her jawline with wild hunger. He gasp loudly and stopped when he reached her breasts. Katherine moaned, pulling herself even closer. It was the most exquisite, most intoxicating feeling she had ever known. He tugged softly on the tender, sensitive buds, and she groaned. The euphoric sensation filled her eyes with tears of delight. His movements were slow and calculated, making her beg for him to take her. He had a sensational smile on his face, but she could feel his hands trembling as he tried to hold her tight against him. "Kat, my Kat." She could hear him whispering her name over and over again as he panted and gasped for air. His manhood pulsed, scorching heat against the smooth, silky skin of her abdomen. It felt hard, pressing eagerly toward the Promised Land. His extended hand moved between her thighs and slipped into the silky curls parting the swollen lips. One long finger slid slowly into her, and she moaned as she struggled to find the strength to gather her senses. He was detonating a fire in her hot furnace, and she could not stop the blazes. Heat spread through her veins, burning every pore in its way. Patrick moaned deep in his throat; he lost complete control of his faculties as he slipped his throbbing staff into her heat. At first, he pushed slowly, and his breath shuddered. With an anguished moan, he drew back and thrust deep inside her virginity's sensitive thin line. Katherine froze as a sharp pain shot across her veins. She cried out. Then, the acute pain faded just as fast as it had come, and bliss took over, setting her on fire. She took a sharp breath, and he groaned in ecstasy. His muscles were locked, and his body shuddered with wild passion. He remained still, astounded by the shocking sensation and sensitivity of the moment. She, too, was stunned and enthralled with the incredible sensation. She had never expected anything so powerful. As soon as the pain subsided, the sweetness of the moment enveloped her. Patrick watched as she shifted slowly and saw the tranquil reaction in her beautiful eyes. When he felt her relaxing again, his movements started back, soft and slow, and she anxiously joined in. Gradually, they became faster and more intoxicating. He was amazing, and she didn't want him to stop. Their lips were locked in a frantic, wild kiss, making both of them moan with exhilaration. If there were such a thing as paradise, it would have to be right where they were at this very moment. With every move, she gasped with pleasure at the extraordinary sensation. He muted her sounds by setting his lips at the hollow of her throat, and she was lost as their souls fused, and their bodies joined in a triumphant bliss. She wrapped her legs around his waist, pulling him even deeper into her as she dug her fingers into his back, and he let out a growl of fulfillment. Ripples of tension gripped him and compressed his heart until it exploded in burning lust. "Oh, Kat!" he cried. The taste of his musky scent gave her incredible joy, and she wanted him to know that. She pulled his head toward her until his lips met hers again, and she kissed him, hard and demanding, as a loud climax shattered both of them. When it was over, a tremor of elation shook her very soul. She wanted him to stay right where he was forever, in pure and utter satisfaction. There was a long, happy silence for a good while. Then, she heard his voice coming out of the silence as a soft murmur.

"I've never felt anything like this before," he said. "This is the most amazing sensation, the most incredible feeling that I have ever known. There is nothing in this world that compares to the feelings you arouse in me. I feel bewitched by you. I promise to love you forever." He rolled over onto his side and took a deep breath. She lay on her back and smiled, completely content. Time seemed to stand still, and she closed her eyes, totally relaxed, thinking of the pleasure of his touch. She was startled when he pulled her with a rapid move on top of him. He was smiling, and his eyes looked happy, thrilled. "I love you, Mrs. Wingham," he said with a broad smile on his face.

"I love you too, Mr. Wingham," she replied with a soft chuckle. She was utterly and irrevocably in love with Patrick. He made her very essence quiver, and her body burned as if she were literally on fire. Nothing she had ever experienced in her life had ever felt as good as making love to him did.

"What are you chuckling about?"

Katherine threw her head back and laughed out loud with extreme joy. "I am thinking about how completely and utterly happy I am," she said with a deep sigh of contentment and gave him a long hot kiss that sent a burning sensation throughout his body, setting every nerve on fire once again. He wrapped his arms around her and rolled over, pinning her underneath his hot muscular body. His mouth came down on hers with intoxicating desire and rocked her to her very core. Her lips parted, giving him access, and like a thirsty man in the desert, he sipped her sweetness from the oasis of her mouth. His breathing was deep and uneven, and the kiss became a searing inferno as his hands moved to her breasts. His fingertips stroked her hard nipples, and she sobbed, molding her body against his, withering away in the sweltering, intoxicating feeling. His mouth moved slowly from her lips, down the silky column of her neck. Tears welled up in her eyes, as pleasure coursed through her veins when his tongue pressed intimately against the pulse at the bottom of her throat, and time stopped. The exquisite feeling made her gasp. He moved painfully and slowly down to her breast and took one nipple into his mouth; he slowly and thoroughly paid homage to the other.

When his mouth reached her soft belly, Katherine shut her eyes, struggling for sanity, but his slow torture didn't stop there. It continued as he tasted and savored each part of her body until her focus shattered. When she opened her eyes, their faces were a paper's width apart. She gazed at the most beautiful, sexy, blue eyes, and he looked right back into her stunning sapphire eyes. It was an astonishing fusion of colors. His smile was magnificent, and his breath was sweet against her face. How could she have such exquisite, inconceivable, and blistering feelings when she got close to him? Could this go on forever?

She pushed him softly, and he fell on his back right next to her. Their gazes were still locked. She propped herself up on one elbow and placed her palm flat on his chest. She gently stroked his muscles, taking her time to discover every detail of every inch of his body as he lay back in utter bliss, moaning at the touch of her fingertips. She leaned forward, and their lips met in a greedy kiss as her hands slid below his lower abdomen and pressed gently, making him growl and writhe in her hands.

"Kat, stop," he groaned. He lay on his back, shaken by the emotions that flooded through him like a burning volcano. Heat washed over him like a tidal wave. His scent was refreshing and musky, and she was startled when he rolled around, taking her with him and pinning her underneath him again. He was hard and ready to possess what he knew was his and his alone. He wanted to give her a shuddering release over and over again. Her body arched beneath his, and he drove into her slowly, methodically, claiming her with a shuddering gasp followed by a low groan of wild passion. Her eyes welled up in utter and absolute pleasure. The release enfolded both of them in total ecstasy, hammering their senses and setting their bodies into a blistering fire.

"You excite me beyond belief." He panted as she reached up and kissed him, pouring every ounce of passion she had left into the kiss. His breath quickened, she closed her eyes again and got lost in a world filled with love and desire.

"Mmmm," she half murmured, half gasped. His arms were still holding her tight as they lay utterly spent.

Katherine fell asleep in his warm embrace, and he stayed awake watching her sleep. It is the first time he could think of his life as perfect. He always had a good experiences, but it was unfilled in many ways. But now he felt happy, content, whole. She was now his wife, to love to hold and protect. It was the last thought he had before sleep claimed him.

Sunlight spilled through the windows, bathing the room in bright colors. She was still overwhelmed and completely lost in the sweet thoughts of the previous night's activities. Her face flushed, sensing her husband's touch. A warm smile touched her lips as she watched this Adonis of a man still sleeping, the gentle rise and fall of his chest. He was the man who owned her soul, heart, and love until the end of time. Her thoughts were interrupted by his deep sigh. He turned toward her, the covers fell away, and her breath held at his gorgeous naked body. She leaned over him and pressed a passionate kiss on his lips. Her hand floated to his chest, slowly tracing downward when her hand dipped below his waist, his pulse rumbled in his ears as he strained himself to take a level breath.

He was now fully awake and extremely aroused. He rolled over and covered her body with his full length. She gasped as he possessed her body with the same hunger and eagerness as he had the night before. Their gasps turned to moans, and their orgasms seemed to go on forever as he continued to move against her. It was a long time before either one could utter a single word. One thing was real; they would never have enough of each other, a special assessment by both of them.

The hot water poured a tranquil sensation over muscles unused to the kind of activity both had indulged in the previous night and the early morning hours. Sharing the large tub, they closed their eyes and emptied their brains from other thoughts but each other. She pulled herself close and grazed his mouth with her lips and down his neck. His eyes popped open as he arched upward toward her. He could not be near her without touching her or holding her. He worshiped her, and she adored him. Folding her in his arms, he kissed her with intensity. She was now his wife to hold and protect. Without thinking, his hands touched her abdomen.

"What is it?" she asked, softly gazing into his eyes.

Water dripped slowly from her hair down to her face slipping between her parted lips. She looked startling beautiful. The corners of his mouth lifted into a needy smile. He wanted nothing more than to lick the droplets away. "I want you to have my baby," he said breathlessly, his hand still on her abdomen.

She covered his hand with hers, their eyes still locked. Katherine gasped at the desire she saw there. "I was thinking about the same thing, wondering if you would think that it is too early for that."

"No! I want kids today, right now," he replied, and they broke into a hearty laugh.

She moved suggestively against him. "Let's get started," she said encouragingly, and he was more than happy to accommodate her. They knew that they were inseparable; they knew that their future was set in stone as their bodies joined in a slow sexual thrust that took their breath away. Katherine sucked her bottom lip between her teeth in ecstasy, and he lost himself in her mouth and body. When they found their release, he gazed into her eyes. He observed a look as if she were watching a bright star in the universe that lit up her face like the sun.

They spent their honeymoon in Brighton's small village, a fabulous seaside resort in East Sussex. The small private house that Patrick arranged was on a remote part of the beach. It was beautiful with a romantic atmosphere that wrapped around the area like a cloak. Only a painter's hand could've brushed on canvas this piece of paradise with such warmth and skill. They spent their time horseback riding across the beautiful green fields and holding hands and walking for hours along the warm water. Their time together was a fairytale, right out of a storybook. They could have stayed there forever, but it was time to return to London.

They stayed busy getting to know each other for several weeks, but they kept the time relatively uneventful. Once Katherine became familiar with the household, she took over. Patrick watched her with amusement. She did remind him of his mother. He left everything in her hands, and he stayed busy with the Viper group. Andrew had requested Paul to get the best of the best and try to close some of the more critical cases that were still open in Whitehall. Paul assigned the jobs to the Viper group. The meetings at the club were that of strategic planning. This type of work was not very different from what they used to do while in France. Their expertise helped to unearth the required documentation, resolve the issues, and mark the cases closed. Andrew was extremely thankful for the help he received. He offered an ongoing position for the four, and they accepted.

Christmas was coming bringing more than the holiday joy into their home. Katherine was with a child, and they were both lost in perfect comfort and ecstasy. They decided to move to their country estate. This way, Katherine would be close to her mother and his family. They spent many hours walking in the gardens and sitting at their favorite bench by the man-made pond. She would read a book; Patrick would lay down with his head against her abdomen, enjoying his son's ir daughter's gentle kicks from inside her. He was elated. He cupped the back of her neck and lifted his head; he met her lips, putting every bit of his heart and love into the kiss. She moaned, knowing that she would taste these lips every day for the rest of her life. The thought left her bursting with extreme delight.

"Lady Katherine, push!" the midwife's voice thundered in the quiet chamber. "I can see the head, please push one more time!"

The last contraction was more rigid than the previous one. A loud groan escaped Katherine as she pushed hard, and her mother's fingers were tightened around her small hand. "I am right here, honey, you are doing fine. I love you." Patrick paled at the sounds coming from the woman he loved. He was standing outside the chamber with his family, waiting for the baby and holding his breath.

"Lady Katherine, push! You are almost there," the midwife called out one last time.

Katherine groaned deeply, and the baby slipped into the midwife's waiting hands. The loud cries of a baby filled the room. Patrick's heart fluttered, and he burst into the room, unable to wait a minute longer. Katherine cried out when she saw Patrick. "You have a boy, my lady – a beautiful, healthy boy," the midwife announced proudly.

Patrick and Katherine broke out into a bountiful mixture of laughter and tears. The midwife cut the cord and lifted the baby cradling the head with one hand. She handed him to the nursemaid to clean and turned to finish caring for Katherine.

"Let me him! Katherine called out. The nursemaid hurried and placed the swaddled baby in Katherine's open arms. She looked down at the small baby, and tears poured down her face. She held him close, and her lips pressed a soft kiss on the tiny forehead. Patrick at a loss for words, stood there numbly as he watched both with so much love that he thought his heart was going to burst.

"He is beautiful!" he murmured. The family stood around, smiling and making sweet comments about the newborn.

"He looks like you," Katherine said, looking up at her husband. The idea that he was the reason for that incredible smile in Katherine's face was invigorating. With her arms stretched toward him, she handed him the baby. He sank into the nearest chair. His hands were trembling, and tears blurred his vision. He swallowed hard, his voice quivered. He folded the baby gently into him, as though still uncertain he was his to keep, love, and protect. The gratification on his face was palpable; there was a visible swelling of his chest. He sat quietly for a long moment staring at the angelic face. His breathing slowly returned to normal. He looked at his wife, and reaching over, he grasped her hand.

"I would like to call him William if that's all right with you," he finally said, gazing between Katherine and her mother. Katherine felt tears welling in her eyes at the sound of her brother's name. Duchess Weldon's eyes filled with tears of joy, and they both nodded in agreement. "All right then. William Henry Wingham, it is." Patrick's voice was now stable and proud. Everyone in the room cheered at the announcement.

"That is a lovely name," she said, watching the two most important men in her life.

. . .

Spring arrived, breathing life into the flowers. The trees were on fire with an abundance of new growth. The birds took turns during the day, always singing. They sat on the mansion's front terrace and gazed at the vast meadow that sloped away from the house. They were both somewhat mesmerized by the tranquil scene. The roses' and clover's scents came to be the very essence of the beautiful days spent at the country estate. The flowers were in bloom, and at sunset, their lovely scent settled on the fields and came drifting up to the terrace where Katherine and Patrick watched their son play before bedtime.

Twilight was coming, and a fresh breeze blew across their faces. After a moment of gathering their thoughts, they stood up, and Patrick lifted his son into his arms. "Bedtime for you, William," he said. His heart was full, looking at the simple smile on his son's face. He reached over and gently pressed his open palm on Katherine's abdomen, his fingers softly flexing over it; she was with a child again. She looked up and took in his gaze. Contentment shined in her eyes, knowing that he owned her heart and soul, and he would always be there to love and protect what was his to the end of time.

The End

ABOUT THE AUTHOR

College, and the corporate world kept Lilian's writing on the back burner for a few years. It wasn't until later on in life that she decided to sit in front of the computer and finally put her thoughts on paper. She lives in Atlanta, Georgia. She is an avid reader and loves novels that feature characters draped in passion, mystery, and adventure. She is especially fascinated with the concept of immortality.

Lilian is the author of the Immortal Rapture Series, eight paranormal, captivating, romance novels. A young British girl Arielle Lloyd with special gifts and an immortal man Sebastian Gaulle find their way to each other and want nothing more than to pledge their undying love to the world. For five centuries Sebastian has sought the one soul who can fulfill his dreams of everlasting love. Then he meets Arielle, whose heart calls out to him like no other. She is also the author of a short novella written for an author collection, Waves of Passion.

Note to Readers

Thank you to my fans. It is the most rewarding and surreal experience to receive your wonderful feedback after reading my book. To the future readers, thank you for loving books and making my book your choice.

Other book by Lilian Roberts

Arielle Immortal Awakening

Arielle Immortal Seduction

Arielle Immortal Passion

Arielle Immortal Quickening

Arielle Immortal Journey

Arielle Immortal Fury

Arielle Immortal Struggle

Arielle Immortal Resolve

Waves of Passion

CONTACT INFORMATION

My website: lilianroberts.com
My Twitter: @lilian3roberts
My Blog: lilianroberts.blogspot.com

www.ingramcontent.com/pod-product-compliance
Lightning Source LLC
Chambersburg PA
CBHW070840260626

47170CB00007B/2448